Within
and
Without

Deborah Maroulis

Within and Without

ISBN-13: 978-0-6483472-5-5

To anyone who is scared but does the thing anyway.

A Note from the Author...

Dear Reader,

Thank you so much for picking up *Within and Without*. Before you continue, I want you to know how important this book is to me. Teens worldwide experience the things Wren does every day, and her voice represents hope for a better future. While I hope you see and like the humor in the pages, I want to make you aware of some of the stronger content. Wren has an eating disorder that sometimes skews her view of the world and the people around her. For that reason, I want to add a content warning, even at the risk of spoiling a plot element. If you are interested, please keep reading. If you feel you don't need them or would like to remain surprised, stop here and accept my sincerest thanks.

Please be advised that there are elements of eating disorders, anxiety and depression, and sexual activity and assault.

If you or a loved one has experienced any of these and need to reach out, please consult one of the resources listed in the back of the book. Again, thank you so much for reading, and I wish you all the best.

Sincerely,
Deb Maroulis

Chapter 1

The boy I've secretly loved for the last three years is parking in Granny's driveway. The tires of his blue 4x4 roll to a stop, and warbled song lyrics promising a good time boom over the vineyards.

Dear fashion gods, now would be the perfect time to send me something flowy and flattering.

Nothing.

I sink into the porch swing as my heart matches the thump of the beat echoing against the wrap-around porch. I suck in my gut and lift my heels so my legs won't smoosh against the bench—a trick I learned to instantly look a size smaller. My hands smooth over my jeans in the hopes the fashion gods might reconsider.

Again, no such luck.

The driver's door swings open, and Jay leaps to the ground, sauntering up the graveled driveway to the porch. To me. Now all that's separating us is a white picket fence and sixteen years of my inability to be normal in a social setting.

I'll take Dying Alone for $200, Alex.

He's abandoned his usual work boots and flannel for a tank top and canvas slip-ons. He's obviously not supposed to be working—so what's he here for? Probably been in town with his friends doing friend-ish things. As he works the gate latch, the muscles under his fair skin flex, sending the hundred-degree temperature up another

1

ten. He's easily the most attractive being on the planet I wish I had the nerve to talk to. I did try once. But we don't discuss The Dark Days.

"Jay!" his dad calls from the path by the garage. "I'm back here." Jay stops and turns. They meet at the gate and his dad nods to me. "Hi, Wren."

"Hi, Mr. Dressler." He runs the part of Granny's business that makes wine.

Jay glances my way, every brown hair crowning his head and freckle sprinkling his nose exactly where they should be.

"Hey," I say to Jay. To my horror, my voice cracks.

He nods in my direction, staring a second too long before turning back to face his dad. Probably thinking *the awkward is strong in this one.*

"Reporting for duty, Sir." Jay fake salutes, then leans against the fence and slides his hand in his pocket.

"Jay Dressler, you get off my fence unless you want to spend the rest of your summer hammerin' in all those nails you're weakening." Granny appears around the backside of the porch, wiping her hands on a dishtowel.

He stands up straight and bows to her like a lord asking a lady to dance. "Beautiful as always, Mrs. Cerridwen." He flashes a smile a cartoon hero would be jealous of.

"Oh, now." Granny shoos him with her towel. "You go on. And call me Granny, just like everyone else around here. Not going to tell you again." She wags her finger at him and winks.

Winks.

"Anything for you, Granny."

Jay's dad attacks him with a playful headlock and turns toward the back of the property.

"Come on, let's go to my office and put you to work." Mr. Dressler waves to Granny with his free hand as the entangled duo stumbles toward the winery offices. Granny plops next to me, her shoulder pressing into mine.

"That boy could charm the stink right off a skunk, don't you think?"

"Granny, that's gross. No one talks like that." I laugh at her weird analogy.

"I do." She pats my leg with each word, sending jiggles across the wide span of my size-12 thigh.

I swallow, forcing the dread rising in my throat back into my chest. My eyes dart to the driveway checking to see if Jay's there taking in every wobble. Thankfully he's not, but my heart radiates sad thumps like waves in a pond and sinks anyway.

I stand, tugging at the ends of my shirt—every self-inflicted fat joke hitting me in the face at once, reminding me who I am. The girl who wears over-sized concert t-shirts and mom jeans, not skinny V-necks and short shorts. Skinny V-Neck Girl can say hello to anyone without screeching like a beached whale—the way I did when I tried to say hi. I run my hand over the rolls pouring over the top of my jeans and make a note to binge whale videos after dinner, if I don't die from embarrassment first.

Granny smacks my hand. "Leave your shirt alone, Wren. You're beautiful."

I give her a weak smile, but I know the truth. Skinny V-Neck Girl won't think twice about a boy like Jay saying hello to her. But Beached Whale Girl will replay that awkward scene every which way, just like I'm doing now. And will probably do forever.

Oh, hi random blushing for the next fifty years.

I dig my earbuds from my pocket and set my phone to play the grittiest song I can think of. They say you have to bleed to know you're alive and, if that's the case, I gotta move so I won't bleed out right here on the porch. I inhale the scent of earthy vines and sweet blossoms of the grounds and blow it out.

"I'm going to walk around, Granny."

"See? That country air'll get you yet!" She waves the dishrag, and its breeze mocks me for not being brave enough to wear shorts.

"My old house is literally thirty minutes from here. It's the same air I've always breathed. It's science."

I cringe at my sarcastic tone but swallow and lift my chin anyway. After spending the morning parkouring over boxes of Home

Shopping Network's finest, trying to *Tetris* the Fed-Ex boxes with my concert tee collection and nearly beheading one of the hundreds of dolls lining the walls of my new room, I can't deal. A tiny crack settles in my heart when I think about the possibility of never going back to my old room and the way things used to be. And every one of those dolls looks way too much like my mom for comfort. Granny seriously needs a good talking to by a Freudian specialist or something.

I managed to save the Mini-Mom before it plummeted to its death, but sacrificed my phone screen in the process. Mom is too into her own thing to notice my broken phone. But now every time my fingers run over tiny fissures on the screen, I'm reminded of my new excommunicated Child-of-Divorce status.

Granny stands and smooths the hair away from my face. "Well, science or not, the town may be close, but this is still farmland and the air is fresher. You're only staying here for a little while. Until your mom settles down."

I can't tell if by settling down she means Mom finding us a new place to live or her new Single and Ready to Mingle lifestyle. The way Granny avoids my eyes I don't think she knows either.

In between swiping right on her dating app and sipping wine with her new book club, Mom promises we're only staying at the vineyard until our old house sells. Since my so-called dad decided to play house with his side ho, Mom's always leaving to drink chardonnay with her bitter single friends. And I'm stuck at Granny's, miles away from everything, shriveling up like the grapes left on the vines after harvest.

*****

I swipe play on my phone and trudge toward the path at the back of the house. As I round the corner, Mr. Dressler lingers in front of the winery office, drilling Jay with directions. His shoulders hunch, and he stares at his shoes as his dad points his finger in Jay's face. I narrow my eyes and secretly wish for a thousand wasps to take up residence in Mr. Dressler's office, then duck behind Granny's Apple Salad tree at the end of the porch. If I were Jay, the last thing I'd want is some screechy girl watching my dad yell at me.

I lean over and inhale the tree's crisp scent mixed with spun sugar. Somehow, Granny grafted branches from three different trees onto this one and uses the fruits to make applesauce sold at the winery's gift shop. Even though her parents left the farm life during the Dust Bowl, the call of the earth never quite left Granny.

I'd never tell her, but I hate Granny's applesauce, even though it's "world famous"—whatever that means when you live in a small town. Something about the texture makes me queasy. And who can deal with all that sugar? My hand instinctively pushes into my belly. With each swipe, I measure which part of the pooch pokes out farther. I wrinkle my nose and blow out a breath, as if I could will the sugary smell away.

Everyone says we have the same pale skin and dark hair, but it's obvious that Granny's green thumb must've skipped a couple generations.

After Jay and his dad go inside, I slink down the path towards the massive oak, the air heavy with summer heat. Climbing on the swing Grandpa made years ago, I pretend not to hear the creak of the rope. I push myself back with the tips of my toes, surprised they barely reach the ground. I crinkle my forehead—someone raised the seat. I stare at the winery office like I can will myself to inherit Superman's x-ray vision.

The office door crashes against the wall as Jay hurries out hefting a garbage bag. He stomps to the outside cans, muttering something to himself, but I can't make out what he says.

I wish Robin were here. She'd just sidle up to him and start a conversation for me. People are always drawn into her easy personality and witty jokes. She flips her hair and smiles, and it's like the sun decided to rise for a second time—why we're even friends is a mystery to me. Well, except we've been friends and neighbors since wearing princess dresses to the grocery store was cool.

As Jay wipes his hands on his khaki shorts, I push back on the swing like I can disappear in the shadows. Like I need the added label of Stalker Girl.

Okay, so about The Dark Days...

On the last day of school, Robin bet me I wouldn't be able to work up the nerve to say hi to him. Every day, he and his fifty million friends trek through the hall—conveniently located by my sophomore English class—on their way to the parking lot.

That last week, she said she was tired of me staring at the hallway, waiting for him to pass by, that I needed to learn to go after what I wanted. When I balked, she used my love of mini-mart cheese fries against me and bet me an order that I couldn't choke out a hello before he made it to his truck. So I had to try.

I mean, cheese fries. Calories be damned.

After the bell rang, I stood on the classroom side of the closed door, peering out the tiny rectangle window and listening for his laughter. As soon as I heard it, my heart pounded in my ears and my tongue seemed to swell twice its normal size. I closed my eyes and tried to breathe, concentrating on the in and out cycle. Robin stood behind me, her hand on my shoulder, silently cheering me on.

Before I knew what was happening, Jay's voice boomed down the hall, and Robin's comforting hand turned into a launch pad. Under her momentum, I pushed the door harder than I needed and plowed it right into Jay's face, knocking him off his pristine pair of checkered Vans. As he checked his nose for blood, I turned fifty shades of humiliated and muttered something about never eating cheese fries again, bolting toward the main doors. Between fits of laughter and tears, Robin offered to get the fries anyway as she drove us home. But the only thing I swallowed that day was my dignity.

Now I'm sitting on a tree swing, Jay Dressler fifty feet away from me. I dig out my phone and start to type.

So, no big deal. But Jay is standing in front of me.

OMG where are you?

*Well, we went to the county courthouse for a simple
ceremony because we didn't want anyone making a big deal...*

Srsly

*On the swing at Granny's and he's sweeping and
literally no one has ever written a song that
could possibly encompass all the feelings I'm feeling rn*

Nervous?

Okay, so maybe someone can.

Ur hopeless. Say hi!

*Already tried that. Puberty struck hard.
Voice crackage. People signing petitions
demanding I be donated to science...*

K, getting back in the pool now.

Sigh...I hate you for not being here.

Love U too!!!

Sighing, I adjust my earbuds and tuck my phone into my pocket. As I fake swing, toe on the ground and barely moving, a shadow from the rose garden catches my eye.

A thin but muscular boy turns over dirt around the outer rose bushes, mixing in some of Granny's homemade mulch. Despite the heat, he's wearing faded blue jeans, a plaid button up with rolled sleeves over a white t-shirt, and laced-up work boots. A backwards baseball cap covers his dark hair.

As if he can sense my stare, he stops and plants the shovel in the dirt. He rests his forearms across the top of the handle as his eyes

7

find mine. Something about the way his lip curls sideways makes me want to be seen, so I put my hand up to wave. But then his eyes shift to the garage and his smile quickly fades. I follow his gaze to where Jay's sweeping the driveway, shaking off his shoes with every few strokes of the broom.

Jay raises his chin when he sees the other boy leaning on his shovel, stops sweeping, and strolls closer to the rose garden. I sit straighter and cut the music.

"Well hey there, Pawn."

"It's pronounced Panayees." He emphasizes the long "e" in his name and wipes a sleeve across his forehead, drying the sweat from his olive skin. "I didn't know you worked today." He crosses his left boot over the right.

"Actually, I'm supposed to be off, but my dad made me come in. He needed me in the office." He sniffs and spits, a wad of phlegm lands just shy of Panayis's feet.

Okay, so maybe he isn't *always* charming.

"Yeah, I'm sure that trash isn't taking itself out," Panayis says. "Let me know if I can help or anything." His lips upturn at the corners. After adjusting his hat, he digs his shovel into the ground, blending the mulch into the earth.

"Okay, Pawn, I'll be sure and do that." Jay's eyes find mine, and he rolls them and smiles.

For whatever reason, I roll my eyes, too, and smile back. Apparently, his tiny acknowledgment of my existence gives him my undying loyalty. Our eye contact makes us partners, if only for a second. Like maybe I could be Skinny V-Neck Girl. Or, at least, a girl who deserves taking part in sparing glances and mutual eye rolls with a guy like Jay.

I push myself off the ground, shooting an apologetic glance toward Panayis, and my foot hits a protruding branch under the swing. My shoe falls into the grass, and as I reach for it, I slip off the swing and stumble off the seat onto my knees. The swing wobbles behind me, coming to a halt in the small of my back.

If only Invisibility Cloaks were real.

I bend to grab my shoe but a hand is already there. Jay steadies my arm and guides me onto the swing. Kneeling, he slips my shoe onto my foot and stands, blocking the sun from my eyes. Pretty sure if he smiled right now, the sun would glint off his front tooth.

"You okay?" he asks.

Jay is talking to me. And I pick now to forget all the words ever invented. Can't even screech.

"Are you all right?" He balances himself by resting his hand over mine on the rope. The pressure sends shock waves down my arm and into my heart like a romantic CPR resuscitation.

"Um, yeah, good." Monosyllables—a good start. I blink a few times to make sure my facial muscles are still working. "All good."

He smiles and stands. "Good. Hate to see a pretty girl throw a shoe and all."

Horse humor. I can do this.

"And the shoe kit's all the way out in the barn. A shame." Blood starts delivering oxygen to my brain again.

"Thank goodness I'm here to rescue you."

"A true Future Farmer of America star."

Panayis clears his throat and Jay purses his lips. He tips his imaginary white hat.

"Always at your service, M'lady."

"You too!"

His smile fades only for a second, but it's long enough. His dimples are reserved for someone other than a girl like me.

"Well, be careful on that swing. Don't want you to fall off." He saunters back to the office.

"No, because that would be embarrassing."

Beached Whale Girl? Check. At least I can tell Robin I've earned those cheese fries.

Chapter 2

I wait for Jay to finish sweeping so I can make an unassuming exit. The last thing I need is for him to see me trip over a root or something after making a fool of myself on the swing. Granny's puppy barrels through some leafy plant, chasing after a white moth. When he tires of it, he lies on the cool grass, nipping at the tiny bugs zipping in and out of the blades. Furry tufts, the color of black licorice, cover his entire body except for a round spot on his chest. That part is a nearly perfect white circle.

The office door slams, and Jay's back inside. Safe from his view and certain I've spent enough time outside to satisfy Granny's obsession with my oxygen intake of "fresh country air," I loop around the deck and pick up my copy of Gatsby on the table next to the swing. All I want to do is plant myself on the old Victorian couch in the front room and get lost in the pages of 1920's New York. I jiggle the door handle, but it won't budge.

Well played, Granny.

An excited bark followed by a small whimper escapes the creature at my feet, and I reach for the handful of wiggly puppy. I settle myself onto the pillowed chaise while the puppy roots for a comfortable spot in my lap. Guess he gets a pillowed place, too.

Just past the porch, hydrangeas inch their way to the top of the railing, clusters of blue flowers among the lily pad leaves. Down the front stairs, smaller bunches of colorful plants and flowers decorate the path to the driveway. Sweet honeysuckle and citrus from the nearby lemon tree fill the air. I sneeze.

Beyond the industrial garage, where all the equipment is kept, there's a newly replanted vineyard. All the sticks that'll one day grow into vines poke through little white boxes that protect them from hungry critters, crisscrossing the fields. But where most people see new life, I see tiny milk carton headstones marking the grave of my social life.

Mental note: make one of those prison calendars to keep track of the days of my family vineyard sentence.

Funny how the kids seem to do the time when it's parents who do the crime.

Plus, after the awkward encounter with Jay, I'm doomed to be the youngest cat lady ever to grace a country porch.

"Might as well make the picture complete." I settle into my fate as the puppy sniffs the cover of my book.

"It's not a bad picture," says a rumbling voice.

I peer over the pages, more shocked at the intrusion than I should be. Workers are everywhere this time of year. But instead of some random person interrupting my reading, Panayis hovers at the bottom of the porch, leaning over a muddied shovel.

"Oh, hey." I sit straighter. Heat floods my cheeks at being caught sprawled all over the chaise like a melted ice cream cone.

"Not bothering you, am I?" He brings his hand to his chest. "I'm Panayis."

I shake my head. "Yeah, I heard you say your name when…earlier." The last thing I want to do is bring up the swing debacle.

He starts up the stairs, and then stops and stares at the shovel like it materializes out of nowhere. Turning, he sets it in the flowerbed, propping it up against the porch railing.

"My dad wants me to deliver something to Ms., uh…" He shrugs and checks the bottom of his boots.

"Call her Granny. Everyone does."

I glance to make sure my thighs aren't spread across the whole seat, although I'm not sure why I care.

"Right. Granny. You'd think with a name like mine, I'd be better at pronouncing stuff." He tilts his head as he swings each boot forward and onto the porch. His lips curl, sending a small twitch to his eyebrow and a wave of something I can't name down my spine.

The familiar panic sets in. The one where I'm talking to someone not related to me and it isn't Robin.

"I didn't know anyone else was around the front part of the house." Heat rises up my neck to my cheeks, and I tug at the loose hair around my face to hide the red splotches I know are glaring as badly as the lights on a movie marquee. "I'm Wren, Granny's, well, granddaughter." I motion to the squirming puddle of fur on my lap. "This is the new puppy, and I just realized I don't know his name." I internalize an eye roll at myself. "I guess I never thought to ask."

His smile crinkles the edges around his eyes. "Fengari and I are already old friends." He steps forward and scratches behind the puppy's ear then retraces his steps to the doorway.

"Fen-who-ee?" I raise my eyebrows. Granny's last cat was literally named Cat, and her two cows were named Sirloin and Beef, so complicated animal names around here are a new one.

"Fen-garr-ee." He draws out the pronunciation. "It means moon in Greek."

"Huh." My eyebrows knit together and I tilt my head. "Why are we naming puppies after space planety things?"

He presses his lips together and squeezes his eyes shut. His shoulders shake from silent laughter. I chew on my lip, half-proud—okay amazed—I made someone laugh and half scared he's laughing *at* me instead of *with* me. I realize my heel is tapping against the deck, so I rest my arm on my leg to steady any unauthorized fat jiggles. After a minute, he opens his eyes and blows out a breath.

"I'm guessing you're not into science much?" The green and yellow flecks in his eyes dance as he waits for my reply.

"Why do you say that?" I can't stop the grin spreading my lips into a crooked line, so I turn my head and study the flower beds. The only guy I want to be flirting with is in the office on the other side of the property.

"Oh I don't know. Maybe it's the space planet things that clued me in."

"Fair point." I nod. He nods back.

Sounds of distant cars passing by and machinery whirling in the vineyards take up the space between us. My heart pounds the way it does when panic sets in, and I curse the lack of my small-talk ability. The more I try to think of something to say, the more blank my mind becomes. He probably thinks I'm rude or disinterested or maybe something more, but it's nothing I can control. Which makes everything worse. But he's fidgeting like he's about to go, so I have to say something.

"Why do you work here?" I cringe, and he blinks in surprise. "I mean, when did you start working here? I don't think I've seen you before." I blow out a breath and raise my hand. "Hi, my name is Awkward, and I have a problem with words. Well, just the speaking kind, really. The written ones aren't so bad." I put my finger over my mouth to stop the spewage. "Sorry. I also specialize in incoherent rambling. You were saying?"

He blinks a few times and clears his throat. I can't tell if he's annoyed or amused. Perfect for my blood pressure.

"My dad is Alex, but you probably know that." He shoves his hands in his pockets and then quickly slides them out again, inspecting the frame of the front door, brow furrowed.

"Oh yeah. Your dad's from Greece, right? I've met him a few times." I nod more enthusiastically now. Probably too much. "I get the Greek thing now."

"Yeah." He narrows his eyes and smirks. I'm pretty sure I'm the color of a red velvet cake at this point, but he ignores it and continues. "He moved to California with his mom when he was a kid. Never went back. His family made wine there, I think. The stories change depending on the number of cousins and bottles consumed."

I smile at his rambling. At least I'm not the only one. He drops his eyes, his cheeks rosy under his tanned skin. Sympathizing, I wait for him to recover. In the quiet, his gaze wanders over the bushes along the walkway leading up to the porch. He glances at the front door, then turns to check the driveway.

"How 'bout you? You working here, too?" He stares at his feet and mumbles something I can't understand.

"Not if I can help it. I'm stuck living here for now."

"You're not a fan of outside." He gestures to the yard and vineyards beyond. Fengari yips so he bends down and scratches behind his ear.

"Not so much. In fact, the less fresh air, the better." I blow out a burst of insistence.

He smiles, resting his gaze on mine. Sounds from the kitchen send Fengari off to investigate. After a few steps, the puppy notices his tail and jumps in circles trying to catch it.

"Where do you go to school?" My face is less hot and I settle into the pillows.

"In town, same as everyone else." The muscles in his neck tense and relax as he swallows.

"Really? I don't think I've seen you."

He raises an eyebrow and shrugs. "Maybe you will now that we know each other."

"Maybe."

Mom's car barrels down the driveway, shooting gravel every which way as she stops abruptly in front of the gates. Great, I'll probably be the one sent out with a rake to smooth the divots. Granny is super obsessed with her gravel. Says it doesn't grow on trees, whatever that means. Um, maybe because they're rocks?

Mom glides down the path and up the porch in her red stilettos, her new "thing" as she calls it. She stops in between Panayis and me and eyes him up and down.

"Well, hello there." She's practically purring. I cock an eyebrow and lower my chin.

"Ma'am." Panayis smiles and nods slightly, the way a cowboy does to a lady in an old movie. She waves him off.

"Oh please, I'm no ma'am. Way too young!" She presses her hand to her chest and laughs like he's the funniest person on the planet.

"Yes, ma'am, um…" His eyes dart from her to me and back again, but all I can do is shrug and watch in horror as she scares off the only person who'll probably ever talk to me around here. She lifts her shopping bag so it's eye level and shakes it.

"Well, I'm going to put these inside. You two have fun." In a lower voice, she adds, "Not too much, though!"

"Mom! Really?" I slide into the pillows and wish for a Dorothy's-not-in-Kansas-anymore-sized tornado to wipe the porch, and me, out of existence.

Panayis chokes out a cough and steps aside just in time to miss her grand exit, tapping her heels and swinging her bag all the way around the porch to the side door that opens to the mudroom.

"I don't even know…sorry." I cover my face with my hands, peeking through my spread fingers and shake my head. He rubs his eye with his palm and laughs.

"She's having fun is all."

"Sure, if by fun you mean torturing me." I adjust myself into a sitting position and draw a pillow over my lap. He nods and winks. I clutch the pillow tighter.

"Could be. I should get this to Granny." He slides an envelope from his back pocket. "Papers my dad needs her to sign or something."

"She's in the kitchen, I think. But you'll have to follow that." I nod toward the clicking. Fengari trots over and sits on Panayis's boot.

He smirks. "I'm going to have to brave it. Nice talking with you. I hope Granny lets you, um, hole up in your room soon…?"

"Yeah, me too." I pick up my forgotten book, surprised at his odd combination of formality and jokes. With a nod, he ambles to the side kitchen door, puppy on his heels.

"See you around."

I stretch out on the long cushions and open Gatsby. Then close it again. Panayis is cute, even if he's about as awkward as me. And the way his mouth curls into a grin when he plays with the dog makes me stifle my own smile. I soften at the idea that there might be someone interesting to talk to for the next week of exile until school starts. But then a loud rumble sends the nearby birds into frenzy, reminding me of what I really want. A shiny, blue four-wheel drive truck backs out of the driveway, a cloud of dust blanketing the air, and me, in its wake.

Chapter 3

The first day of school promises to be about as exciting as listening to Mom turn a joke into a lecture, but at least I'd talked Granny into dropping me off at Robin's instead of the buses—where all the underclassmen and other losers like me who don't have a car are deposited. And after finding out my mom's "still sleeping" and wouldn't be taking me to school, I can't deal with that level of humiliation on the first day of junior year, too. Granny tried to catch me a ride with Panayis, but thankfully, he'd already left.

Robin and I turn into the parking lot with some deep voice blaring out of her radio, crooning about straw-blond angels and small deaths.

"Where do we park?" She turns down the music like people do when they're searching for something. "We need to find a spot that won't kill our social life."

"How about over there? I think that's Maggie's Corolla." She's the vice president to Robin's president of the junior class. Tall with long, blond hair and more like Robin in that she's friends with just about everyone, including Jay. "We like her, right? Even if she's a tad too Top 40?"

Robin rolls her eyes as she steers into the spot. "Not everyone likes to listen to depressing The World Doesn't Get Me music. Some people actually want to participate in high school."

"No, I want to participate. Just as more of a supporting character. Maybe a walk-on, like one of those people in a movie who accidentally bumps into the main character as they traipse in awe

17

down Broadway for the first time."

Robin side-eyes me and smiles. "I worry for what's in your head."

"You and the other voices." I shrug. A throaty laugh escapes her lips. I've so missed hanging out with her. It's good to have her back after the year-long week I've had at Granny's *getting settled* or whatever, even if I'm able to experience a random smile from Jay every now and then. And even if it's because I've injured myself somehow.

I miss being able to go across the street and lose myself in the voices of Robin's brothers and sister arguing about who has car privileges or who's supposed to be doing the dishes. Since the day she cartwheeled into my bedroom on my fourth birthday, the same day my parents and I moved in to our new house directly across from hers, Robin dazzled me with her flair. She and her dad came over to introduce themselves and help carry things in from the moving van. She said whatever she thought the moment she felt it, and still does. It takes me about two weeks, a Google search, and a dozen typed and deleted tweets to find the perfect comeback.

Robin shuts off the engine to her mom's old Honda and waves excitedly to Maggie who's waving back just as enthusiastically. Across the aisle, Jay and his friends are laughing about something. My heart skips a beat. Robin adjusts the rear-view mirror to check her hair and makeup. When she's tousled her fiery-red hair in all the right places, she hands me her lip stain.

"Here, put some on. It'll bring out the blue in your eyes."

"Um, no thanks. I can never get the lines right." I don't usually wear much makeup. The colors always seem wrong and make me feel like one of those roving billboards.

"It's not even that hard. Come on…" She sticks out her bottom lip and tosses the tube so it bounces off my chest and lands in my lap.

"Fine, but if this ends badly, I'm blaming you." I open the tube and sniff its contents like it's spoiled milk and then flip down the visor to reveal the mirror. Following Robin's lead, I check my hair. The tips eek over my shoulders in a brown wave. I like the way it feels on my back.

"Oh, found Maggie. Look where she is…" Robin teases. "Want to go say hi with me?" She turns off the engine and grabs her bag.

Every day before and after school, Jay and his throng congregate around his truck, listening to the latest country anthems belt from his stereo, while I rush by to Robin's old Honda two rows over. I wait there for her to finish with student government, watching him and his crew fake fight while the girls around them fake scream about getting fake hurt.

I smear on some of the lip stain. Robin's right. The plum color makes my eyes go from gray to bright blue, and my mouth appears fuller. But the last thing I need is fuller anything. Familiar tugs draw my lungs into my chest, and a small voice whispers how ridiculous I am. I try rubbing the excess off with the back of my hand but only succeed in staining that, too. As I wipe my hand on my pants, my eyes search the mirror, hoping to see more Skinny V-Neck Girl, but only Beached Whale with plum lips stares back.

In the reflection, I notice Panayis hoofing it from the other side of the parking lot onto campus. Weird I hadn't noticed him before, but usually I'm too busy trying to not bump into chairs or squeeze into my desk.

I hand the tube back to Robin and grab my bag. "I want to get a good seat."

"Wait a sec, Wren," Robin says. "Let's go say hello. See what everyone's been up to. Then you can say hi to Jay." She bats her eyes.

"You only want to go over there because Sitta is right next to Maggie." I walk my fingers up her arm and grin. Her freckles disappear as her cheeks redden, and she presses her lips together and scrunches her nose.

"We texted all last week."

"What? You didn't tell me." My mouth hangs open as I regard her new, slightly more badassness. I'm constantly in awe of her brevity.

She wrinkles her brows and tucks her chin—Robin's classic I'm Sorry face. "Didn't want to jinx it. And I know you're not exactly a huge fan of the cheerleading type."

"Hey, there are laws that explicitly state how soon a best friend must be informed when the girl you've liked for literally ever starts talking to you."

She shrugs and grabs her phone.

"Laws, Robin." I tap my own phone and raise my eyebrows.

"Okay, so let's go over and get all swoony together."

"Ew, not when you put it like that." I wrinkle my nose.

"How you can like someone who listens to that pop country crap they call music, I'll never know."

I ignore the jab because I kind of agree. "Yeah, after my spirited fall into the depths of oblivion the last time I saw him, I'll be lucky if he acknowledges me." I laugh so she thinks I'm mostly joking, but truth be told, the way my heart's doing laps around my stomach, I'm anything but.

"Wren. You stumbled off the swing. You didn't fall face down into a pit of mud or anything. Relax and smile. It'll be fine." Her eyes scan my outfit and she shakes her head. "Just hide your hand. Looks like you've been bleeding or something. And for the love of your social life, don't use your ear buds as a way to get out of talking." She rolls her eyes and climbs out of the driver's seat, closing the door on my objections, not waiting for me to catch up.

"Great," I say to the empty car. I click play, adjust my social armor and slink off to join her.

As I shuffle toward the group of students huddled around the tailgate, I can't stop staring at Jay. He's wearing his hair in messy spikes that he keeps brushing back and forth with his hand. Over his crisp white t-shirt drapes an open button-up with the sleeves rolled just below his elbows. The front of the t-shirt is tucked into his faded jeans to show off his belt buckle. He's wearing the same canvas shoes from the vineyard. I shake my out hair and adjust my book bag on my right shoulder. My heart pounds over the sound coming from my ear buds.

I stop next to Robin and wave an awkward hello to the group, accidentally interrupting some girl's dramatic retelling of whatever show she'd seen the night before. Robin says she's the kind of girl who always has a boyfriend and laughs a little too loud at his jokes. She's pretty, though, and a cheerleader. That guarantees her some sort of social status among the High School Elite.

Robin and Sitta are smirking at each other, so I turn my music down and my attention toward the boys talking about yesterday's practice. They're complaining about some play that went wrong, and Jay's listening and standing there, all hot. His eyes settle on mine and the summer heat shoots up about a thousand degrees.

"Hey," he says. "I saw you the other day where my dad works. Out by the office?"

Crimson heat creeps up my cheeks. "You saved my shoe." More monosyllabic nonsense for the win.

"Your dad works for her grandma, right?" Robin rescues me. "She's staying out there." His eyes shift toward her as she speaks, and I know I have to say something. I swallow my pride and nearly my own tongue.

"Yeah, my parents are getting divorced so my mom and I are staying with Granny for a while," I say. Robin jeers a TMI in my direction, but I can't stop the verbal vomit. "You talked to Panayis. You know, about stuff." I make a mental note to schedule an appointment for the soonest available lobotomy.

"Yeah. You're Wren, right?" The corner of his lip curls as he brushes his hair forward with his hand.

Robin pushes into me with her shoulder and then turns away to join the other girls. Recovering from the shock that Jay Dressler knows my name, I hide my stained hand under my bag.

"Yeah, that's me." I raise my eyebrows and do a little presentation wave with my other hand.

I really need to make that appointment.

He tightens his lips into a grin, and a seed of panic bursts in my chest. I'm exchanging actual words with someone I've barely talked to, and even then they were hardly coherent syllables. I run my hand over the front of my shirt, smoothing any lumps that'd make my stomach appear any bigger than it already is. I will my tongue not to swell and press on.

"Do you like working at the vineyard?"

His grin shifts into pursed lips and a wrinkled brow. I swallow hard, watering the seed of panic now growing into a full-on hedge. He slides his phone from his pocket and taps it a few times, then rolls his eyes as he stuffs it back into his pocket. I should've asked something else. Something less parenty.

"My freakin' dad," he says.

I'm not sure what to say, so I just stand there taking up space.

"Doesn't even ask if I have plans. Just demands I show up to do his shit work whenever he feels like it." His eyes shoot to mine. "Yeah, sorry. I don't mean to bag on your grandma's place."

"No, I get it. I kind of hate being out there, too." *Times a million.*

"Really? Sucks then, to be out there, huh?"

"Parents." I shrug. "Can't live with 'em, can't file emancipation without a good cause."

He tosses his head back and laughs. "True story." He leans in close like he's about to tell a secret. He smells sweet and tangy at the same time, toothpaste and boy deodorant. "Well, I may like it a little more now that I know you're going to be there."

I smile, careful not to show too many teeth. How am I seriously not bursting into flames right now? The first warning bell of the year signals it's time to head to campus.

"Where's your class?"

"Umm, I think it's in the English building. I mean, that would make sense because I have American Lit." I squeeze my eyes shut and internally cringe. He just laughs and says I'm funny and he'll find me later.

The group breaks up; some of the girls travel in a pack toward the math building, others straight into the bathroom for a lip-gloss check. Jay jogs to meet some of the guys heading toward the quad. I sidle up next to Robin and head to the opposite side of campus. She stares sideways at me with a cheesy grin.

"Nice walk-on moves, movie extra," she says, picking up my casting reference from earlier. And this is why I love her.

"Well, I'm not getting my union card just yet." I grin back, tucking my chin into my chest to hide it. I'm afraid if I smile out loud, I'll jinx it. I mentally place a hold on my Virgin Cat Lady Starter Kit in the hopes that our interaction isn't a onetime thing.

"I think he likes you, girl. And I'm so proud of you. Despite the TMI session, you didn't say anything too stupid." She purses her lips and raises an eyebrow, her eyes following Sitta and her long brown ponytail surrounded by her pack. I push her arm and laugh.

"So, how'd that go?" I nod toward Sitta as she rounds the corner of the science building. Robin's freckles disappear again and her pursed lips stretch into a wide grin. "That good, huh? Nice moves, yourself." I hold out my fist and she pounds it with hers.

"You should come and sit with us at lunch today instead of hiding in the library. See if he talks to you again."

"I don't know. The library has pretty good Wi-Fi." I grin and she rolls her eyes. "Besides, he's probably just messing with me."

She throws her arm around my shoulders and steers me toward the English building. "Well, you won't know unless you come and sit with us."

But the boy I never thought I'd have the courage to speak to and I have something in common. Suddenly, impossible doesn't seem so unmanageable any more.

*****

When the lunch bell rings, what's left of my breakfast hardens into a ball of jagged rocks in my stomach. There's no way I'll be able to eat anything, especially if I'm going to be sitting at the same table with Jay. With my luck, I'll choke on a carrot or something.

I find Robin inside the girl's bathroom by the cafeteria, our usual post-class meeting place. In front of the mirror, she smooths her hair into a ponytail. Her book bag is lodged between her knees, and she's holding a bobby pin between her teeth. I lean against the wall by the sinks and sigh—and grin. She glances at me and furrows her brows.

"Moody much?"

"Sshhhh…" I laugh and kick at the air in front of her. She spits the bobby pin from her mouth and uses it to pin her bangs back. She runs her hand over her hair one more time, searching for stray fly-aways.

She scans me up and down and tugs at the bottom of my shirt, straightening its folds. Her hands brush against the jeans button digging into my skin, and I imagine her hand sinking into its crater. I suck in as hard as I can, but it's not enough.

I push her hands away and fluff the shirt over my pants, covering the way my jeans slice my soft middle. "I got it, thanks."

She rolls her eyes, and gestures to the mirror with her arm sweeping out. I take her place in front of the mirror and double check, in case she missed anything. The lip stain has faded, thanks to my incessant lip chewing, and my hair's not too frizzy. I glance at her lean legs and flat stomach through the mirror. Her perfect outfit complements her creamy complexion without even trying. That's all she's trying to do for me. I put my head on her shoulder.

"Sorry, I guess I'm just nervous."

She smiles and pats my hair over my ear, the sounds of the bathroom now a crunchy echo. But sometimes a crunchy echo is all a girl needs.

"How is your mom?"

I sigh. "I don't know. She hasn't really said much. She's into her phone more than me." I attempt to laugh at my lame joke, but a strangled sound escapes my throat.

Robin waves her hands and shakes her head, her flaming-red curls swaying back and forth. "None of that. Besides, the more time your mom is preoccupied with finding Mr. Right Now, the more time we get to hang, right?"

I nod, but the lump in the back of my throat stays.

"Are you ready, then?"

"I guess." I face her for final inspection.

"You look good. You got this."

Robin's motto is to chill, to not over-analyze everything—pretty much my exact opposite. But based on the morning's events, I admit she might be on to something. I've always chosen to keep to myself.

And whenever I choose, I have her and my books.

Jay's consistently at the center of some group, and it's never occurred to me to try to penetrate that circle. The idea terrifies me more than having to decide whether to answer my phone.

Seriously, people just need to text.

Jay likes being around people. He says what he thinks when he wants to. Sometimes, before I fall asleep, I picture myself standing in the group, laughing at someone's joke. Even better, everyone laughing at something I'd said. There are high-fives and girl hugs. Borrowing tiny outfits and group mini-golf outings ending in shared milkshakes where calories don't matter.

In reality, that could never be me. I'd rather talk about how Gatsby represents the death of the American dream or why the stars look alive but are already dead when their light reaches us. Talking about what I'm wearing to the game makes me want to shred my own skin.

But being around Jay is different. I've never wanted to talk to anyone like him before, but the butterflies flying around in my stomach tell another story. I guess what they say about opposites is true. Adjusting my book bag, I nod to Robin.

"Let's go."

We shuffle out of the bathroom and across the hall to where the upper-classmen sit. I survey the tables to see where the group is and, as usual, Jay is right in the middle. Sitting next to Jay, Amsel wears his football training jersey, and Sitta fills the seat at the edge of the table, an empty space conveniently right next to her. The rest of the table overflows with other Future Farmers of America and members of the Lettermen Jacket and Pom-Pom Society.

If this were some prime-time CW show, the table would be slightly off to the left of the frame, filled with muscular guys tossing a football over skinny girls eating nachos. But with one of the best Agriculture colleges right up the road and wine country just west, kids here are into more than Friday Night Lights.

Robin steers us toward the empty space by Sitta with Maggie sitting across. *Great. I can listen to them talk about homecoming or something else just as mind-numbing.*

A few steps away, the library doors open, calling to me. Robin's already immersed in extreme hand gestures with Maggie. She'd never know if I disappeared…

But then Jay smiles and waves me over.

I mentally scold myself for my bad habits. Not five minutes ago, I'd resolved to experience more and analyze less, and here I am, pretty much sitting on Daisy's white couch complaining about the heat when I should be embracing it. I suck in a breath and straighten my spine.

I force my feet to move one in front of the other and stand across from where Jay's sitting. His eyes meet mine as my shadow crosses his lunch and his lips curl on one side. He's talking, but my heart's pounding in my ears and everything sounds like the beach. Even though my nerves are having their own little parade through my stomach, I smile back and wave hi.

"Dude, move over. Let Wren sit there." Jay pushes Amsel and motions for me to sit next to him.

Next. To. Him.

Robin surveys the seating arrangement and says something about being treated like a second-class citizen, and then returns to Maggie for a round of head nods and *ooh gurls*. I maneuver around the table, careful not to knock over a garbage can or accidentally set something on fire. Glancing at the space between the table and its connected bench, I use whatever's left of last year's geometry to calculate how I'm going to fit. Who had the brilliant idea to solder seats to tables? Have they not noticed the various sizes people come in?

If I could manage to work myself onto the bench, I'd buy a lottery ticket.

Amsel scoots over, and I silently will him to make enough space for me to fit. The other girls use up exactly zero space at the table with their skinny hips and flat bellies. Wishing I could suck in my thighs like I could my stomach, I hoist one leg up and manage to get it to the other side without breaking anything. Clutching the table, I lug my other leg over the bench and knee Amsel right in his kidney.

He jerks up straight and jeers at Jay.

"Sorry." I wrinkle my nose and shrug.

"He's fine." Jay cocks his chin toward Amsel who scoots the other way. My left side smooshes against Jay's, so I rotate toward him, making a little more room. The waves crashing in my head subside, but my heart's racing.

"It's tight quarters, but you don't have to move if you don't want to," Jay says. "You can stay close to me." He adjusts his sleeves and leans in, leaving almost zero space in between us. I force air in and out of my lungs. "Glad you're here."

"Thanks." Small-talk panic sets in. My hands shake as I open my lunch and attempt to unwrap my sandwich. As I fumble with the baggie, Jay asks if I'm planning on going to the scrimmage game on Friday.

I've actually only ever been to one football game; Robin's brother played in school, and I went with their family when she and I were freshmen. Most of the time, I had no idea what was happening, and the chilly air made the metal benches so cold my legs ached. I ended up watching the pom-pom squad playfully push each other and laugh too loudly as they vied for attention from the players. Between the band's thumping and the crowd's cheering, I left the game with a gigantic headache.

"Yeah, probably," I lie.

"Cool. You should. I'll be there to watch Amsel kick some ass." He tosses his head back in approval to Amsel and another guy down the table.

I have no idea what kicking ass means in a football game, but I nod and smile. I nibble at the edge of my sandwich, way too nervous to actually eat anything. I catch Robin's eye, and she smiles before turning back to Maggie and Sitta.

"You know, you could sit with me if you want," he says.

My face must be the color of the bread on my sandwich because Jay's smile disappears.

"I mean, sit with us." Jay eyes dart across the table. "That's if you want to." As he talks, he presses his knee into the side of my leg. I nearly choke on a stray crumb. He smells really good. Like Halloween candy after it mixes together in the bowl.

"I want to. Yeah, I totally will."

A smile spreads across Jay's face as he blinks in slow motion. Or maybe I'm about to pass out and it only seems slow. I blow out a breath of victory.

Even though I'm experimenting with spontaneity, my analytical side won't quite shut all the way up. How did I go from Invisible Girl to sitting next to the cutest boy at school?

He stretches, leaning back and extending his arms out into the aisle, elongating his form and flexing his muscles. I may have actually sighed out loud, but I'm hoping that was just in my head. He picks up his massive sandwich, meat slices hanging from the sides, and chomps nearly halfway through it.

I spend the rest of lunch listening to the different conversations around the table. Maggie and Robin tell Sitta about what student government is proposing for this year's homecoming while she tries to Insta-art her cafeteria fries. Amsel attempts to distract Maggie from her conversation by stealing fries from her plate.

They've been dating since last year and are pretty much joined at the hip—or mouths. I'd even heard a rumor they're applying to all the same colleges. Jay talks to everyone, although he doesn't really talk about anything, more small talk. I catch him glancing at me a few times. Or maybe I'm the one doing the staring; I can't be sure.

The bell announces the second stretch of classes. Pre-calculus is next.

Jay stands and straddles the bench. "Where are you going?"

"Math. Where souls go to die."

He laughs. "I'll go with you. My class is down that way."

I blink.

"We should talk later. Do you have Snapchat?"

I can't remember where the math building is. I can't remember what Snapchat is. I inhale but super slow so he doesn't notice all the air has left the atmosphere. "Um, yeah. Give me your phone and I'll put in my number."

Never in my life have I asked for a guy's phone. This risk-taking philosophy might pay off.

"You give me yours." He reaches for my phone. I want to avoid a repeat of the Great Summer Swing Incident as much as possible.

"Here. I put it under Sexiest Man Alive, in case you're wondering." He hands me back my phone, shoves his hands in his pockets and grins.

"Of course you did." *Of course you are.* I snap a picture of him, type "dork" over it, and send it to the number he just entered. "Now you have my number, too."

We arrive at the math building way too quickly. "I'll talk to you later, that is if I survive this class. I English way better than I math." I sigh at the Door of Doom.

He smiles and shakes his head.

"Obviously. And yeah you'll hear from me!" He does a little hop and steps backward, then turns and jogs toward the library building. I stare after him—mouth hanging open—until he's out of sight, not believing what just happened. I need to text Robin immediately. I open my phone as she rounds the corner.

"Thanks for waiting for me," she says. In the rush, I forgot we have pre-calc together. I mumble an apology and slink into class. "It's okay. Not like you had a hot guy escort you to class for the first time ever or anything."

"Thanks for adding the first time ever part." I sit in the middle of the room next to where she drops her book bag and spend the period trying to concentrate, but all I can see is Jay's crooked grin as he handed me back my phone. Sexiest Man Alive.

Even though she's sitting right next to me, I send Robin a text:

I need you to tell me everything
you know about football.

Chapter 4

"Why do we care if the ball goes between the posts again?" I unbuckle my seatbelt as Robin rolls her car down the vineyard's driveway exactly thirty minutes after school lets out and an hour earlier than I'd be home if I'd ridden the bus. She lets out an exasperated sigh and shifts the gear in park. She leaves the engine running and the air blowing, a luxury I'll miss as soon as I go inside. No air conditioning in the Farmhouse.

"We don't really care where the ball goes." She moves her hand between us, pointing to me and then herself. "We are there to hang out with actual people and bathe in the high school experience you've managed to avoid for the last two years. The team cares because that's how they get points and win."

"Bathe? Gross." I slide down the bucket seat and rub my eyes. "Football is complicated."

"No, it isn't. You just need to get out of your head and enjoy yourself." She pulls down her visor and checks her makeup, swiping a finger under her eyes.

"Okay then, peopling is complicated."

She ignores my whining. "And, if things go all right, maybe you'll end up with a date. The Grape Festival is coming up soon." She side-eyes me and grins.

Since our town is all about growing grapes and making wine, it hosts this huge event every year to showcase all the varieties. There's even a parade where all the old guys wear silly hats and ride around in tiny cars spraying silly string everywhere. Grade school kids and clubs make murals with grapes, and the county hands out blue ribbons for the best jam. Most of the kids don't go to those things unless they have to for family or whatever. Almost everyone spends their time at the carnival and concerts, and usually after dark when the families with younger kids head home.

When we were younger, we'd see the high school couples screaming together on the Zipper and sharing cotton candy and kisses on the Ferris wheel while we waited in line for the kid rides with our parents, and even though we made fun of their face-sucking, I secretly hoped one day it'd be me.

Over the summer, Robin found a Dear Diary I'd written when I was twelve about my dream date at the festival, complete with the huge stuffed animal prize and fun house hide and seek. I chased her over my bed and into the backyard, but by the time I got it back from her, she'd read most of it. And she hasn't let me live it down.

"That's not funny," I say, but we're both grinning.

"It's a little funny." She tilts her head and smiles a huge, toothy grin.

"It's just a stupid story I wrote a million years ago. It doesn't mean anything."

"Ugh, I hate this song." She grabs her phone and clicks the shuffle button until bass bumps against the windows. "And it isn't stupid. I kind of want someone to win me a huge stuffed animal, too. Even if the bear's ugly, the idea of it is romantic."

"Oh wow, you've got it bad, don't you? Since when are you willing to let someone spend money on you who isn't your immediate relative?" She's all about splitting everything equally.

"We aren't talking about me." She cocks an eyebrow and waits for me to speak, a Robin Special. Out of the corner of my eye, I see Granny come out of the kitchen and onto the porch, drying some dish with one of her embroidered towels. It's her way of asking why we're sitting in the car or maybe to turn down the music. Either way, I shift so my back is to the house, forcing me to answer Robin.

"Fine. Yes, I would love to be that person holding hands on the

Ferris wheel or whatever. It's just never going to happen, okay?" I notice the miniscule size of her lap. Her legs barely cover half the seat while mine dominate the whole thing, even when I sit up straight. There's no way I'm going to sit comfortably next to anyone bigger than a size two. I mean, that's a whole different definition of snuggling. No thanks.

"Yesterday, you would've said the same thing about Jay walking you to class or sitting next to him at lunch." Robin covers my hand with hers. "Junior year is your year, I can feel it."

"It's going to be our year." Even though I'm not so sure, I squeeze her hand and smile. But if it is all happening, I'm going to have to become more comfortable with myself. I can't see Beached Whale Girl staring back from the mirror. I need a plan, something stricter than just keeping track of my calories. Time to actively seek Skinny V-neck Girl.

And mean it.

As Robin backs her car out of the driveway, I slump into a chair at the kitchen table. Granny stands by the stove with a huge bowl cradled in her left arm. Her right hand rapidly mixes ingredients—whatever they are. I smirk at her outfit—a flowered long-john shirt under her too-big overalls, giant cuffs rolled up below her knees. Slippers replace her rubber "vineyard" boots, and her hair is tucked into a messy bun.

"Hey, Granny. What're you making?" I scoot the chair, and its legs grate against the refurbished barn-wood floor. Faded wallpaper and family pictures that go back decades dominate the walls. A few empty spots stick out like missing puzzle pieces in the barrage of photos. Probably removed because my dad's in them.

I pick a small apple from the bowl on the butcher block and bite into it, immediately cursing myself for not thinking before shoving food in my face. In his pen, Fengari chews a rubber steak, barking at it every time it squeaks.

"I am making dinner." She grins over her shoulder. Benny Goodman plays in the background, Granny's feet sidestepping to the beat as she empties the bowl into two baking pans and slides them into the oven.

"Granny, that's a cake."

She nods and winks. "I always knew you were the smart one." She rinses the bowl and dries it. "Cake has milk, eggs, all kinds of healthy stuff, and sometimes you just need a good cake for dinner."

Cakes also have sugar. Lots of it. Exactly what I need. I clench my jaw. The apple sits like a brick in the pit of my stomach. "Where's Mom?"

"She left you something." She nods at an envelope on the table.

The note says she's going out of town for a few days. That's code for she met someone online and wants to "see where it will lead." Since Dad left, my mom's been into "finding herself as someone other than a mother and wife." And every trip she and her online date-of-the-week takes makes the possibility of moving home seem farther away.

That explains the chocolate cake. I let my shoulders drop and survey the kitchen. How did my mother come from a house like this?

Almost everything in the farmhouse is old-fashioned. The only modern piece in the kitchen is a small microwave. It sits on the tiled counter next to a crock filled with old cooking utensils. Repurposed glass shelves line the window over the sink, reflecting the shadows of the small trinkets she's collected or dug up over the years. Her favorite holds center stage—a rusted, old-fashioned skeleton key she'd found while clearing rocks out of her garden beds.

Granny always said I could have it when she died. That it's her legacy or something. She likes to brag she'd found the matching chest filled with treasure somewhere in the vineyards but refuses to show anyone. Says the map will be in her will, and we can dig it up under a full moon when she's gone. She's morbid like that, always promising things and making funeral plans. Can't deny the mystery is a little fun, though.

"It's good to have you here." She brightens her smile like she's showing me how to feel. "Dinner"—she nods slowly—"will be around six."

It's not in me to smile back, but I nod and trudge to the stairs leading to my room.

I've been assigned the smaller of the upstairs bedrooms, right across the hall from Granny's. Even though I've managed to carve a space for my band t-shirts and Converse collection, I long for the deep purple walls of my own bedroom, lined with signed concert flyers. I especially miss my old bed that knows where to give and hold when I shut out the world.

Avoiding the stares of the doll museum on the far wall, I throw my book bag onto the antique coverlet, sending bits of dust confetti into the stifled air. Decorations for my own private pity party. I open the window for hope of any sort of breeze and wrench my journal from under the bed. Grabbing a pen, I wiggle myself into the upholstered chair.

Methodically, I recount each bite of food I've swallowed since this morning.

Turkey slice, 60 calories.

Half a slice of bread, 40.

Apple, 95.

With cake for dinner, I'm done for the day. As I enter it all into my journal, my phone buzzes.

One Snapchat.

I'll take social life for $300, Alex, and hold the pity party reservation.

I open it and a picture of work boots flashes on the screen. *U been running thru my mind all day* is written over them, followed by the cheese emoji. My heart leaps as I bite down on a smile. At the same time, I shake my head because of the cliché pickup line. I want to save the picture to show to Robin, but Jay would know if I did. Since I don't want to add to my awkwardness, I memorize it before the time runs out.

After a panicked moment of not knowing how to respond, I think what would Skinny V-neck Girl say? Got it. I remove my pencil pouch from my book bag, snap a picture of the scissors, and send it back to him with the caption *cut it out* followed by the eye roll emoji.

My heart is a kite among the clouds.

I stare at my phone until the red triangle turns into a red square. I slowly count to ten, trying to not be too eager but willing a response just the same.

I touch the screen, and a picture of Jay puckering up next to a goat's cheek pops up. The caption reads *text you later!* I let myself smile a big, toothy smile and fling myself onto my bed. Sure, it's a stupid pickup line, but it's my first one. Maybe I will get that Ferris wheel moment after all. I shove my journal back into its hiding spot and plug in my phone to charge. Too excited to stay in my cramped room, I grab Gatsby and head to the porch.

Concentrating on the billboard eyes on the book cover, I open the front door and smack into something solid. The novel topples onto the porch, and I lurch backward to avoid falling, only to stumble over the threshold of the doorway. Panayis grabs my arms and steadies me. My hair covers my eyes and sticks in my lashes and mouth. He bends down to my eye level and brushes the hair out of my face.

"Are you okay? I'm really sorry. I didn't expect anyone to come out of the door so quickly," he says.

"Um, yeah. Should've paid attention to my own eyes…sorry. I guess I'm excited." I cringe. Again with the TMI.

He raises his eyebrows, a question in his eyes.

"Excited about reading outside." I lob a cheesy thumbs-up at him and smile. "I'm okay now, you can let go."

His eyes land on my arms, still in his grip. "Oh, oops. I just wanted to make sure you weren't going to lose a shoe or something." His lips curl up at the ends as he lets go. I take a breath and attempt to smooth back my hair, willing myself not to turn all blotchy red as the Swing Incident rears its ugly head.

"You saw that, did you? Leave it to me to put the awkward in any situation."

He bends down and picks up my book while I settle into a spot on the old, velvet chaise lounge on the corner of the porch. Granny believes in using "real furniture," so we're stuck covering everything with sheets and pillows to keep it clean. And really, the sitting on a sheet is a thousand times better than velvet when it's a hundred degrees. He closes the front door and leans his shoulder against the jamb.

"Why are you excited to come outside? I thought you were allergic. Fresh air and all?"

"I don't know, actually. I just couldn't concentrate upstairs, so I came down here." I don't know why, but telling him about Jay feels weird.

A sheer curtain blows through the open living room window and flicks the edge of the chaise. It swells and then flips on itself before the curtain falls back inside. Since there's no air conditioning, Granny keeps the windows wide and the fans on high all summer and into October, when the weather finally cools.

The warm chocolate scent of the baking cake wafts through the window, and a low rumble escapes my gut. I push my hand into my stomach, hoping to quiet it. Panayis's eyes dart over my mid-section, but thankfully he doesn't say anything.

A slice of chocolate cake with icing has 235 calories, and I doubt I can get away with not eating. Better to eat half and deal with it later.

"AP English?" He nods to my book. I shrug, not wanting to admit I'd started it for fun. "I read that last year. Good story, although I always felt like Daisy doesn't get enough credit. I mean, if you think about it, she holds everyone's fate in her hands, yet she is always portrayed as the victim."

No one ever wants to talk about books, not like I do. There may be friendship potential here yet.

"Well, maybe she doesn't realize her own power." Even though I'm sitting down, my legs feel shaky and my breath quickens. Probably hungry is all—I can get through it. I flex my leg muscles, willing them to relax. "Maybe she's used to having men take care of her, so she just assumes that's the way it should be. Strong woman weren't universally accepted yet." I shrug, and he narrows his eyes. Probably thinking too much book, and not enough reality TV talk. "Yeah, I don't know where that came from, sorry."

"Don't be. I think you're right." He stares into the garden. "Maybe strong wasn't her thing. After all, it was the 20s. The beginning of the women's movement."

My lips curl slowly into a smile. Then I remember his glazed-over expression when I talked about Daisy. Not that I care, but I want to avoid nerd status just once in my life around someone my own age. "What are you doing here, anyway?"

He switches porch sides and props himself against the railing at the end of the chaise. "I came to see about your first day of school."

Only the best day of my life. A grin leaks from the side of my mouth. I fall onto the pillows and let out a contented sigh.

"I saw you a couple of times, but you were with other people, and I didn't want to interrupt." He works his jaw, clenching it tight and releasing it.

"You should've said hi."

"You were sitting with Jay Dressler at lunch. I didn't want to intrude."

"You know him?" I lean forward.

"Yeah."

"I'm glad you saw it, because I was beginning to think I was dreaming. Of course, the only thing keeping me from the deluge of a dream sequence is the fact that I wore clothes and no one was pointing and laughing." I roll my eyes and he smirks.

His eyes focus on the garden, and his gaze hardens. After a moment, he exhales and folds his arms over his chest.

"You should give yourself more credit." He taps his fingers against his arms as he stares at his shoes. "I mean, you seem like a nice person, and I'm sure if you wanted to, you could have a lot of friends."

"I'd totally have more friends. And would. Except people. Peopling is hard." I throw my head against the seat and drop my hands to my sides.

"Got it." He makes a checkmark in the air. "Adding people to the things to avoid list. Right up there with fresh air."

I nod and smile. He's changed from his school clothes to faded jeans and a t-shirt, along with his backwards hat. The short sleeves hug his arms around his biceps and material stretches across his chest.

"What about your day?" I suck in and straighten my back.

He nods, his face brightening. "Actually, all right. Classes don't seem too bad." He cocks his head and slowly curls his lip into a crooked grin. "Thanks for asking."

I clear my throat and tuck my legs under me, taking a sudden interest in straightening my shoelaces. "Oh yeah? What are you taking?" I sneak a glance to find he's fully facing me. I suck in another breath. I've never really talked this much with non-Robin people, but he makes it easy. Especially if books are involved in the conversation.

"A little math, a little English. The usual." He reaches over to pick up my copy of Gatsby and thumbs through the pages.

"Ugh, math. So gross. Which one are you taking?"

"Calculus," he says. I groan and he laughs. "Not a fan?"

"I could write a five-page paper on why I hate math." I point to the book. "Give me a good story over a word problem any day."

He smirks. "I mean, I could help you sometime…if you need it."

"Um, sure, that'd be great." I raise my eyebrows and nod, but the shaky feeling in my legs and stomach is back. Instinctively, I reach for my phone but remember it's upstairs charging. My heart skips thinking there might be a message waiting from Jay. "I don't usually talk this much. Guess you have a future in couch therapy."

"I'll send you my bill." He winks.

I wait for him to say something more, but he just stares, head tilted. I raise my eyebrows at him for a response, but he remains straight-faced. As much as I like talking to him, my mind is upstairs dying to check my notifications for any possible Jay-messages. Then, I remember how he and Panayis were that day on summer break. They didn't seem too friendly, and I know they don't hang out with the same people at school. In fact, today marks the inaugural sighting of Panayis on campus.

"How do you know Jay?" I ask.

His relaxed frame stiffens and the smile in his eyes fades.

"I knew him when we were younger. Why?"

"Oh." I sigh when he doesn't offer any more details.

"Are you guys…?"

"No. I mean, maybe?" I shake my head. "No." I chew at my bottom lip. Because hey, I'm probably some huge Snapchat joke he and his friends are playing, so no is definitely the safer answer.

"Oh." His thick brows knit together.

"He asked me to come with him to a football game."

Panayis scoffs, and then sits in the rocker on the other side of the porch, crossing his foot over his knee.

"What?" Hair bristles on the back of my neck. It's like my mom just told five-year-old me that I can't have the toy she promised for being good at the grocery store. I mean, I don't know if there's anything to scoff at, and who is he to act this way?

"He's got a reputation is all. And he's in trouble with his dad a lot—from what it seems around here. I mean, I don't know."

Jay did mispronounce Panayis's name that day, but that's how guys tease each other. Robin's brothers did that stuff all the time. They call each other all sorts of things. And Panayis was the rude one that day. Kind of like now.

"I don't know. Haven't heard that." I pinch my lips together.

"I mean, it's whatever." He stands up.

It isn't whatever. This is Jay, the maybe possibly potential first date of my life. "What's up with you two anyway?"

He glances at me and then out to the garden, working his jaw in tight clenches. He's staring at one of the rose bushes, its branches full of little buds and more branches growing wild near the bottom of the plant. After some silence, he nods toward it, ignoring my question.

"That bush needs to be pruned."

"Well, whatever it is, sorry. I didn't think he would even know I exist, but, you're right, it's whatever." I stand and clasp my hands together and stretch them in front of me, then roll my shoulders. Panayis is just someone working on my family's farm. He doesn't understand what he's saying. And who cares about a stupid rose bush?

"Yeah." He straightens up and smiles, although the crinkly parts around his eyes aren't there. "I should get to those rose bushes." Fine. He can have the rose bushes while I check my phone.

"Well I have homework, so I'm going in." I gather the book and stand.

"Glad to hear you had a good day anyway." He waves from the path to the gate.

"Next time say hi at school." I smile, too, but my voice remains flat.

Upstairs, I crash on my bed and throw my book on the chair. I open my phone and there are three new alerts. Two from Robin and one from Jay.

Chapter 5

Before I can open the message, Granny sticks her head into my room.

"Dinner time," she sings. She points to my phone. "Put that thing away and come sit with me. We can eat outside if it's cooler."

I sigh and shoot a longing glance at my phone as she shoos me downstairs. "It's just as hot outside. We might as well eat at the table." Plus, the last thing I want to do is eat cake while Panayis cuts roses. Marie Antoinette much?

After the chocolate cake dinner, of which Granny cut me an extra-large slice citing something about full bellies making for good sleep, she settles in the downstairs living room for her evening show on PBS, Fengari at her feet. I excuse myself and hustle upstairs.

From my doorway, I can see my phone's screen lighting up. But the chunk of cake churning in my stomach weighs heavier by the second. Instead of flopping onto my bed, I close the door to the bathroom separating Granny's room from mine and embrace the dark. I turn on the faucet, the sound of running water overcoming the TV voices from downstairs. I imagine the trickle carrying my failure of eating the whole slice down the toilet.

Timing is everything. The flush has to cover the splash but also clean up the mess. And flushing more than once might bring unwanted attention.

Pre-marital-woes Mom had curves in all the right places, but once she married my dad, her curves turned into bulges. Since the divorce, if she isn't chatting online with her soulmate of the month, she's butt-lifting the Brazilian way or pinning weight-loss miracles to her digital corkboard. Now that she's losing the weight, people tell us we look like sisters. She eats that crap up like it's on her cheat day. All I see is my head on her middle-aged body.

Robin is super thin. One time, she let me borrow one of her belts that matched my outfit. I could barely latch the catch in the last hole, but she insisted the belt would be fine. I was afraid to sit down the entire time I wore it. I could almost hear it screaming at me to let it die with dignity. Since then, every time I stand next to her, I feel like some out-of-control blob, my shadow waiting to devour her sinewy frame.

Shaky, I push myself up and lean over the sink, the cool of the water giving me sweet air to breathe in. I rinse my mouth and wipe the sweat sheen from the back of my neck, then sink to the floor. I push against the counter to quiet the ticking muscles in my back.

I run my fingers over my too-wide nose; let them slip down to my cheeks and further to where my abdomen pops out under my waist. I straighten my back and suck in, hoping the pooch will lessen. No such luck. I slouch to my normal posture and run my hands over my backside and around the bulges at the sides of my legs. The worst part of me. All I can think about is the cake sludging through my veins and attaching itself to the thickest part of my thighs like chicken fat on a raw breast. Hopefully I'd stopped it in time.

Flipping through the afternoon TV talk shows a year or so ago, I settled on one about some girls and how they'd kept their weight down. I listened to one of the girls describe exactly how she would make herself sick after she ate so she wouldn't absorb the calories. She looked good, too. Shiny hair and a pretty smile.

I finally knew how I could avoid my mom's you-don't-need-to-diet face as she blended kale and blueberries for herself and ordered pizza for me. The last thing I wanted was for my body to turn out like hers, and I knew that if Robin ever loaned me clothes again, I definitely didn't want to hear them scream.

If the Ferris wheel dream ever did happen, I'd have to figure out how to avoid chocolate cake dinners for good.

In my room, I slide my journal from its hiding place and enter 352. Then I cross it out and write 176, plus activity. Satisfied, I tuck it away quickly, in case anyone barges in without knocking as my mother loves to do. If she were even here.

I sit in front of the open window and finally check my phone. The one message from Jay is another goat, but this one is standing on top of some chicken coup. Cute, but it's nothing that couldn't have been sent to everyone.

Dang.

There's about four bajillion messages from Robin. I'd texted her before dinner to tell her about Jay's Snapchat. Her motto may be to stay easy going, but she hates to be kept waiting on any sort of guy gossip. The last one reads:

IF YOU DON'T TEXT ME BACK RIGHT NOW,
I WILL TELL EVERYONE ABOUT THE TIME
YOU MADE US PEANUT BUTTER AND CHEESE
SANDWICHES AT YOUR DOG'S BIRTHDAY PARTY
WHEN WE WERE FIVE.

Sorry, eating dinner. Just one random pic is all he sent. We can talk about it in the morning on the way to school. And you're the one that ate it so go ahead.

I follow up with a few emojis and put my phone down.

43

Then pick it up.

I open Snapchat in case it's not working and forgot to notify me of any incoming snaps.

Nothing.

Not even a new story. I chew my bottom lip and set my phone on my pillow.

Who knows why Jay's talking to me, but the circus in my stomach performs like Barnum and Bailey on steroids every time I think about it. Analytical Me says maybe he's being nice because of Robin. Or because Granny is his dad's boss. Maybe the silly Snapchats really are just a joke for him and his friends. A small wave of panic electrocutes my heart and jolts down my spine.

If I were a joke, I might die.

Just then, my phone cries out a cuckoo, my tone since I started my latest book.

just got out of the shower, tired from
work. what ya doin?

Another lightning bolt hits my heart, sending a different wave of feeling down my spine. I pick up my phone.

OMG Robin he just texted me.

          Don't text me, talk to him!

With a steady burst of courage, I reply something about finishing dinner and bingeing videos on my computer. *Duh, Wren, where else would you watch them?*

Haha that's cool. Im bout to knock out.
stop by my truck in the morning.

          Um yeah okay

I feel about as casual as a twelve-year-old at a pop concert.

K g'nite. A smiley face emoji pops up.

Good night.

I follow the text with a sleepy face emoji.

LOL.

Throwing caution and my social media cred to the wind, I screenshot the conversation and send it to Robin with a message that reads, Sweet Dreams!

*YOU WILL TELL ME EVERYTHING
IN THE MORNING.*

I grin and slip into my pajamas. I settle into my bed and stare at the ceiling, avoiding the eyes of all the dolls on the opposite wall. They sit there all day, eyes boring into me like hundreds of tiny Mom spies—and she's the last person I want in the middle of my conversations with Jay.

He wants to see me. At his truck. In front of everyone. My heart beats hard, and I have to breathe deep to get enough air.

I open my phone and set my alarm thirty minutes earlier than I'd originally planned to wake up. I'd need the extra time for my hair and maybe even a little makeup, if I could pull it off. Class joke and tomorrow's punchline or not, I'm all in.

Chapter 6

For the first time in my high school life, I'm awake before my alarm chirps. My breath comes in short bursts. It feels like there's a knot of desire and dread winding its way around my lungs, like two coats of oily paint, their colors swirling around each other but never blending. I lie on top of my sheets, mentally scanning my closet for something to wear.

There's nothing but t-shirts and Granny's old linens to choose from, and togas made out of old-lady lace is so not in right now. Guess I'll be rocking that Grunge style one more day.

I peek into Mom's room after my shower, hoping she left behind some sort of light-colored lip gloss or an eyeliner that won't give me raccoon eyes. To my surprise, she's in her bed, dead asleep. A bit of hope pops into my chest and asks the dread-knot to dance. Maybe she'll drive me to school so Granny won't drop me off in the truck that backfires coming out of second gear.

"Mom, you're here!" I shake her arm, and she rolls onto her back, eyes closed and mouth open. Mascara streaks line her face, and remnants of red-lipstick smears stain her chin.

Totally knocked out.

I shake her shoulder. "Mom, you need to wake up. I have school."

Her right eye squints open as she moves her tongue around her mouth and swallows. She smells like sweet perfume and an alley behind a liquor store. I cover my nose with my hand.

"Rough night?"

"Panayis offered to have you ride with him to school." She smiles and stretches. "I mean, makes sense, right?"

My eyes about bug out of my head. Awesome. Driving into the parking lot in his beat-up truck and trekking across the aisles to get to Robin. Alone. Or worse—he might tag along. Panic creeps into my emotional cocktail.

I'd almost rather take the bus.

"Don't you have to go to work?" A stupid question because, I already know the answer.

"Took it off—mental health day. Had to after dealing with attorneys yesterday. You understand." She adjusts the pillow under her head.

Hope leaves Dread-Knot on the dance floor, and Panic asks to cut in.

I want to say no; I don't. Nothing makes sense anymore because we live here and not at our real home, and I've never seen her like this before, but there's no point. She'll tell me I'm being selfish and acting like a child or something just as insulting. I bite down the words with clenched teeth.

"I guess."

"That's my girl. Okay, have a good day." She rolls back, tugging the sheet over her head as air grates against the back of her throat. I head for the door before she exhales, grabbing her makeup case off the dresser on my way out. Letting me use her stuff is the least she can do.

When I'm ready, I head downstairs where Granny sits at the table, sipping coffee. "Well, aren't you gussied up this morning. Got a hot date?"

My hand shoots to my cheek as it burns and my eyes go wide. "Maybe?" I bite the inside of my mouth to stop myself from grinning.

"Oh, really?" she croons. "Who's the lucky gentleman caller?"

I roll my eyes. "You can just say guy. It's not 1900 or whatever."

She stares at me flatly, blinking purposefully. I press my lips together and study my cuticles. If I say it out loud and it doesn't come true, if the whole thing really is some sort of joke…

"Just some guy. I don't want to jinx it."

"If you say so." She shoots a glance toward Mom's room then points to a bag on the counter. "Thought you could use a lunch. Packed you some leftovers." She smiles but there's worry behind her eyes.

"Leftover cake?" I know I'll throw it away as soon as I see a trashcan, but the fact that she's awake this early and put food in a bag for me to eat at school warms the frost in my bones. I lean over the back of her chair and wrap my arms around her, putting my head on her shoulder. "You're the best, Granny."

She pats my arm with her free hand. "Same to you, kid." She nods to the driveway. "If you head toward the mailboxes on the side of the road, you'll see Panayis waiting for you. Or if he's not, give him a few minutes."

And I have to hike ten minutes to my ride. At least I can count it as activity.

"Good kid, that one, offering to drive you like that." She narrows her eyes and a mischievous grin slides across her face. "Say, it's not Panayis you're getting all dolled up for, is it?"

"Ew, Granny, no." I wave my hand like I'm swatting a gnat. "Not in a million years. And please don't say doll." There's too many of those in my room twinning with a person lying in her bed who I never want to be.

SOS
I've been abandoned by my loved ones and am being forced to drive to school with a relative stranger.

I'm sure it's not that bad.

Can't you come get me? I'd take the bus but it's already gone.

There's no time!
I'll see you when you get here.

I hate you.

Love you, too!

I shove my phone in my pocket and huff. Adjusting my backpack over my shoulders, I resist the urge to kick the gravel as I slog down the driveway toward the road. Literally the most important day of my high school career and I'm already sweating.

No truck. No Panayis.

By the time he arrives, my mascara will probably be racing the eyeliner down my cheeks. I'm nearly to the mailboxes when a beat up, blue and white striped truck veers off the road and drives right past me, sending dust and baby rocks flying through the air and all over my clothes.

Perfect.

I cover my mouth with my hand and step to the side, nearly landing in the ditch dividing the road and property. As I catch up with the truck, its brake lights come on and it skids to a stop, sending another big cloud of chalky dust into the air. I squeeze my eyes shut and wave my free hand in front of me, like that's going to keep me from smelling like road just in time for the biggest morning of my life.

I consider going back to the house and saying I'm sick, because I so cannot deal with this. Can I call a timeout? A do over? No? Okay.

In the cab, Panayis crawls over his seat and pokes his head out of the passenger window. "Stay there! I'll pick you up where you are."

I give him a thumbs-up instead of the finger I really want to use. Not at him, so much. More at the whole morning—which is a big ball of suckage. It's not his fault, really, which makes it ten times worse.

He hops back over his seat and behind the wheel, throws it in reverse and gasses it, stopping with screeching brakes and splattering gravel right in front of me. Jumping out the driver's side, he rushes around the front of the truck, sort of mumble-talking the whole way.

"I'm so sorry. I didn't see you. You all right?" His words are short bursts of friendly fire, and my outfit is collateral damage. He holds his hand out like he's going to grab my elbow or something, but I turn so he can't. I'm not officially mad at him, but his dirt-bath-slash-carnival fun-ride isn't helping.

"Can we just go?" I huff as he opens the passenger door. Throwing my backpack on the floor, I climb in and try to undirt myself as much as I can. As he backs out to the road, I flip down the visor to check what's left of my makeup and sigh. "You don't have a mirror?"

He shakes his head. "Nah, not in Bubba."

"Bubba?" I raise an eyebrow.

He pats the dash as he picks up speed on the country road leading to town. "Bubba may be old, but he hasn't let me down yet."

"Unless you're lip gloss." I press my lips together, the grit and color feeling more like a scrub than a look, and do my best with my reflection in the side mirror.

"I'm really sorry about that. I was trying to hurry, but I just made a mess of things."

His tone makes something tug at my heart a little. I wave him off like it's no big deal, even if he drives a truck named Bubba and is a maniac on dirt roads.

"It's whatever. But next time, I'm wearing a helmet," I say. He knits his eyebrows together and turns onto another long road. "Hopefully you're not as bad on actual blacktop." I give him a weak smile as he shoots me a glance.

"I'll try my best." His voice is flat but his eyes say he's joking. For some reason, him joking around when all I want to do is be at school makes me want to scream. "You're all dolled up. Is this your New Year New Me vibe?"

I wince at his choice of words. "Please, don't use that phrase."

"What, nice? Vibe?" He steals glances in between watching the road, and the right corner of his mouth curls up.

"Dolled up. You sound like you're a hundred and two years old." And just like Granny.

"Did you or did you not make an extra effort today?"

"Maybe." I stare at my knees and shrug.

"Well I'm so sorry but I'm trying to show you I noticed and it's nice, but from now on I won't make any commentary on your outward appearance. Don't want to be sexist or makeupist or whatever it is I am that's offending you."

I flop my hands on the seat and sigh. The tug in my heart becomes a squeeze, and it twists so it's hard to breathe. Why? I have no idea, but one of us in a bad mood is enough. I throw my head back and roll it to face him.

"You're right. I'm sorry. You're going out of your way to be nice and I'm being a jerk," I say. He raises a hand from the wheel in protest and opens his mouth to talk. I point to the steering wheel. "Put that hand back, Mister. Ten and two." He side-eyes me but lowers his hand. I nod and cross my arms, pressing my lips together like I'd just proven a quantum theory or something. "I accept your compliment as it stands, no -ists about it."

A low rumble escapes his lips as his shoulders and belly shake. "Gee thanks."

The squeeze on my heart lessens a bit, but my foot taps a mile a minute. I need to get to school. Like, I never thought I'd say those words, even to myself. And aside from pushing his foot harder on the gas, there's no way we're arriving any faster than Panayis drives. I need to relax.

"How about some music?"

He grimaces and inhales sharply. "That might be a tad difficult."

For the first time, I notice the entire dashboard. There are old, weather-cracked knobs and switches to control the vents in the center and on the sides and a gaping hole where the radio should be. "Bubba doesn't like music?"

"Someone jimmied Bubba's door and stole the stereo last year. I never replaced it. Didn't need it." He nods to his earbuds connected to his phone next to him. "But now that you're riding with me, I might think about it."

I try to smile, but the idea of daily rides of the Bubba-mobile makes me cringe instead.

"You don't have to, I have my own earbuds." I click on my phone to scroll through my songs.

"Yeah, but then we can't listen together. What do you have on there?" He tilts his head toward my phone.

"I don't know, probably nothing you'd like."

"Try me."

"It's not your typical stuff. Robin makes fun of me, calls it 'in my feelings crap.'" I air quote the last few words and roll my eyes.

"I'm sure it's not that bad." He shoots me a glance. "As long as it's not a bunch of kid TV stars- turned-pop-'artists,' we're good." He air quotes "artists" with one hand.

"Wow, didn't know you could be so judgmental." I pretend to write a note on my phone. "Note to self: never bring up child stars who make music to Judgment Boy driving Bubba."

"Wait, no…" His face pales and his eyes go wide. "I'm kidding. I mean, if you like that stuff, I mean music…" He swallows hard.

I bite my lips together and tuck my chin to hide my smile, but a snort escapes and now I'm going to die of embarrassment. I cover my face with my hands and groan.

"Guess the joke backfired," I say through my hands. Death is imminent. And my last breath will be in a truck named Bubba.

Panayis snickers and pats me on the shoulder. "That's what you get for trying to put one over on me."

"Yeah, well, at least I don't listen to country, like Jay."

He sits straighter, and his smile fades like an old poster beaten down by the sun. Great, I forgot they don't like each other. My eyebrows draw together, and I blow out a breath. Just because he doesn't like Jay doesn't mean I shouldn't be able to say his name without him acting all weird. Whatever, he's going to have to deal.

"What, you like country?" I ask.

He tilts his head and shrugs. "The newer stuff, yeah. I guess." His eyes focus straight ahead, and all the earlier levity sinks like the proverbial lead balloon.

"Cool." I bite my lip and peer out the window. He turns the wheel and houses begin to line the streets. We're close to school now, so it won't be much longer. I can escape this old truck and focus on what's…I mean, who's waiting for me when we arrive.

Chapter 7

Robin's car sits on the opposite side of the sparsely filled lot, and more than anything, I wish for one of those transporters from some science fiction movie so I don't have to tramp over there like some freshman. And in this heat, the film of dirt I'm wearing—courtesy of Bubba—is turning into paste as it mixes with sweat. Panayis couldn't even bother to drop me off. Okay, I didn't actually ask, but he should know that's where I'm headed.

"See you here after school?" he asks as I slam the passenger door. I tug my hair around my face, wishing for a huge hat and sunglasses to hide behind.

"No, but thanks. Robin's taking me." I wave a half-hearted thank you and avoid eye contact with the world's moodiest guy.

"Okay, see you back at the vineyard." He shuts his door and heads the opposite way.

On the other side of the lot, I duck into Robin's car, thankful hers is the only one in our section. The entire side where Jay parks is empty, but it's still early. My black t-shirt is fused to my body with the muddy glue, and the already thick air makes it hard to breathe.

I close the car door and adjust the air vent, letting it blow straight on to my face and into the arm holes of my shirt. Lowering the visor to check my hair, I await the barrage of questions she's about to throw at me.

"What was that?" She points to Panayis entering the cafeteria.

I lean against the seat. "New carpool, apparently." I shrug as she laser-stares through his back. "More convenient for Mom, I guess."

"Oh." She doesn't say much, but I hear what isn't said, and I'm grateful. "Anyway, never mind me. Just sitting here waiting for my best friend to tell me what happened."

"It's already hot. How is it already so hot?"

"Wearing black doesn't really help the situation." She pokes my shoulder. "Tell me what he said."

"But I love this shirt. And basically, all I own is black, so I'm screwed." I turn and face her. Robin's eyes bug.

"Wren, you put on eye liner. And lip gloss." She jumps up and down in her seat and makes tiny clapping hands. "Am I finally rubbing off on you?" Her smile slides into stern curiosity, and she rests her hand on my shoulder. "Are you feeling okay?"

"Is it still there? After this morning, I'm amazed."

"Why, what happened? Do I need to hunt down Old Truck Guy?" She cracks her knuckles and cranks her head, loosening her shoulders.

I smile and shake my head. "His name is Panayis, and no. Just a country road mishap is all."

"Okay, but why are you wearing makeup? You hate makeup?" She digs through her purse and seizes a sheer pink gloss. "You're right; you do need a touch up. Here."

"Seriously, I have no idea what I'm doing." She hands me the gloss and I do what I can to touch up what's left of my face. I hand back the tube and throw myself against the seat, sliding down as far as my jeans will let me. All my thoughts and insecurities trample over each other. She'll know what to think. What to do. "Like, what even happened? And does Jay know he's talking to me and not someone else way hotter and funnier?" I close my eyes and cover my face. Robin pushes my shoulder.

"Shut up. Now tell me everything."

I peek from behind open fingers. "You realize that makes no sense, right?"

She fake laughs and acts like she's about to throw something at me.

"Okay." I raise my hands in surrender. "Anyway, you saw the whole conversation last night. Do you think he's serious or just messing around?" A slow boil of panic rises from my stomach and up my throat.

Before she answers, a familiar rumble vibrates my seat. I close my eyes and swallow hard to keep my somersaulting heart in place. His truck swings into his usual parking spot, beats shaking all the windows. The music and vibrations vanish as he turns off the ignition. Peering into the visor mirror, I notice him jump out of the driver's seat.

He shakes out his pants, and then runs his hand through his hair a few times. I swallow to keep my insides from shooting out of my face.

"If you're going, I can go with you," Robin says.

Normally, I would've expected her to be by my side simply because she always has been when I needed her. But this time, I stumble on my typical auto-yes. She's been there for every first day of school, every clumsy social gathering. She's even been there when I've needed to escape my parents' relentless arguing. I've always depended on her to bail me out of awkward situations by doing the talking for both of us.

I want her to know how important she is to me and how grateful I am for her help. To understand that I need to try this on my own. It's the only way I can survive being a joke, if that's what I am.

"I'm good." I flip up the visor and open the door to the other heat wave across the aisle.

"Who are you and what have you done with my best friend?"

One by one, the spaces near Jay's fill up, and low greetings of head nods and "What's up" replace the morning quiet. As a group forms at the rear of his truck, I rest against the back of the car and catch his eye. He tilts his chin at me and winks. My heart and stomach trade places, and I lift my hand to wave.

Before I can raise my hand all the way, he spins and leaps on Amsel's back. Like a farmer tackling the prize hog. Not to be outdone, Amsel gallops around in circles, holding on to Jay's legs. My smile and my hand fade back into their resting positions, and my pace slows so I can drink in the whole scene from a distance.

Maggie, Sitta, and some other girl in a cheer uniform stop just before the bed of Jay's truck and watch the duo's antics. Amsel gallops around the girls, making whooping and braying noises. Jay's hand loops around his head like he's swinging a lasso. The girls scream and laugh. Jay jumps off of Amsel's back and loops his lasso arm around Cheer Uniform's shoulders. Amsel grabs Maggie's waist and whisks her up onto his back, galloping around Jay, and the girl he's got his arm around—who's left a boulder where my stomach used to be.

Robin sidles up beside me and nudges my arm with her shoulder. "C'mon, let's go inside. It's too hot out here anyway."

I shoot her a weak smile and force one foot in front of the other. The vice around my lungs make it hard to breathe, heat or no heat. We follow the noisy group to the school campus, as they make their way to the quad.

Maggie yells for Robin to hurry up and points to Sitta, who's sneaking glances at Robin every few seconds. Waves of sympathy radiate from her, and like radiation, they make me sick. I know she'd give up a flirt session for me, but I can't do that to her. It dawns on me I never asked about her and Sitta and how it's going.

Selfish and a joke. Cool.

Nodding to Robin to go ahead, I dig my ear-buds from my pocket.

"You sure?" she asks. I nod again and crank up whatever song can be loud enough to drown out the hitch in my breath as she jogs to meet Sitta and Maggie.

Robin's wearing a breezy white blouse over a blue tank top with khaki shorts and blue sandals. I tug at my own baggy t-shirt and silently curse my worn-out sneakers. Of course Jay isn't serious about talking to me, not the way I dress. Hell, even he dresses better than me. Suddenly the makeup I'd spent so much time on feels like a mask, heavy and plastic.

I slip into the bathroom after the last bell, knowing it'll be empty.

I close the door to the last stall and kneel in front of the toilet. Holding my hair back with one hand, I plunge the other one down my throat until there's nothing left. As I lean over the toilet, a wave of familiarity envelopes me. The bitter taste and sweet release of control.

*****

First period flies by, mainly because my brain is anywhere but. Second period, the teacher's voice buzzes in the background of my constant replay of Amsel's braying and Jay's whooping and giddyups. I stare out the window where birds fight over shady spots in the trees. Robin texts me in third period, promising a girl's mani/pedi later. Inspecting the chipped blue polish on my nails, I gratefully respond yes.

When the lunch bell rings, I meet up with her for our usual morning review in the bathroom. I complain about the heat, and Robin grumbles about how cold the classrooms are. Neither of us mention what happened before school. She goes to her usual table in the cafeteria, and I park myself in my usual corner of the library, happy to have the protection of my back against the wall, watching the crowd.

For the thousandth time, I replay the morning's scene, but this time it occurs to me I might be overreacting. At the same time, I can't help feeling like I'd done something wrong, and it bugs me that I can't figure out what it is. Jay and I aren't friends, not really. But he did ask me to drop by and see him in the morning.

No.

His actual words were to stop by his truck. Maybe that's what he says to everyone, and I'm reading more into it. Heat flames my cheeks, and I instinctively bring my hands to cover my mouth.

This is exactly why I avoid people. I close my eyes and shake my head, as if that can erase all these feelings. I dig through my backpack and find my book and aim to bury myself in empty words for the rest of the period.

When the bell rings, I pack up my books, hoping my thoughts will stay shut away for the rest of the day, too. On my way to pre-calc, I feel a tap on my right shoulder. I turn to my left expecting to see Robin. Instead, Jay's a bit behind me.

"Boo," he whispers as he leans in on his crooked grin.

That smile. All the feelings I thought I'd thrown up that morning rush into the center of my brain. My heart sends small electric shocks to my ankles and toes, and I flex them to make sure they won't fly out through my Converse.

"I'm terrified." My voice is steadier than I thought could be possible. "You got me."

"Oh I do, do I?"

You have no idea.

He struts ahead and turns so he's facing me as we head to class. "What shall I do with you, then?" he asks. I shrug, caught in the sparkle in his eyes. "Let's meet tomorrow at lunch. Where do you hang out?"

I nearly trip over my own feet.

"In the library. I read." *Shut up, Wren.*

"Cool. See you." Without waiting for a reply, he turns and jogs to his class. I stop in front of my own door, my mouth hanging half open.

"Um, something you want to tell me?" Robin appears at my side and stares toward the doorway Jay high-fives as he enters.

"I have no idea." I open my mouth to speak again, but then close it. For some reason, I can't tell her he asked me to meet him. *Tomorrow. In the library!* Just in case it turns to crap like this morning. And I'd rather not see her pity face again. Plus, I know she can't afford the amount of mani/pedi dates I'd need if that happens again.

We sit, and my mind drifts to my corner of the library. I try to envision Jay and I chatting non-stop and being shushed by the librarian and not caring. Me playfully hitting his arm as I laugh at his jokes and him sneaking a touch here and there, trying to hold my hand.

My phone vibrates in my pocket.

What did he say?

Robin stares as I read her text. Who am I kidding? I need my best friend. I text back.

> *Dude. Major planning sesh after school. You're taking me home.*

*Only if you never say sesh
again.* 😒

I exhale and stow my phone under my leg in case the teacher roams the aisles. Biting my lip, I do a different math problem and count the minutes until tomorrow's lunch.

*****

> *Are you sure about the shorts?*

Yes.

> *I'm not sure about them.*

You tried on a thousand things.

> *But there's probably something better.*

Wren.

> *Robin.*

Then wear something else.

Like what?

*Wear the shorts. They look good
on you. How much weight have
you lost anyway? I keep meaning to ask you.*

I don't know. I don't really count.

Exactly 14 and a half pounds, but if I tell her that, she'll figure out how much I weighed before. Better not risk it.

What about the top? It feels…not me.

*Why did we spend all afternoon at the mall
if you're not even going to wear what you bought.*

I'm fickle?

*Then wear one of your death-rager
band shirts. He'll recognize you better
anyway.*

Ha. Ha.

*You can do this. Just be yourself.
Except maybe don't sarcasm too much.
He's not big on wit.*

Wow, that's nice.

I just mean he's into…not words.

You mean he's into Cheer Uniform?

You mean Ashley? She's nice,
and it's not her fault.

I know. But let me be petty about this.
It's literally the only time I get to be
petty about another girl.

I worry.

You and the other voices.

Good night, Strange Child.

Fine.
If you need anything, I'll be sitting up,
counting the hours until tomorrow.
Me and the clock.

I can't see this. I shut off my
phone already.

Sigh, good night.

Chapter 8

The next day, I jump out of my seat before the lunch bell finishes ringing. Halfway to the library, I remember that I need to meet Robin in the bathroom. I make a quick u-turn, my face burning with anticipation of being alone with Jay at lunch and the memory of him parading through the parking lot with his arm around Cheer Uniform…I mean Ashley. Whatever, I like my name for her better. I check the time and heave a loud sigh as I push through the door.

Robin's at her usual place in front of the mirror, smoothing back her hair and complaining that it's taking an eternity for it to grow out. I mutter a few uh-huhs, but my tapping foot against one of the pipes gives away my true thoughts.

"What's wrong with you?" she asks. "You're all jumpy." She turns to me and tilts her head. "You nervous?"

"Not."

Robin stares at my foot.

"Maybe."

She purses her lips and raises her eyebrows like she does when she sees a puppy or other cute furry thing, which annoys me because, hello, not a puppy. She reaches out her arms. "Need an encouragement hug?"

"Hi, my name is Wren and I hate touchy feely. How ya doing?" I hold out my hand for her to shake, but she rolls her eyes and goes back to the mirror and her hair.

"Suit yourself."

The door swings open and Sitta glides through, her thin frame and long ponytail perfectly backlit by the outside light. I tug at the bottom of my shorts, willing them to grow another inch or two.

"Thought you'd be in here." Sitta traipses past me, spins, and leans her back against the stall divider. She nods hello to me and smiles at Robin, whose freckles disappear into a rosy blush.

"Trying to encourage Wren to relax about her lunch date." Her eyes shift from me to Sitta. "Hi." A weird grin I've never seen before spreads across her face. She extends her hand and Sitta takes it in her own and squeezes it. Then they just stay like that, grinning and staring. Suddenly, this bathroom is too small for three people.

"Yeah, so I'm going to go," I say.

Robin snaps out of her trance and gives me a once over. "Cute status achieved. Remember, you'll be on your turf. Books give you super strength, right?"

"Sure." I can't help but grin at the image of sucking power from bound paper.

"I like your top." Sitta stands next to Robin as she laces their fingers together. Robin's eyes go big for a second, then her whole face contorts from surprise. I'm pretty sure I'm reflecting the same thing right back.

"Thanks." I consider the two of them standing side by side all blushing and cute. I'm happy for Robin, but it feels weird to share her with someone else. Especially in our place. Yeah, it's a high school bathroom, but it's *our* high school bathroom. I swallow and force a smile.

"You guys have fun, too." On my way out the door, I add, "Don't do anything I wouldn't do."

Giggles follow me out the door.

*****

The library is empty. By empty, I mean no Jay.

I sit in my usual spot and dig out my book with shaky hands. I force myself to inhale a long breath to slow my pounding heart. I read and reread the same paragraph about fifty times, glancing at the turnstile in front of the desk every other word. I do my best to calm down so as not be a sweaty mess of frizzy hair and tapping feet when he finally shows up.

I adjust myself in the chair. The shorts creep up my legs and feel like a tourniquet around my thighs. I fluff my shirt over my stomach and attempt to tug the shorts farther down my legs without making a scene. I dig a carrot stick from my lunch bag and nibble, counting the number of chews before I force myself to swallow. Beached Whale Girl really wants to go back to the bathroom to ease the pressure mounting from the butterflies, but I stay in my seat, shoulders relaxed and forehead smooth—what Skinny V-neck girl would do.

I glance at the chair and table across the room. The light's better there. I'm halfway to it when I stop and eye my original place. The view of the door's better back there, which means he'll be able to see me. Lowering myself back into my usual chair, I reopen my book and force my eyes to stay on the page instead of shooting to the turnstiles every time summer heat blows through the open doorway.

"Hey," a voice says from behind. All my energy's in the front of the room, so I jump a little. "Oh, sorry." Panayis turns a chair backwards and straddles it, facing me.

"Oh, hey." A lump forms in the back of my throat, but I manage to smile. "It's okay." The outside heat sweeps over me, and Jay slides through the turnstile. My heart pounds, hot crimson creeps up my neck and circles my ears. "I'm just reading."

"Uh huh. You haven't turned the page the entire time you've been sitting here. I've seen you plow through pages faster than a Greek kid devours a cheeseburger on Easter."

I stare blankly.

"You know, Lent? No meat for forty days? Never mind." He rolls his eyes and nods to the book. "What part are you on?"

Jay's eyes land on mine. I'm a deer in headlights, and my whole life is passing before my eyes. He nods to me, and then sees Panayis. His smile fades, and he stops dead in his tracks.

And we have impact.

His brows furrow only for a second, but it's long enough to shoot a hole through my heart. He scans the room again, eyes darting to the faces at the tables and by the stacks, his hand wringing at his waist. He points to his watch and mouths he'll see me later. Then, like a hit-and-run, he slides through the turnstile and out of sight.

So much for the romantic meeting in the corner of the library. So much for my juicy tell-all with Robin in pre-calc. So much for my social life. Panayis stops talking and stares at me, waiting for an answer.

"I'm sorry, what did you ask?" I choke on the last word like it's the last one I'll ever utter.

"I asked what part of Gatsby you were on."

"Oh. Well…" I glance at the page, because I'd forgotten the book completely. "Um, this is the part where Nick invites Daisy over to meet Gatsby, but she doesn't know he'll be there."

"Right, where he knocks over the clock and breaks it. Time stops and all that. Great part."

"Sure, great part." So much for sucking strength from stories. Jay left, and my time went on without me, moving from the hopeful future to the bitter past, leaving me with no memory to savor.

I manage a small smile and nod, the color draining from my face as fast as it rose. His fingers drum a soft beat waiting for me to continue. When I don't, he clears his throat and stands, straddling the chair.

"Well, you said to say hi the next time I saw you at school, so…" His voice becomes as distant as my thoughts.

I raise my eyebrows in silent response. He stands there all tall and taking up space. Space where Jay should be right now, not some ride-share guy who has the worst timing of anyone on the planet. Seriously, his lack of timing should be studied. My foot taps and my leg shakes, but I don't care. If I don't move, I'll explode.

"Anyway, I'll leave you to it. Lunch is about over anyway." He turns the chair around and tucks it under the table. "See you at the vineyard."

I wave a quick turn of my hand and press my lips together as I gather my book bag. *Some lunch date that turned out to be.*

My phone vibrates in my pocket.

Trying to make me jealous haha

I clutch my phone to my chest and let out a huge breath. It may not have gone the way I wanted, but at least he's still texting me. My first instinct is to text Robin, but I remember her Sitta-shaped heart eyes as I left the bathroom and decide it's probably best not to bug her. I can tell her in class.

No haha…sorry, he just showed up. I didn't mean for that to happen.

I didnt know u guys were friends

We aren't, really. Just saying hi.

Kk we can try meet up another time

Yeah, I'd like that. Sorry again.

I shove my phone in my pocket, unsure of the feelings swirling inside me. I don't know why, but I feel like I messed up somehow. Like Jay's leaving is my fault. And poor Panayis. He doesn't deserve to be thrown under the friend-zone bus. But I did it anyway.

I'm turning into one of those girls I make fun of. The suckiest part is I don't care. Maybe I judged them too harshly before. This dating thing is way harder than I thought.

I wave to the librarian at the door and make a mental note to ask Robin for clothing help next period. Beached Whale Girl is not going to ruin this again. There has to be a Mini V-Neck Girl in me somewhere.

My phone vibrates.

I have a feeling you're worth the wait.

Outside the library, I throw my sandwich and the rest of the carrots in the trash and head to the bathroom to unswallow any calories I've consumed.

Chapter 9

FatKat: *Anyone here?*

Girl: I am

Cherry: Hey

FatKat: *Do you guys purge, because I have a question?*

Cherry: What is it?

FatKat: *I have a spot on my cheek, it's red and kind of bruise-ish. I'm not really into makeup but I need to cover it because...gross.*

Cherry: You probably burst a blood vessel. Maybe don't throw up so hard?

FatKat: *I didn't know you could do that.*

Cherry: Yeah it's not like the movies

Girl: Just get a thicker concealer. There's a ton of makeup tutorials on YouTube that show you how to apply it

FatKat: *Wow, thanks. The more you know, I guess. Ooh gotta go.*

Cherry: Peace

*****

I close my laptop as Granny cracks open my door. Her outside overalls and long-sleeved shirt are replaced with an old-fashioned, cotton house dress—something I'm not entirely comfortable with. To me, Granny has always been more muck boots and sunhats than sleeveless sundresses.

69

"What are you doing all cooped up on a Saturday afternoon? Seems a waste of a sunny day." She opens the door all the way and stares into the closet. "Do you have enough room in here? I can probably move some of this stuff out."

"It's fine."

"Nonsense. A girl needs room to fluff out all those pretty clothes." She sits on my bed, forcing me to scoot over.

"I don't really have that much—just shirts and jeans."

"Didn't you and Robin just go to the mall? I swear I saw you dragging in a big bag of something." She reaches for my leg and squeezes. "You're going to need a whole new wardrobe if you lose any more weight."

My heart thumps two beats at once. I'm not sure if I'm happy she noticed or freaked out, because I feel the same as I always have. I suck in my stomach out of habit.

"Granny, I…"

"What's that on your cheek?" She points to the spot I'd been asking about online, and I swallow hard. My hand shoots up to cover it.

"I don't know. I woke up and it was there." I smile and shrug, hoping I appear way more nonchalant than I feel. I'm not even sure broken blood vessels heal. I glance at my laptop, wishing I could Google it.

"You are such a pretty girl. And smart, too. You can do anything in the world that you want, you know that?" She smiles and pats my leg. "Back in the Stone Age, we girls didn't have as many options as you and yours do. I hate to see you waste all that opportunity sitting up here alone in this room."

"I'm doing research." I pat my laptop. "For an assignment."

She pushes herself up with her arms and straightens slowly, groaning as she moves to the door. "These bones don't move as quick as they used to." She turns to me, mischief reflecting in her eyes. "Say, why don't you take Fengari outside. He needs to run around a bit, and he's too little yet to go by himself. What do you say?" She's smiling, but she isn't asking. Not really.

"Sure, give me a few minutes to finish up and put on my shoes."

She's already out the door, her hand waving as she starts down the stairs. From the living room, Mom's voice floats to my room.

"She's fine up there. That's what teenagers do these days. She's probably talking to her friends on her computer."

"Nonsense. That girl spends way too much time alone. She needs to be around people and have some responsibility."

I wiggle my foot into my Converse. It's bad enough I have to be outside with the bugs and the pollen, no way I'm going without full foot protection. Downstairs, the couch creaks and heels clack on the wooden floor into the kitchen.

"Between the move and…everything, Wren's dealing with enough. She doesn't need to care for your dog, too. Maybe you shouldn't have gotten another one if—"

"You watch your tone with me. You may be grown enough to be a mother, but you're back under my roof now. That girl needs help, and you're too busy running around to see it. Now if you don't like what I have to say, do something about it."

I stop halfway down the steps and sit, and wait for them to finish bickering. They mix together about as well as homemade salad dressing. But if Granny's oil and Mom is vinegar, what am I?

The hallway is filled with pictures of versions of Mom. At the bottom of the stairs, she poses as a baby, clapping her hands and staring at them. Granny said they had to put scotch tape on the palms of her hands to play with so she wouldn't cry. The pictures climbing the steps act as a Mom timeline—baby at the bottom and a blushing bride at the top. In the middle, where I'm sitting, Mom is a teenager, permed hair and big bangs. Long nails and flawless skin. Thin arms and flat stomach.

She told me once she struggled with how she saw herself. How she always felt awkward when people stared at her, like they were judging how she shook the floor when she took a step. Just one glimpse and I can tell no one stared at her because furniture shook as she moved.

The door slams and, after a minute, a car starts outside. I work my way through the living room and into the kitchen. Granny is at the sink, scrubbing some pot, muttering under her breath. Knowing better than to say anything, I creep out the same door as Mom, scooping Fengari from his pen on my way.

I sit on the swing under the tree as the puppy pads around on oversized paws and sniffs out a stick. He drags it to a shady spot and begins to chew.

Panayis ambles toward the house from the vineyard, shovel in gloved hand. A vice squeezes my chest as he nears. I search for a quick getaway, but there's nowhere to go. It's bad enough I have to make small talk with him on the way to school.

I know it's not his fault Jay didn't stick around that day in the library, and I'm the one who told him to say hello when he sees me, but I can't help being a little pissed at him. I'd finally worked up the nerve to be alone with Jay, new outfit and all. And there's the tiniest of chances we're on our way to becoming something other than people who have the same friends.

Seeing him exit the library once he'd seen Panayis sitting at my table proved I'd never be anything other than the awkward side-kick to my popular best friend. I *am* the equivalent of a movie extra— walk-on for life. Except now that I've had the chance to audition for the lead role, being in the background isn't as appealing as it used to be.

"Hey," Panayis says.

"Hey." I stare at my shoes.

He leans over the fence that separates the driveway and the back lawn. He smiles at Fengari whittling down his stick.

"Should he be chewing on that? I mean, are tree branches healthy for dogs?" He's all smiles, and that makes me want to throw something at his face. How can he be so happy all the time?

"I don't know, Panayis, I left my *How to Raise a Puppy* book in the house." I immediately want to retract my words, but I'm my mother's daughter. I raise my chin and match his gaze, heart pounding a little too hard. He literally steps backward.

"Okay, well, have a good day then."

My throat closes, and I'm pretty sure I'm going to choke on my own stupidity. Mom left in a huff after fighting with her own. Why is that my goal? I deflate into a slump.

"Don't… I'm sorry, I'm just not having a great day, and now I have to be out here to babysit the dog and I guess I'm even a failure at that." I push the swing backward as if I could move farther away from my own awkwardness.

He swings the gate open and the dog wags his tail at the sight of his friend. As Panayis kneels to pet him, Fengari rolls over, stick in mouth, and stretches out for a belly rub, clearly showing even he has more game than me.

Not that I need game in this situation. Like I care what some random guy thinks.

"Do you want to talk about it?" Panayis glances up as he scratches dog belly.

That day in the library, Jay's face changed when he saw me talking to Panayis. Part of me is excited I have the power to make anyone's face make that expression by talking to another guy. Maybe there's a speck of something inside of me that promises I can be more like the girls Jay usually hangs around with.

Skinny V-Neck Girl's voice is there, but Beached Whale Girl overpowers it.

Don't be stupid. Guys like Jay don't waste their time on girls like you. Guys like Jay may ask to borrow a pencil or have their paper handed in for biology class, but they don't meet girls like you in the library.

Panayis kneels in front of me, trying to get Fengari to run after the stick. A wave of guilt washes over me like a lukewarm bath.

"Nah," I say. "No therapy couch needed today. Just the shock of starting junior year and having to move here is all. I just want to go back to my own house, you know?"

He stands and brushes the dirt from his knees. "Yeah, I get it. I felt like that when my mom died. Even though everything seemed all right, I really wanted it all to go back to normal."

The world shifts a little and my eyes widen. The wash of guilt becomes a tidal wave, and heat pricks my neck and cheeks. "Oh. I didn't know about your mom. I'm sorry." My breath catches on the last word.

"Why do people always say they're sorry?" His lips slide into a flat smile. "It's not like anyone can do anything about it."

I don't really know what to say, so I stare at the green, appearing and disappearing under the swing. The breeze rustles the leaves above us, and Fengari barks at the blowing grass hiding his stick.

"I didn't mean to kill the conversation," he says. "I just want you to know that I understand how you feel." His usual bright hazel eyes are watery, reminding me of a summer dip in a secret lake.

"You're right. Saying sorry is kind of stupid." I laugh under my breath. "I just wanted…" I sigh. "I don't know what I wanted. I guess to say it's not fair she died." He smiles but says nothing. "When did she?"

He sits on the ground in front of the swing, and Fengari trots over and plops on Panayis's folded leg. "When I was eleven. Happened kind of fast. One day she's making kourolakia and the next day she's not." He runs his hand over the grass.

"What's kourolakia?"

"It's a Greek cookie. My mom used to make the best." He smiles as if wrapped in the memory. "I used to help her in the kitchen." Pulling at the grass, he cocks his head sideways and squints, eyes against the sun. "I could show you how to make them sometime."

I close my eyes, afraid to breathe in case the imaginary smell of cookies adds pounds. Sound crashes in my ears like waves on the beach, and my chest heaves as I push air out of my lungs.

"If you want, I mean." His voice sounds different, far away. I suck in a breath and blow it out, trying to slow my heart and not seem like a freak who can't handle a simple conversation about a cookie. He lays his hand on my leg, and it's everything I can do not to jump off the swing and run away. "You okay? We don't have to. It's just an idea."

But this isn't a simple conversation. His mom died, and there's so much love and hurt and kindness in his smile. My own mother disappears in her leased Jetta when things spin out, and I fall apart and take it out on everyone within a ten-mile radius. I open my eyes, try to conjure a smile not seen in a fun house mirror and give him the answer he deserves.

"No, that sounds fun. I'm always up to learn something new. Of course, with minimal effort and a lot of complaining. And if I don't set anything on fire."

"I'm sure you'll be fine. I can supervise—and keep an extinguisher nearby, just in case." His smile changes and it's not as lonely. My breathing returns to normal. He leans on his elbows, shifting out of the light toward the shade of the tree branches. The formality he usually wears melts under the late summer sun.

"Thanks." I fake kick at his leg as I swing toward him.

He stares at the grass. "I do most of the cooking at home now since my dad works so much around the vineyard. I like it. Makes me feel closer to my mom." He shifts his gaze toward me, eyes searching mine. "Is that weird?"

"No, I don't think so. It's a nice way to remember her." My own mother hasn't cooked once since she and Dad split. At least Granny knows where the stove is, even if she does fry everything or coat it in sugar. I shiver.

The afternoon passes as Panayis plays with the puppy and I supervise from my spot on the swing. A cuckoo clock chimes in my pocket, jolting me out of my thoughts. Panayis stands straight, eyes wide, and Fengari yips at his hand, which holds his stick.

"My ringtone. I guess it's a little loud." My cheeks heat as I reach for my phone.

A text from Jay.

What ya doin'?

Panayis and Fengari fade into the background, and my heartbeat pounds in my ears like drums. I check the time and I'm shocked to see how much has gone by. I start to type but then delete it. I can't tell him the truth, that I'm having fun with his sworn enemy as he plays with Granny's dog. That it's been an hour and it feels like it's been fifteen minutes. I can't risk him thinking something is going on with Panayis when it's harmless hanging out.

Nothing. Just
hanging out with
my dog lol. You?

Found out I gotta work for my
dad next week. Maybe you could
keep me company lol?

I blink a few times to make sure my vision's working. I'm not exactly sure what keeping company means, but no one wants an awkward person asking stupid questions. I bite my lip.

Why is this so hard?

My eyes shift to Panayis. With him, everything is so natural. I don't have to think about anything. Well, except cookies, but I can plan around those. I sit straighter and clench my jaw. I just need to get to know Jay better—spend some actual time talking to him.

Sure, that'd be great.

Cool. Hey, a bunch of us are going to
the Grape Festival. Are you going?

I feel myself turn about a hundred different shades of purple and am pretty sure I'm going to reenact the end of that movie where the superhero baby explodes into a flaming monster. This is it. Okay, it's not the official Ferris wheel date I'd written about in my journal, but it almost is. And could be.

I type *I'll see you then* but immediately erase it. I replace it with the *cool* emoji. Can't seem too eager, even though I'm already willing the sun to go down and time to speed up.

"Did you win the lottery or something?" Panayis turns so his back is to me. With a stick in hand, he coaxes Fengari to attack it. As he jumps, Panayis tosses it toward the middle of the lawn. Fengari leaps after the stick, rolling over it as he clamps down.

I feel you, dog. "What? Why do you ask that?"

"You're smiling ear to ear."

And we're back to old people speak.

"Ear to ear? Really?" I stand and stretch, stiff from sitting on the wood plank for so long. He shrugs. "A friend asked to get together."

"A friend, huh? I see." His tone darkens.

I glance toward the house and make a point of visibly checking the time on my phone.

"Yeah. Well, I'm going to go and see when dinner will be ready. I'll probably be forced to set the table or something, but I'll risk it." I roll my eyes at the thought.

"And I should finish up with that shovel before it gets too late." He points to the forgotten tool leaning against the fence. "See you later, Wren." He smiles, and the corners of his eyes crinkle in a way that make the back of my neck hot.

Before I can think too much about it, I shove off whatever that was as quickly as it comes. I wave a goodbye over my shoulder and head toward the house. No time for distractions if the festival is only a week away. If I want to be ready for my potential Ferris wheel ride, I have to focus on dropping whatever poundage I can manage. I can't afford to worry about why Panayis is so easy to talk to or why time flies when I'm with him.

This is the time to focus on channeling Skinny V-neck girl.

And for that, I need makeup. And an outfit not black and t-shirt-ish to pick out. Once I'm on the porch, I text Robin.

> *Cancel whatever you're doing tomorrow*
> *after school… I have news.*

Chapter 10

After four rejected outfits, I settle on the first one Robin picked out. Ignoring her smug expression as I climb into her backseat, I try not to seem surprised Sitta's riding shotgun. Eyes glued to her phone, she throws a half-hearted wave in my direction and keeps scrolling. As if Robin can read my mind, she glances in her mirror and meets my eyes.

"I picked up Sitta first. Didn't think you'd mind." She wears a new expression, something between pleading and bliss. A flicker of unease sparks in my core, but I shrug it off. Just because I've never had to share Robin before doesn't mean I shouldn't try.

"Makes sense. I mean, she lives on the way, right?" I stare out the window at the endless rows of yellowing grape leaves as Robin nods. "And I'm way out here in Isolation-ville. How many times did you have to fill your gas tank to make it this far?"

Robin shakes her head as she accelerates onto the paved road and leans toward Sitta the way someone does when they're telling a secret. "She's a tad dramatic, but I'm guessing you figured that out."

"Hey. Right here?" I point to myself but neither of them notices. They're too busy shooting heart eyes at each other. I mutter under my breath. "That's cool. Okay."

Robin turns on some pop station and I glower at her. When she notices, I raise my eyebrows all innocent and she mouths, "Please." I huff through my nose and focus on my own phone, rummaging through my most recent playlist. If I can't listen to it, I can at least visit the titles. For the rest of the ride, an awkward silence fills the space in between the vibrant beats and shimmery squeals blaring through the speakers.

This sharing my best friend thing may need practice.

Robin nods to the parking lot attendant and maneuvers her car into the spot he points to with his orange flag. We unfold out of the car and make the necessary wardrobe adjustments after the long ride. The outfit Robin chose for me is a blue, frilly sleeveless blouse that ties in the front and a pair of faded jean shorts. I thought they fit all right in my room, but now that I'm standing next to two girls who are a million times smaller and fresher than me, I can't help wishing for more fabric. I'm thankful I wore my Converse—at least my feet will be comfortable.

"Stop fidgeting, you're fine." Robin narrows her eyes in my direction as I adjust the knot of material barely covering my belly. Throwing my purse strap over my shoulder, I pay careful attention to how my arms rest against my sides so they're not too wide, and try to keep my thighs from pressing together too hard.

Music from three different spots blare and blend together at the gates, and the enticing aroma of fair food beckons everyone inside. Robin and Sitta match strides in front of me, holding hands as they saunter toward the entrance.

"Guys, we need to buy tickets first." I point to the booth beside the turnstiles and security check. Robin glances at Sitta then at me with the same expression she makes when her mom makes liver and onions for dinner. Like liver, this can't be good.

"Oh, um, Sitta already bought us our tickets."

"Cool." I shove the wallet I'd been digging out back into my purse and turn toward where they're standing. Robin's liver and onion look spreads and crinkles her forehead.

"I mean, she bought our tickets." She moves her pointed finger between the two of them. "We can wait here." She swallows and her expression turns the smile she's attempting into a grimace. That familiar feeling of being too big, too conspicuous envelops me like an old winter coat.

"Oh, right, of course." I try to laugh but it comes out a strangled breath. When it's just me and Robin, it's easy because we know exactly how we fit together. I always buy the bigger size fries because, even though she says she won't want any, she sneaks them off my tray. And she knows what mood I'm in by which band I wear on my t-shirt. But now, there's someone else standing where I should be and everything's off.

Robin should be with who she likes. I'm just not so sure where that leaves me. Wait, yes, I do. Standing in line by myself to buy tickets. There is an upside, though—totally saving money on fries from now on. Like I eat them, anyway.

Digging my wallet out, I shuffle to the line and stand behind some greasy guy wearing a tank top two sizes too small. I keep my eyes on my shoes and my arms crossed around my midsection the entire time. Over the music, I hear a familiar voice whooping and shouting.

Jay and Amsel are standing by one of the bandstands, cheering on the girls tap dancing for scholarships and pleading for world peace as contestants for the next Miss Lodi Grape.

Pageants? 1985 called and wants their misogyny back. At least name it something someone would be proud to wear on a banner in public.

Regardless of what my brain thinks, my body stands straighter, and I readjust arms and thighs for minimum spaceage. I shoot a glance to Robin, but she's already noticed and sending me secret pointy hand gestures. Something warm and familiar melts away the winter coat feeling.

We may be entering this strange world of dating, but some things will forever be the same.

Once inside the gates, we wave to the boys as we pass them and roam through the maze of sausage vendors and hot tub sale booths toward the rides. Well, Robin and Sitta wave. I sort of flap my arm like a broken wing and laugh, except instead of the cute giggle I'm anticipating, this throaty breath of a 30-year smoker coughs its way out.

By some miracle, Jay smiles and waves back. I bite my lip in case any other weird sounds have plans of escaping and catch up to the girls. As we pass the Ferris wheel, Robin elbows me and nods, grinning and bobbing her eyebrows. I roll my eyes, but my heart speeds up at the thought that tonight could be the night my middle school self's dream comes true.

*****

Omg what if he ignores me?

He won't.

We've been here ten minutes.

Exactly. ONLY ten mins
Give him a chance to find us.

Why didn't we just talk
to them earlier?

Idk, these are the rules. And also,
I'm literally standing right next to
you. There's this magical device called
your mouth you can use to communicate with.

I stare at Robin with my lips pressed together and eyebrows raised, then jerk my head toward Sitta, who's blissfully unaware of this whole conversation. Robin mimics my expression and does this tiny shrug, daring me to argue. I sigh and put away my phone.

We're in line for one of the tamer rides—the Whirl-A-Car, where you spin your car in circles while the whole track moves around. The biggest person usually sits in the inside seat for maximum spin potential, so I stand at the front of our group. When it's time to climb on, Sitta steps in front of me, dragging Robin behind her.

"Um, I usually sit on the inside."

"I'll crush you. Sit by Robin." Sitta climbs in and Robin follows like the world didn't just shift off its axis.

"You going or what?" Some carny guy's barking at me from the control box. I fold myself into the seat and Robin lowers the bar over our legs. I scoot as far away from her as I can, feet planted firmly in opposition to crushing my life-long friend. I can see the headlines now: Teen Sweethearts Crushed by Deadly Girl Claiming to be Best Friend.

The ride starts, and Sitta's already cranking the wheel. I grind my feet harder into the car's floor, holding my breath I won't slide over. I'm clutching the bar, expecting a fight to the death, but instead of sliding, I'm staying put. I keep my eyes shut the whole time, not wanting to risk this gravitational miracle. When it's over, Robin and Sitta slide out, but not before eyeballing me up and down.

"That was different," Robin says. "You feeling okay?"

Every time I bring up my weight, she gets weird and shuts down. Since this is kind of a big night for us both, I decide not to say much. "Yeah, just not used to being on the outside. Kind of freaked me out."

She side-eyes me like she doesn't totally buy it but stays quiet, probably for the same reason I am. Then she's all elbows in my ribs, tapping me on the shoulder.

"What is your deal?" I step to the side as she points to the game booth across from the ride's exit. Jay's leaning against the stand, one ankle crossing over the other and holding a stick topped with a huge pile of pink cotton candy. I bite down on a smile, mostly sure the vibrations running through my body aren't left over from the ride.

He searches the crowd, and when he sees us, his face brightens. He waves as he makes his way toward us. Robin and Sitta keep going, but my legs refuse to move like they're encased in cement. My breath quickens and my nostrils flare, searching for oxygen to reach my brain. And then he's in front of me, perfect dimples framing his perfect smile.

Dear Powers That Be, please let me not say something stupid.

"Hey," he says.

I nod and clutch my hands together. *Dear Powers That Be, please let me say something.* I'm not panicking because Robin'll be chiming in any second. Except she doesn't. My eyes search our surroundings and settle on her on the other side of the booth, giggling and waving.

I shift my weight from one foot to the other, pursing my lips together.

"This is for you." He pushes the pink cloud toward me, and its sweet, sticky aroma makes my mouth water. I swallow and breathe through my mouth. Awesome, now I'm a mouth breather. "Can't go to the carnival and not have cotton candy."

"Festival, not carnival." Oh good, my voice decides to show up, and it wants to play a round of etymology. Can I die now?

"What?" He gives a little laugh and rustles his hair with his free hand. My body's in full fight or flight mode and he's standing there offering me candy. With a concerted breath, my hand awkwardly grips his before grasping the stick.

"Oh, nothing, it's stupid. Thanks for this." Cotton candy isn't that many calories, but the sugar in one serving's like two days-worth. There's no way I'm putting any of this in my body, but I'm not sure how I can make that work without seeming ungrateful. Especially since I've made such a positive impression so far.

"No, I'm interested. What's the difference?"

I give him an "are you serious" stare.

He nods. "Really."

"Well, carnival roughly means a party to store meat, not that it's an actual party—more like a gathering, and festival has more to do with the whole feast. This one's all about the grapes, so no meat. Hence festival." I squeeze my eyes shut hoping the word vomit stops and something large will knock me in the head so I can contract some sort of short-term amnesia. "Thanks for the cotton candy. See you later."

"Wait, what? I'm not going anywhere."

I open one eye. "You're not?"

"Nah, smart girls are kind of hot." He smirks, sending a mix of hope and fireworks through my veins.

"What is?" I open the other eye.

"I've never heard a girl talk about a meat party before."

My lips curve into a shy grin. "That would be your take away."

"I like meat, what can I say?" He smacks himself on the forehead. "That didn't come out right."

"I know what you mean." I push his arm and chew on my lip. His ears turn pink at the tips as he studies the sky, shaking his head. For whatever reason, his awkwardness sets me at ease. I guess I'm not the only one who says stupid things when they're nervous. I'm about to say something about checking out the rest of the festival together when Amsel throws his tree-trunk arm around Jay's neck, the rest of the group piling around us.

"Ooh, cotton candy!" Robin grabs a huge chunk and shoves it into her mouth.

"Hey, ask first." Even though I'm mostly grateful I have less caloric worries, I turn away, protecting the cotton candy from her thief hands. Amsel reaches over Jay's back and grabs another handful.

"Thanks." He tosses a grin at me and releases Jay from whatever wrestling move he's performing. He offers a piece of his loot to Maggie, the obligatory girlfriend percentage of whatever he drags back to his cave. "What're we doing next?"

Maggie jumps up and down as she swallows her bite. "Let's go on the Ferris wheel!"

"Great idea!" Robin smiles at me and waggles her eyebrows. I close my eyes and try not to die on the spot. When I decide death hasn't come for me, I open them. She's grinning from ear to ear. Shaking my head so only she notices, she shrugs, grabs Sitta's hand and inches toward the line.

I'm well aware this Ferris wheel fantasy is sort of stupid—a childhood dream date before I knew what high school was really like. And the only reason the idea's hung around this long is because Robin mercilessly enjoys torturing me with my pre-teen journal's flowery language and gaudy descriptions. But, as ridiculous as it is, imagining being stranded at the top, the lights of the entire festival on display—with Jay and his perfectly placed dimples—makes my entire body tingle.

I turn to him and shrug as casually as possible. "Want to?"

Instead of agreeing like I hoped, he checks his watch and sucks in a breath through gritted teeth. "I have to put my goat to bed before they close that part of the fair…festival." He presses his lips into a humiliating grin. A gigantic lump forms in the back of my throat. I nod over and over. I should've known this would happen.

"Sure, whatever works." My voice is 50-decibels higher than usual, and I'm blinking way faster than any non-alien needs to.

"Raincheck?"

Not risking another voice-crackage, I nod emphatically and tap his shoulder with a sideways fist. Making my escape, I shoot him a double thumbs-up, well three if you count the half-eaten cotton candy. He waves, a weird expression on his face.

I've endured years of Robin's teasing and wasted hours dreaming of this moment, never really expecting anything to come of it. After all, girls like me don't score dates like that. Beached Whale Girl playing dress up in Skinny V-neck's clothes. That one moment I let down my guard. Allowing hope to enter through the cracks—who am I kidding? This isn't even a date. He probably bought the cotton candy for himself and changed his mind.

I wrap my arms around my middle, tears threatening to release a tempest on my face. The best thing I can do is forget this night ever happened. I turn and start my search for the booth selling drive-thru lobotomies with a side of amnesia.

Chapter 11

Head down, I zoom by the line everyone's in. Robin calls my name, but I only move faster, hunched over, willing any kind of invisible powers to kick in. My phone buzzes in my back pocket, but I ignore that, too. Let her have her fun.

One of us should snag the kiss at the top.

Leaving the rides and games behind, I trash the cotton candy and wipe at the hot tears as fast as they come. The fact I'm crying at all makes me angry, and with that, more tears. Mom is the one who weighs her self-worth with dates, not me.

I wind in and out of cranky toddlers and tired moms and half-wasted dads, not caring where I end up. Face painting, corn-hole, and tired patrons sitting at the footsy-wootsy massage stations used to be charming. Now all they are is a labyrinth of reminders that I should've burned that journal entry a long time ago.

I pass booths selling everything from plastic storage to horse vitamins. The air is crisper as the sun goes down, and a half moon keeps watch. Gangly freshmen wave awkward hellos to each other and then scurry off to find reinforcements. The scent of hay mixes with cigarette smoke while music from one venue bleeds into the next.

I make a right turn and come face to face with the food court. Sweet French fry grease, stale beer and mustard swirls in the air. Billows of barbeque smoke float from the local sausage factory's grill, mesmerizing hungry fair-goers. I breathe in what can only be described as what the gods receive at Camp Half-blood's meal times.

My mouth waters, my body begs for the numbing comfort chewing provides. The stand on my right has no line. I rush to the counter, digging money from my wallet.

"Can I help you?" It's one of the FFA kids that sits at Jay's table. "Hey, I know you, right?"

I force a watery smile. I croak out "Wrong booth" and flee down the alley as fast as my shaky legs will carry me. I joke in the chatroom about how if no one sees you eat them, calories don't count. But in truth, it's too…personal. Too raw. He can't see me order.

My stomach clenches at the idea of food. Surveying the grounds, I see a bathroom sign in one of the pavilions showcasing this year's wines. I dart through the tasting crowds into the quiet peace of the bathroom, locking the door behind me. And empty everything into the bowl.

A knock on the door jerks me from a daze, and I pick myself up from the bathroom floor. Keys turn in the lock and the door opens.

"Everything okay in here?" An older woman in a green jumpsuit offers me a kind smile. I run my hands under the cold water at the sink, and then dry them on the back of my shorts.

"Sorry, don't know how that locked." I dodge the question in her eyes as I weave around her and out the door. Some 90s ballad whines on the overhead speaker, and forty-somethings in tight jeans swirl red liquids in stemmed glasses. Avoiding their eyes, I exit the pavilion the opposite way I came in.

The smell of hay and animal feed dominates the air, and a string of yellow lights marks a path to a line of trailers. Smell aside, the air is nearly still and offers peace from the reckless attitude of the festival. As I follow, the hum of a generator replaces the music, and intermittent braying provides a melody for the electric buzz. As I round a corner, makeshift pens separate show animals—sheep, goats, pigs, and cows, all grouped by size and kind. At the end of the line, Jay's sweeping stray wood shavings into a pen, talking to some girl doing the same thing to the pen across from his. I freeze.

Awesome. Now he's going to think I'm a stalker. A lunatic stalker with a vocabulary disorder.

I have two options. One, I can saunter down the aisle all "oh hey, fancy meeting you here" status. Or two, retreat as fast as I can through the pavilion, possibly knocking over a few wine-drunk moms and injuring several small children along the way. Neither is good. I settle for Option 1.5.

Turning on my heels, I make my way back toward the music. But before I reach the corner, a deep voice echoes off the makeshift pens.

"Come to see the carnival?"

Busted, stalker party of one. I whirl around, tilting my head, trying to maintain any semblance of innocence. "What?"

"Look around. A meat party if I've ever seen one." Jay's chest contracts and releases as he chuckles, like he's forcing it or something. His laugh is usually more of a "haha" sound. I steal a glance at the girl across the aisle. Is he showing off for her? But she's still sweeping, back turned. Then a thought occurs to me and my eyes go wide.

"The animals. They aren't...you don't...?"

Jay leans his broom against the side of the pen. "No, not these. Just messing around." He saunters toward me, his scent a welcome break from the animals. I lean in a little closer. "Once you name them, it's kinda hard to eat them."

"Tell me about it. Once, Granny named some of her cows she planned on slaughtering and couldn't do it. Gave all the meat away." I shiver. Score one for vegetarians.

"What are you doing way over here? Come to find me?" His voice sing-songs.

I choke on a swallow. "What? No." I curl my toes inside my Converse and roll my ankles.

"That's convincing." He purses his lips, turning his grin into a smirk and winks. My curled toes nearly melt right out of my shoes.

"No. It's just, I needed a break from all the music and screaming, so I followed the quiet. Didn't know I'd end up out here." I swallow again.

"I thought you'd be on the rides with everyone else." He shoves his hands into his jean pockets and gestures in the direction of the rides with his chin.

"Oh, nah. Hard to be a third wheel in those seats." *Bring up the fact that you're a loner. Nice job.* Squeezing my eyes shut, I exhale through my nose. "I mean…" I rub the back of my neck.

"I know what you mean. Come on, let's ditch these smelly things." He bumps my shoulder with his and strolls toward the pavilion. When I catch up, he offers me his bent arm. I loop mine through his, and we stay like that all the way to the games.

We pass one where people are shooting water guns into clowns' mouths, trying to make their fake horses win a race. The next is a mini-bowling game that's more skeeball than anything. Jay stops at the big booth in the middle of the row. Huge plastic buckets are attached to a slanted board, and people are tossing softballs in, willing them to stay.

The guy running it is in a lumpy royal blue t-shirt, the thin kind where you can see everything going on underneath, and cargo pants balanced carefully underneath his protruding stomach. A large money apron acts as his belt. "Three balls for five dollars! Win the beautiful lady a prize!" He points to some large alien heads and a life-size stuffed collie hanging from the roof of his booth.

"Yes, I'm good at this one." Jay digs around in his pocket, pulls out a bill, and hands it to the blue t-shirt guy. When the guy sets the balls on the counter, Jay picks up one in each hand, carefully tossing and catching them, like he's practicing a world-famous pitch or something. "Let's make a bet. I win and you go out with me. I lose and I go out with you." He flushes. "Wait, that came out wrong." He rocks back and forth on his heels.

I bite my lip, trying not to laugh, and shake my head.

"Let's go with the first part. I win and you go out with me, k?" His eyes crinkle in the cutest please ever recorded in all of history. I cross my arms and shrug, tilting my head in what's probably the worst attempt ever to act nonchalant. It's all I can do, though, because if I try to speak, I'm pretty sure whale noises would be all I can produce. Not only did Jay ask me out, but he's trying to impress me by winning me a stuffed animal.

"Playing with your balls again, Dressler?" Amsel strolls up behind Jay, patting his back. Jay elbows Amsel's ribs and tells him what he can do with his own balls.

"You guys are disgusting." Maggie pushes Amsel, who catches her in a half-wrestling move, half- bear hug. She shrieks, but in the way girls do when they're happy with the attention. Jay and I exchange a glance and roll our eyes.

"Okay, here it goes." Jay tosses one of the balls toward the bucket. It lands inside with a thud, rolls around and then out, dropping on the ground.

"Ooh, so close!" Blue t-shirt guy says.

Jay tosses the next one, higher this time. The ball hits the bucket, bounces once, and then rolls back and forth along its curve. "Yes, made it!" He holds his hand up for a high-five, which I gladly give. "Told you I'm good at this."

"You did say that." I bite down on a grin, my entire body humming. I nod to the last ball in his hand. "You've got one more."

"Nothing but net." He mimics his last toss. The ball hits the rim of the bucket and bounces to the ground. "Dang. No worries, though. I still won." He runs his hand through his hair and emits a breathy laugh.

"Here's your prize, young man. Congrats to the lady!" Blue t-shirt guy hands Jay a twelve-inch pickle with legs, wearing glasses and a fake mustache. Mr. Pickle is embroidered across its chest. Jay accepts it, confusion clouding his face. Amsel is doubled over, howling with laughter.

"What about the collie?" Jay points to the hanging dog with Mr. Pickle.

"Sorry, son, that's for two or more balls." Giving Jay the once over, he turns toward the opposite side of the booth. "Who's next?"

Jay hands me the toy and shrugs, a sheepish grin on his face. "It's not the collie, but at least Mr. Pickle won't hog the whole bed."

No one's ever won anything for me. Ever. It could've been a stuffed poop emoji, and I'd still be stoked. I hold Mr. Pickle to my chest with one hand and rest the other on Jay's arm.

"Thanks. No one has ever given me a mustached pickle before."

"Coulda got a bigger one if he only had two or more balls." Amsel's bent over again, clinging to Maggie, who's picking at her nail.

"Fuck off, Amsel." Jay extends his hand to me. "Come on."

It's like the next thirty seconds happen in slow motion. I run my hand down his arm. Jay laces his fingers with mine. It feels like sliding into the perfect pair of jeans. I try not to stare. With one foot in front of the other, I match my stride with his. Or maybe he's matching his with mine. When we stop, we're in front of the Ferris wheel—and he's holding two tickets. Then he's speaking in quiet tones, his voice whispering into my hair.

"Since we didn't get to go earlier, I thought we could now."

Somehow, I manage to nod and stay upright. I'm not sure how since my legs have turned into jelly. He squeezes my hand and nods back.

As we inch our way to the front of the line, my eyes rest on the car in front of us. Three kids climb out and the guy managing the ride shoos the next people in line toward it. They snuggle close together, leaving plenty of room on either side. The guy locks the safety bar over their legs, and they cross ankles, locking themselves together, too.

Eyeing Jay's width and my own, I calculate how we'll fit into the car. Visions of me squishing into the side of the car to leave enough room for him while the guy forces the safety bar over my legs flood my imagination. My breath comes in jagged starts.

And then it's our turn. Jay climbs in first and pats the seat next to him. I slip in, grazing the opposite side of the car and, to my surprise, there's a ton of room in between us.

"Scooch over. If you want." Jay rests his arm on the back of the seat, and I slide closer. There's plenty of room for Mr. Pickle on the seat, but I lay him over my middle, hiding my pooch. The car whooshes backward, and Jay's hand falls to my shoulder. "Here we go."

Chapter 12

That happened, right?

Yes. Now go to sleep.

Okay.
I can't. Mr. Pickle is staring at me.

Turn him around.

I am not spooning a pickle with a fake
mustache.

Why am I participating in this?

Because you love me.

I'm glad you got your Ferris wheel
ride. 😶

We didn't kiss.

It's a woman's right to choose.

Omg stop.

Does this mean I can go to sleep now?

You did that on purpose.

😈

He wants to meet up Monday night.
After he gets done working.

You mentioned that, like 12 times on the way home.

Sorry. I'm excited.

#metoo

Fine. Good night.

Mmhmmm.

*****

By Monday afternoon, I'd typed and deleted a thousand messages asking Jay what time he wants to meet, if he still wants to at all. When he finally answers the one I did send, he says as soon as it's dark.

The grape harvest finished early this year, so we'll have the office to ourselves. During dinner, I chew whatever I can't hide by pushing it around on my plate as fast as possible. I jump up a little too aggressively, grating the wood chair against the floor.

"Careful there," Granny says as she dabs at the corners of her mouth with her napkin. "Where's the fire?"

I set my plate into the sink and run the water a few seconds—long enough to cover the plate, then turn it off before Granny gives me another lecture about how expensive it is to run the pump. Living the country life sure has a lot of rules.

"I have a lot of homework." I shoot her a wide-eyed smile. "Don't want to fall behind and sully the family name or anything."

She doesn't reply, but her lips press into a straight line as she narrows her eyes.

At twilight, I stand above the infamous third stair from the top of Granny's landing. Its creak got my mother grounded more times than not. And not because she was sneaking out. Sneaking back in did it. When Granny first falls asleep, she sleeps like the dead, slumping over in her wingback chair, open-mouthed, in front of some loudly crooning 70s variety show on the television.

But Mom never knew what time Granny would wake up and climb the stairs to the bedroom or if she'd abandon sleep altogether and sit up to solve a cross-word. Granny insists that she always knew when my mom would sneak out, but she pretended like she didn't because "all kids need to experience life and learn a few things on their own." Mom says that's B.S. and Granny just doesn't like anyone getting anything over on her. From the way Mom hasn't been around, I'm guessing that apple fell pretty far from the tree.

Granny's rhythmic breaths are now joined by a nasal gravelly sound, a sure sign Masterpiece Theater doesn't stand a chance. My phone vibrates in my pocket. I dig it out and open the lock screen. Robin.

Don't do anything I wouldn't do.
Actually yes, do all the things.

Rolling my eyes, I stuff the phone back into my pocket and make my way down the stairs, stretching my legs over the squeaky third one and rolling my foot softly on the next step, holding onto the railing so I don't fall on my ass. I shush the whimpering Fengari, who wants to tag along, and slip out the back door. I pause once to note the irony of knowing history and still repeating it, but I'm too excited to see the boy outside waiting for me.

The office porch light clicks on and its haloed, a yellow ring circles the building like a beacon directing me to a hope-filled night. I stop under the big oak tree for a moment to collect myself and check that my hair hasn't frizzed out of control in the ten minutes that's passed since I last checked it. I smooth the turquoise tank I settled on from Robin's choices of wardrobe, pop in a sugar-free mint and try to relax my typically serious expression.

Jay stands in the middle of the halo, shadowed by the light pushing toward the edges of the circle, leaving the center dark, like the eye of a storm. His left hand is shoved in his jean pocket and his right tugs at the ends of his hair—messy, but totally hot. His wrinkled button-up hangs loose, showing off an untucked gray t-shirt underneath. He's definitely the storm and I'm definitely not calm.

He smiles, his eyes brushing over and then behind me. "Hey," he says. His gaze finds mine and the right side of his mouth slides into a crooked grin. "Glad you could make it out."

My heart does a little leap, and I bite my lips together to hide my grin.

He hands me a single daisy, his fingers lingering over mine. The light behind him casts a defining shadow on his face, making his eyes seem larger than normal. They sparkle, the blue pooled in the gray reflecting in his shirt. I shiver.

"Hey." I sniff the flower, even though daisies don't have much scent. I brush my hair over my shoulder, tucking my chin, and lift my eyes to his. Excitement whisks its fingers up my spine, and I shiver again. "Sorry, I'm just a little cold," I lie. He crinkles his forehead.

"It's 80 degrees outside."

I shrug. He smiles and loops his fingers with mine. I could stand this close to him with our fingers threaded together forever.

"Let's go inside the office. No breeze."

I follow him to his dad's office in the back of the building. The lights are off, but the glow from the computer's screen saver allows us enough light to see around the room. The wine company's logo of a woman standing in a barrel smashing grapes bounces off the sides of the screen. Jay turns the leather office chair around and sits down. He leans back, his hands lightly gripping the arm rests.

"I don't normally come in here," I say. He doesn't respond, and the room wears the silence like a damp sweatshirt. I can feel his eyes on me. I nod as my skin flushes and the heat rises in my cheeks. "The office is nice."

Smooth. Could I stop talking now?

Jay laughs a low, gravelly sound and clasps his hands behind his head. He crosses his ankle over his knee.

"Yeah, I guess." He studies me, but his expression makes me feel more like a model than a slide in biology. I suck in my belly pooch. "So how come we don't hang out? I mean, we have the same friends, and I'm here all the time."

"Um, I don't do groups," I say. Realizing I sound exactly like my resting face, I lighten my tone and exaggerate a hair toss over my shoulder. "I mean, I don't know. Obviously, my social skills are amazing, especially judging from the extremely smooth way I'm impressing you with my utter coolness."

He grins.

"I don't know if you've noticed, but sarcasm is my second language."

"I noticed." His eyes crinkle at the corners, and he winks. I try not to sigh. "Hey, what happened with Pawn the other day?" He drops his foot back to the ground and rests his elbows on his knees. There's a darker tone to his question, but I wave it off as curiosity.

"Nothing, why? And sorry again. He just showed up." I tug at the hem of the tank, hoping it might swallow me up along with the awkward conversation topic. The last person I want to think about is Panayis.

Jay stands. In two steps he's lacing our hands together and pulling me so we're side by side, leaning against the wall. I stare at the office chair, too afraid to make direct eye contact in case he's actually a mirage, and this whole night's been some sort of weird fantasy, and

I'm actually asleep and holding hands with one of Granny's creepy dolls or something. But the warmth of his body spreads over mine, and I know it's real. He's real.

I might have *real* tattooed on my body after this.

"I thought he might be into you or something." He clears his throat and snaps me back into the conversation.

"What? Into me? Ha. No, we've only talked a few times because he works here." I force out an awkward laugh. "And now I have to drive to school with him and Bubba." My shoulders droop for effect and slide down the wall. He follows so we're sitting on the floor. Grape Lady and her barrel dance back and forth on the monitor.

"Bubba?"

"His truck." I shrug, and he shakes his head.

"Well, I work here, too, so maybe we can talk, too." He swallows so his Adam's apple bobs up and down. "I mean, I'd like that." He turns his face toward mine, folding his leg so that it bends in front of him and touches my thigh. I pray it doesn't sink too far into my flesh and ruin this moment. He traces his finger between the edges of the tank and my shoulder. "I like this." He raises his eyebrows and nods. "Hot."

Well, he's not thinking about my thick thighs, that's for sure. I laugh and instinctively adjust the straps for coverage. My cheeks burn from the attention, and I'm grateful for the dim light.

We talk a little more about school and the people we know, and then I remember I should ask him about his animal at the fair or something he likes. "So you're into FFA? I mean, I'm not that into outside, but it's cool, I guess. Animals and dirt and stuff." I half-heartedly punch the air with pretend pom-poms then drop my hands into my lap. I lean over. "This is not my area of expertise."

Seriously, I'm majoring in stupid when I get to college.

He laughs at my fake cheer. "Obviously you're a natural." I push his arm and he returns the bump—a sure-fire, fourth-grade way to say I like you. My heart is among the clouds. "It's a lot of work raising goats, but it's fun, I guess. A lot of pressure to always be 'on' you know?"

I don't but nod anyway. His gaze shifts from playful to something serious, and it settles into my chest and lungs. My breath quickens.

"There's something about you… And, well, successful social skills or not, I think you are mostly cool."

My lips curl upward. "Mostly?" I lift my hand to my chest in mock offense and turn to face him. His fingers lightly graze the back of my hand and then close around my fingers.

He leans in. "You know, sarcasm is my second favorite way to communicate."

"What's the first?"

Um hello, is this me? How can I sound this calm when Jay's face is inches from mine?

I've never kissed anyone before. At least, no one that counts. One-time Robin dared me to either a) kiss her visiting cousin or b) eat a worm that'd made its way to the sidewalk after a heavy rain. Her cousin was the better choice, although I did consider the worm for at least thirty seconds. I'm no expert, but I'm pretty sure this will be an entirely different experience.

He grasps my hands in his and wraps them around his waist so I'm forced to lean in even closer.

"This is my favorite." His voice sounds like a smile, and he smells like summer sun and dryer sheets. His lips brush over mine and I grin into his mouth. "Damn, girl, that's sexy."

When he releases me, I close my eyes and breathe in deeply, dropping my head to his chest. He folds his arms around me, hands spreading across my back. I'm pretty sure if he lets go, I'll melt into the floor.

"We should hang out more often." Jay shifts his body and leans against the wall. He tugs my hand to follow.

"Um yeah," I say, still stunned by his spell. I press my back against the cool of the wall, keeping my hand threaded with his, not wanting to let go. "I can definitely help you out with that whole socially awkward thing…if you want. I mean, because of my mostly cool ways and all."

He laughs and draws me close so our shoulders touch. Without breaking his gaze, he flips onto his knees and cups my face with his hands.

"I'd like that." He kisses me again, this time parting my lips with his tongue. My breath catches on a sigh, and I sheepishly return the move, not sure if I'm doing it right. But by the way he presses me against the wall and moves his tongue with mine, the more I know our kiss is perfect.

Before we realize, it's super late, and Jay's dad has texted a million times wondering where he is. He brushes his swollen lips across mine one last time and jogs down the driveway toward his truck. I follow him as far as I can see into the dark, and then make my way to the house. Actually, I think I'm floating.

The kitchen lights flood the porch through the French doors, and my flight crashes to the ground. I stare at the back door, daring the knob not to squeak, like that'll magically make Granny be upstairs asleep instead of waiting for me at the table. But, since she's a stickler for turning out a light when no one's in the room, I know I'm totally busted.

Granny sits at the kitchen table sipping from a cup in front of a full tea service. She isn't one to heat up water in the microwave for her tea. She boils her water on the stove and then pours it over her loose tea leaves. Leaving them to steep in a porcelain pot, she wraps the pot in a cozy to encourage its warmth. Tonight, she follows the same routine, except this service holds a cup for me and small butter cookies on a rose-patterned plate. She pours a cup and sets it in front of an empty chair, which she pushes out with her foot.

"Have a cup with me?" Her tone indicates she isn't really asking. She keeps her eyes on the service. "It seems just the night for a snack, don't you think?"

I close the door as slowly as I can to put off the inevitable lecture and sit down. Fengari jumps at the gate separating him from the rest of the kitchen. On my way to the table, I lean down and scratch his head.

"Granny…"

"Wren. I just want to have a cup of tea with my granddaughter." She smiles and sips her tea. "You like Oolong, right? Something warm's always comforting before bed."

Picking up a cookie, I sigh and sit down. I pick at its edges. I'd rather go upstairs and bask in the glory that is this night, one that all other nights wish they could be. It seems like we've been talking and kissing forever. I bite my bottom lip and taste his kiss. I sip my tea to hide my grin. Granny interrupts my thoughts.

"Do you know Oolong means Black Dragon? My mom always loved dragons. She had them all over her house, remember?"

I shake my head and make an effort not to sigh. She waves off the memory.

"You were probably too young to remember her much. Anyway, she sure did love dragons." She sips her tea and peers out the window like she can see through the black night and into her mom's living room. "There was a huge one on her coffee table, took up half the space. Said they reminded her of what could happen, you know?" She leans forward and pats my knee.

Oh. So we're using metaphors. Awesome.

"Sure. Dragons equal dangerous. Got it." I gulp my tea, draining the cup. When I set it down, she lifts the pot and refills my cup. "Thanks."

She ignores my flat gratitude. "Actually, the name of this particular type of Oolong means Iron Goddess of Mercy, although I couldn't pronounce the Chinese if you gave me a million dollars." She laughs like she's told a joke and sips her tea. I inhale then let out a deep breath. "Interesting concept. The Oriental dragon means good fortune, and this particular tea is infused with both the dragon and mercy."

I grimace at her choice of words. "Granny, no one says Oriental anymore. It's Asian."

I'm so not in the mood for a history lesson. I fidget in my chair, itching to lie on my bed and text Robin. Like, if I tell her everything, it's, like, really real, and not some memory I'll replay every day as long as I live. My foot taps the chair leg and shakes the table.

"Regardless of political correctness, the point stands. But, I guess you have to be willing to understand it." She touches my knee with her cup-free hand, stilling it so the shaking stops.

I finish the last of my tea. This time I bring the cup to the sink instead of setting it where she could add more.

"Thanks for cleaning up, Wren." She brings hers into the next room where her office chair creaks as she sits. Her computer whirs to life, which means she's in for a marathon of her favorite Old Lady video games. I exhale in a huff as I haul the service to the sink. After rinsing and drying, I follow her into the room where she's methodically matching and destroying little balls of animated fur. I don't need her permission to date, but having it would sure make my life a lot easier. And besides, isn't that what she's always on about, me going outside and doing teeanagery things?

"Granny. He's nice. I seriously don't understand what the big deal is." I wish my mom were here; she'd understand. If anything, my outing's nothing compared to her new dating philosophy. I lean against the doorway and cross my arms. On the screen, the colors of the balls line up and then explode.

"Wren." She says my name like a warning but keeps her eyes on the game. "Not every dragon brings good fortune or mercy. It'll do you good to remember that." For the thousandth time since we sat down, I roll my eyes and turn to leave. "Just keep your guard up."

"Okay, Granny, I will… I am." I climb the stairs to my room, my mood lifting with each stair taking me away from Granny's incessant dragon-speak.

She doesn't know what she's talking about. Doesn't see Jay the way I do. I push her warning into the back of my mind's closet and imagine stuffing it into a tiny box reminiscent of Pandora's, and shove her words under the pile of geometry equations I'll never use.

Closing the lid on the imaginary box, I do the same to my bedroom door and curl into my chair. Outside the window, the halo of the office light invites me back. I trace the corners of my lips with my finger and shiver. My phone cuckoos; it's Robin.

So, how'd it go? Are you back yet?

Le sigh.

Nice. Did you guys… 🌚

Yeah. 💜

WREN. YOU'RE NOT A KISS
VIRGIN ANYMORE.

Why do you gotta say things
like kiss virgin. Gross.

Just sayin', if you can't SAY it,
maybe you shouldn't DO it.

I can say kiss…just not your weird extra noun.
Hey, does that make kiss a verb?

You're doing the thing again.

The nerd thing?

Yeah.

Fine. Anyway, Granny went all Dumbledore
on me and warned me about dragons or whatever.

That doesn't help the nerd status.
Dumbledore and dragons?

Yeah, her way of telling me to be careful,
protect my heart and lady parts and what not.

Gross.

                                   Hey, if you can't SAY it…

W. 😑
Um, maybe she's not wrong?

                                   What do you mean?

*Well…today at school, Amsel said
something about you to Jay and they were
laughing.*

    My heart sinks.

                                   What did he say?

*I'm not sure, but I don't think it was too nice.
Just be careful is all. I'm not Dumbledore, nor
do I have a dragon, but I do love you and want
you to be happy.*

Happiness existed approximately 4.7 seconds ago. Now, I don't know what to feel. Robin's never lied to me, and despite Granny's lack of ability to understand the remotest of me or my friends, deep down I know she only wants the best. Whatever, it's still unsolicited advice. I press my finger into the pain starting over my right eye. Amsel owns whatever he said. There's no way Jay would do that. The way he kissed me, and the way I felt when he did…that had to be real.

                                   *I'm
sure it's
not what
it*

seemed.
Just a
weird
coinciden
ce. It's
whatever
.

I can't breathe. It isn't whatever. The tea churns, begging for release. Robin's mistaken. He was here. With me.

With me. *Real.*

Just an hour ago, my stomach was alight with butterflies, and now, I'm choking on their corpses.

I open his story on Snapchat, like there'll be some tell-all about his Dating a Nerdy Loser prank. Nothing. Just pics of him and Amsel doing stupid things. The tightness in my chest eases a little, but the idea nags at the back of my brain. Robin has to be wrong. I start a text to Jay but then stop. Instead, I text Robin and try to sound like the earth didn't just jump off its axis.

Did
you hear
what
they were
saying?
lol…

Only a few words. Probably way
out of context

Uh huh. What were those few
words heard way out of context?

Idk, something about why Jay's
talking to you when he could have

105

Ashley.

I suck in a sharp breath as my heart sinks. Freakin' Amsel. Freakin' Cheer Uniform. Freakin' tea churning. A tornado of dragon juice swirls in my gut.

Yeah, I can see how easily that can be taken out of context.

......

What.

Not that part. He said...something else.

Well, if my first kiss really is some elaborate prank, it can't get much worse. Unless...no. He wouldn't.

Did he say I'm fat? Is it about dating a fat girl?

No! There is literally no one on this planet who thinks you're fat.

I huff. Yeah, right. But she's my best friend. She has to say that.

Then what?

Idk, something about you not being one of us. It's stupid.

106

I open my mouth and close it again, furrowing my brows. I've never actually been stabbed, but if words could come in the shape of a blade, "not one of us" slices clean to the bone.

Oh.

Like I said, probably way out of context.
Maybe he meant FFA?

Yeah, maybe. LOL

I'm so not LOLing. I know her too well not to hear the doubt behind her text. As much as I want to know the truth, I'm not about to text Jay and accuse him of things I don't know are true or not. And since I vowed not to let Robin fight my battles anymore, I can't ask her to find out for sure either.

Can you imagine? Yes, that'll be one order of lunatic with a side of Irrational Girlfriend, thanks. Girlfriend. Huh. Guess I'll find out in the morning.

In the bathroom, I close the door and turn on the water. Sounds of electronic balls of fur crash and splatter through the vent. When the tea is gone, I wash my face. In the mirror, Beached Whale Girl stares back.

Chapter 13

The whole way to school, Panayis drones on about some game he and his friends played all weekend while my mind churns the possibility that I've fallen for the classic high school prank. I really should've seen this coming. I've seen every John Hughes film ever made.

On one hand, no one kisses like that and doesn't mean it. And he did ask me to meet him. Twice. On the other hand, why did I kiss him so soon? I don't even know him that well. What does that say about me? Desperate. Pathetic. And it might not be true anyway. Churning.

Panayis drops me at Robin's car, and I dive in the front seat before anyone around Jay's truck can see me. Robin's already talking.

"What?" I ask.

"I said there's probably some misunderstanding. You did nothing wrong."

"Except make out with the guy who may or may not be using me as the ultimate joke. There's that." I glance at the crowd behind us through the mirror.

Amsel's standing on the truck bed shouting something to the rest of the parking lot and pointing to Jay. Who's standing next to Cheer Uniform—does she have any other clothes? —with her arm around his waist. Bile rises to my throat. I grab my bag with a shaking hand and jump out of the car.

"Wait for me," Robin says. Sitta practically skips toward the car, a smile blooming on her lips. Robin flushes when she sees her. "I'm not letting you go in by yourself."

"I'm okay," I lie. "You go over and we can meet up later. I don't want to draw attention or anything." I fake a smile, willing what little breakfast I ate to stay down. She glances at Sitta then me, narrowing her eyes. I nod and shoo her away. "Go be disgustingly cute, you two. And do it over there so I don't have to watch." I wink and, if it's possible, Robin turns a deeper shade of red.

"Okay, if that's what you want. You know I'm here for you. One punch and it's KO for him. I have all that practice fighting my stupid brothers, remember." She throws a couple of punches in the air and hugs me hard enough to give me the strength to walk onto campus.

As I turn that way, Jay makes eye contact and nods hello. His smile fades as he lifts his hand to wave, and then runs it through his hair instead. Clenching my jaw, I hike up my bag, welcome armor against the darting eyes from the other side of the aisle.

"See you later, Robin," I say loudly enough for everyone to hear, and I twist my mouth into my best smile.

In the bathroom, I check my hair in the mirror, smoothing the frizz popping up from the morning fog. Should've brought a hair tie. I'm going to need it.

When the room empties, I close the door and lock the stall. After I place toilet seat covers on the ground, I kneel and stare at the water in the bowl. Cheer Uniform—I mean Ashley—is popular, pretty. Why would I think he wants to be with someone like me?

Because he said so. Last night.

With each wretch, memories of last night come up. His easy smile and the way he shook his head into his lap when he laughed at my jokes. The way he offered me his open hand, closing his fingers around mine, brushing his lips over the back of my flexed hand, teasing my fingers to close around his.

But if all that was real, why does my stomach hurt? Why is the heartbeat in my ears pounding a war cry instead of a love song?

After, I rinse my mouth and check my teeth for leftover residue.

Straightening my shoulders, I resolve to survive the day. I dig my ear-buds out of my pocket and crank up the volume. Something has to drown out the warning in Granny's tea and the pity in Robin's voice.

As I push my way through students checking text messages and trading homework, the sun streaks through the pockets of fog hovering over the grassy areas of the campus. The coming chill in the air makes me hug my sweater and tug the hood closer to my neck. I search for a sunny spot and wait for class to start. Panayis rounds the corner, but before I can turn around, his face brightens. Too late, I'm stuck. I sigh inwardly and match his wave. His lips are moving, but I keep walking, hoping he gets the hint. He turns around and sidles up next to me, matching my pace. I smile half-heartedly and remove one of my ear-buds.

"Sorry, didn't hear you. Music is loud." I hope this'll deter him, but no such luck.

"Yeah, I can hear it. I asked how you were, although I'm guessing not fabulous since you're listening to emo music. Plus you were super quiet this morning. What is that?" He holds the free ear bud and attempts to listen. "Blood like Cherries?" He shakes his head and exhales in mock sympathy.

"That's not even a real band." I smile bigger in spite of myself.

"Fight with Granny?"

There's no way I'm telling him the truth. Not with the way his face changes every time Jay is brought up.

"Yeah, I think she has a master's degree in annoying." I hope my answer's vague enough for him to fill in whatever kind of story he'll believe. "Insert teenage drama here."

He tilts his head and squints his eyes. Then he raises an eyebrow and exhales.

"Okay, don't tell me, then. I'm around if you need to talk." He circles around on his heels and heads in the opposite direction. I stare, mouth half-open. I got off way too easy. I'm about to ask what he means when he turns around and smiles. "See you at the vineyard."

I wave a small circle at him and turn toward English—and run

110

right into Jay's chest. The small flurry in my stomach turns into a brewing storm.

"What are you doing here? The quad is that way." I motion to the middle of campus and sidestep, but he moves in front of me.

"Wait." His left hand clasps the top of my arm, and I stop. "Where'd you go this morning?" He brushes his hand over my shoulder, smoothing back my hair.

I step backward and cross my arms. I can't bring myself to say the truth. "Didn't want to interrupt whatever you and Amsel were joking about," I say, practically spitting the words. His face blanches.

"Why? We were just messing around." He steps closer and slides his finger over my sleeve, leaving tingles in its wake. I shake them out.

"Well, you looked pretty Not Messing Around with Cheer, I mean, *Ashley's* arm around your waist." I hate myself for even saying it. When did I turn into an afterschool special villain?

If this is what romance is, count me out.

I try turning off my music while fumbling with my earbuds, but my hands shake so much, I drop them. They're still attached to my phone, which is tucked into my pocket, so they dangle between us like the truth hangs in the air. He winds the wire around his hand and places the coil in my open palm. He cups his hands over mine, leans his forehead close and sighs.

"Everyone was laughing at Amsel, and she was playing along with his joke."

"What joke?" *The one where it's me?* I swallow hard.

"I don't know. Riffing off something about prom court he'd said earlier." He shrugs and red splotches color his cheeks. "Like we should be king and queen and he's campaigning early."

My head feels like it's going to explode. That's what Robin overheard? Out of context, indeed. I bow my head and move closer to him. "Oh. Well, that's not such a big deal."

Mental note: Kill Robin and her contextualizing skills later.

He grins. "Hence the confusion regarding your no-showage this morning." He closes his eyes and opens them, like a slow-motion blink. "Please don't make me hunt you down like some prey every morning. I prefer kissing you before exercise."

I raise an eyebrow. "Prey?"

"Really hot prey, though." He leans in and brushes his lips across mine. He smells so good that I almost forget to suck in as his hand slides over my side. Almost. "And I really wanted to see you this morning."

"Why?" I tilt my head.

"To give you these." He hands me three daisies tied with a red ribbon. "To remind you of last night." His face softens into a smile as he brushes my cheek with the back of his hand. This time, I don't jerk away.

"Oh," is all I can muster.

"I'm sorry about the misunderstanding because, well, all those amazing social skills you're supposed to teach me." He wiggles his eyebrows, causing tiny electric storms in my veins. "And I really like hanging out with you. Definitely want to do that again." He leans in, his face close to mine, our lips almost touching.

If this is what romance is like, count me in.

I breathe in his dryer sheet and deodorant scent as his lips meet mine. When he releases my lips, he stays close, his smile against my cheek. Someone somewhere yells something about PDA, but it's only background noise. Only minutes ago, I was rushing to class. Now I never want the bell to ring.

"You going to the library at lunch?"

I nod and he says he'll try to meet me there. It's my turn to smile.

"See you later then," I say.

He trots off toward the other side of campus, and I head to English, tucking the daisies carefully into my bag. The fog seems to have lifted, and the sun spreads its light farther into the corners of the hallway. I relax my shoulders and let the warmth embrace me.

*****

During lunch, I wait in my usual spot in the back of the library. I drag out some math homework and pretend to pay attention to it, but my eyes gravitate toward any movement by the door. Any time it opens or the turnstile flips, my eyes gravitate to the front. I must've read the same problem twenty times. Why is Jay taking so long? Something must've kept him in the cafeteria, or maybe he had to see a teacher. Whatever it is, it's probably important.

I almost text Robin, but then stop. She knows everything about me. And almost every memory I have is with her and her family. I've depended on her for a social life, and maybe it's time that changes.

She's more involved in student government than ever, and I'm clearly not cut out to deal with people in a public forum. Plus, she's getting busy, not in a metaphorical way either, with Sitta, and I have something starting with Jay. Maybe keeping this to myself would be good for both of us. Maybe I can at least try to branch out, make a few friends. The thought of what Robin thought she'd heard Amsel say makes me shudder. A few new friends, indeed.

I shove my work in my bag and pick up my journal. I record the sandwich and apple I ate for lunch and stare at the entry. My phone vibrates. It's Mom and not Jay. Heart sinkage.

Hey Love. Have you seen my red skirt?

Did you check the clothesline? Granny's decided dryers are bad for the environment now. Why do you need it?

Got a date with Banker Guy.

She's quit trying to confuse me with all her boyfriends' names and has since resorted to nicknames for easier identification. My role model, ladies and gentlemen.

Where are you going?

Vegas, Baby! Be home in a few days!!!

That's not a date, that's a trip.
But whatever.

Isn't it exciting?! Love you!

A choking noise escapes my throat. At least this time she mentioned leaving before Granny had to hand me another note or make another cake for dinner. I set my phone down and cross out the sandwich from my journal. I deduct the calories from my daily intake and then head for the bathroom. I shove the image of my mother hanging on some gray-haired banker in a bad suit for a free trip to Vegas down my throat and wait for it to come up, cleaning up the mess lunch turned out to be.

As I rinse my mouth, I replay the emotional tug of war I'd gone through in the last twenty-four hours, whipping from the highs of kissing Jay to the lows of fearing my joke status in a matter of minutes. Images of Mom running off with Mr. Next Guy with airline miles morphs into her body and my face, making me shudder. The last thing I want is to be like her, defined by my next date. I dry my face with one of those awful school bathroom paper towels and try to band-aid any makeup still hanging on.

I used to be a girl without drama, and I like that reflection of myself. I'm not about to spend junior year waiting around to figure out whether or not a guy does or doesn't want to date me. Nor am I going to believe every person who thinks they know something about said guy. Panayis has his own history with Jay, but it doesn't have to be mine. And Robin, as much as she tries to protect me, she made a mistake, a big one, that could have cost me an entire relationship.

As much I want to find out why Jay didn't show, I'm waiting for him to find me. Because if he doesn't, I have my answer.

*****

I'm dreaming of a clicking sound. Different than Mom's heels clacking on the wood floor. It sounds lighter than that. Less musical than a fork clinking a plate. A bird on the roof, maybe. But why am I dissecting a dream I'm currently having?

I open my eyes and roll onto my back. The tapping again. Well, just one tap, really. I sit up and check the time on my phone. One-thirty in the morning. There's approximately zero birds around here that would be searching for breakfast this early. Maybe a late-night snack? I press the palms of my hands into my eye sockets then move my hands over my hair using my fingers as a comb.

Another rap at my window, the same noise. I fold myself out of bed and kneel on my chair, peering out like some ancient person screaming at kids to get off their lawn. A shadow moves on the path between the house and the rose garden in front of the east vineyards. A muffled voice whisper-shouts my name.

Sliding up the bottom pane, the whispers are clearer, and this time I recognize the voice. And despite his no-show at lunch earlier today, a slow grin spreads across my face.

He found me.

I can't seem too excited, though, or he'll think he can ghost me whenever he wants. A rule made super clear by Robin and Sitta after school. I clear the sleepy rasp from my throat and lean close to the screen.

"What are you doing here? It's the middle of the night."

"Can you come down? I want to see you." He holds something large and roundish up, but I can't tell what it is in the dark.

"Um, no? We have school tomorrow." I shoot a quick glance over my shoulder at my closed door.

"Please? I feel bad about missing lunch and want to make it up to you." His feet scrape on the dirt, and I'm sure everyone in a five-mile radius can hear us, because there's nothing to muffle sound but crops and cows.

"Just a minute." I shuffle off the chair and to my door, pressing my ear against it to listen for any signs of Granny stirring.

Silence.

Rushing back to the window, I run my hands through my hair and grab my jeans from the end of my bed. "I'll be down in a minute. Stay there." Once I fasten my jeans, I throw on shoes and a hoodie and slink down the stairs as quietly as I can. I slip out the front door, because it's heavier and quieter than the one on the back porch. It's also closer to where Jay is waiting for me.

The cool night air invades the openings in my hoodie. I fold my arms over my stomach and head toward the rose garden. Jay's in the same spot, still holding the big curvy shadow.

"What are you doing out here?" The dark skies and chilly air force my question into a whisper. Like speaking too loud on a clear night like this might break the starlight's spell cast over the vineyard. I glare at his hand and the huge case it's holding. "And what is that? Are you stuffing my body into a suitcase or something?"

His laugh is a burst of air out of his nose. "No, goof, this is my guitar. Come on." He nods to the dark vines and reaches for my hand with his free one, but I back up.

"Uh, I don't think so. You know coyotes and other furry-fanged creatures roam those acres in the black of night, right?"

He steps closer. "Don't worry, I have a plan."

"Says the male lead in every horror film ever made." I clutch my hoodie tighter and he rolls his eyes.

"Fine, we can go to the office." He touches his pocket. "Brought the keys just in case."

When we close the door behind us, he leads me to the back office. He leans his guitar against the desk and settles himself on the floor.

I stand.

"So," he says.

"So." I fold my arms over my middle. Shadows of the grape-stomping, computer screen lady move over his face. When he says nothing, I drop my arms and sigh. "What are you doing here?"

"I told you. I wanted to see you." His lip curls into a half grin, and he pats the floor next to him again.

"I mean, what happened at lunch today? You said you'd be there, but you weren't. Now you show up here all Romance Guy with a guitar and expect me to be Swoony Girl. That's not right."

He slumps his shoulders. "I know, you're totally right. It's just, I kind of freaked out." He stares at his knees.

I'm taken aback. How is him freaking out about this even a thing? "What do you mean, freaked out?" I step closer.

"Last night was intense, Wren." He narrows his eyes and draws his brows together. He sits up, eyes taking in everything but me. "I've never met anyone like you before, and I guess I didn't know what to do." He lifts his eyes to meet mine, and even in the dark, the heat in his gaze melts whatever resistance I have.

"Why? I mean, how?" I shake my head at myself and sit in front of him. "Ugh, I don't know what I'm trying to ask."

"I guess I needed a minute to figure out how I felt. Like, I think we could be something real, you know? I've never really had that before and it makes me nervous." He sits up and folds his legs under him, reaching for my hand.

I stare at him, slack-jawed, unable to move. *Real.* There's that word. Only *he* said it this time. Something flickers in my chest, a tickle. Is this what love feels like? He threads our fingers together. I imagine sparks shooting from everywhere our skin touches.

"Are you going to say anything, because now I'm getting really nervous and I'll probably start babbling incoherently until you speak." He squeezes my hand.

I swallow and blink. "I'm sorry. Can you pinch me or something? I'm not sure this isn't a continuation of a previous dream." I narrow my eyes. "We are awake, right?"

"I have a better idea." He leans in and presses his lips against mine, sending shooting stars up my spine.

I smile. "This doesn't help debunk the dream theory."

He grins. "I'm happy to keep trying." He clasps the back of my neck with both hands and envelops me in a hug, sliding his hands down my back and around my waist, but I wrench away. His eyes dart to mine as he wrinkles his forehead and sits straighter. "Something wrong?"

I want that flickery feeling when I'm with Jay so bad, but Robin's pity face and Amsel's carnival laugh infects every kiss we share. This thing we have is as young as it is special, and I don't want any drama to ruin it. I meet his eyes.

"No nothing's wrong. Exactly," I say. He narrows his eyes and tilts his head. I run my fingers over the creases of his jeans where his knee bends. "I like you, too." I lower my gaze and he cups his hand over mine, pressing it into his leg. "One of the reasons I got mad is because of all that crap with Amsel, and something Robin said, too, but that was just a misunderstanding." I glance at him, expecting him to ask. When he doesn't, I continue. "Anyway, the point is, maybe we can kind of keep this to ourselves for a while until we know where it's headed?"

"You want to see each other but not tell anyone?" He rubs the back of his neck with his free hand. I shrug.

"Kind of? I mean, like you say, this feels different, and I don't want another misunderstanding like earlier. Maybe let's keep it between us, if that's okay." I blink, terrified he's going to charge out the door.

"You mean, like, a secret romance?" A grin spreads across his lips and curls up one side.

I nod. "Yeah, I guess."

He holds out his arms, and I scoot closer and fold myself in. "Cool, we can be like Romeo and Juliet."

I lift my head as far as I can. "You know *Romeo and Juliet?*"

"I paid attention in English once."

"Totally ruins your FFA cred, just so you know." Despite my joke, the flicker in my chest spreads into a full-on flame. He shrugs, moving both our bodies with it.

"It's our secret." He lifts my chin so our mouths meet, and I hungrily accept.

Chapter 14

The leaves in the vineyard yellow, readying their descent to the ground. The wind gathers them in groups, hosting dance circles all over the property. I bundle up in a hoodie to protect myself from the cold creeping in with the darkening early hours.

I stand on the stair landing, listening for Granny's patterned deep breathing as she sleeps in front of some PBS show. With every exhale, I creep down each level, until I can slip out the back door. The office porch light flickers off. Jay waits for me in the office, which has become our usual meeting spot—a place where we can be together without the rest of the world watching. Where Granny won't shoot daggers at me every time he shows up for work, like He Who Should Not Be Named or something.

"There you are," Jay says. "I missed you." He wraps his arms around me. Yes, we're that disgusting couple.

"It's so cold outside." I shiver and snuggle into his arms, closing my eyes and imagining we're standing in front of a fire. "You're so warm."

"Listen, I can't stay tonight. My dad found out Amsel's been doing the feedings for me. If I'm too late, he'll make me work extra hours."

I stick out my bottom lip and cross my arms.

"I wanted to see you, though," he says.

I exaggerate a smile. "That's okay," I lie. "I have homework anyway, and Granny can wake up any time." I toss a half-wave toward the house. "Are you working the pruning chain gang this weekend?"

"No, we have to go up north to show the animals. It's a two-hour bus ride round trip, so I'm off the hook this time."

"Lucky."

He presses himself against me and kisses my neck. We fall against the wall as he kisses me thoroughly on the mouth. My knees might buckle any second, so I grab his shoulders. He lets out a soft moan and presses his hips into mine.

"Jay," I say between kisses. He pushes my leg open with his and straddles me over him. "Wait."

He steps back, breathing hard. The hunger in his eyes hardens. "Something wrong?"

"No. I don't know. It's happening kind of fast." I roll myself off his body and lean against the wall.

"Aren't you having fun?" He slides his fingers down the side of my arm, then clasps his hand around mine.

His smile melts my nerves and I smile back. "Of course."

He leans in for a kiss, and I lift my mouth to meet his. My hand still in his, he wraps his arm behind my back and coaxes me toward him. My arm pressing into my back, I arch into him. Keeping his mouth on mine, he brings his other hand up to my chest and plays with the opening of my shirt. I step back.

"I thought you had to go." My breath comes in short bursts. Part of me is screaming to shut up, but the other part isn't sure it can handle what'll happen if he stays.

Instead of leaving, he bends forward, kissing my neck and flicking his tongue down my collar bone. All of a sudden it's too fast and too dark and I can't breathe.

"Jay, stop. I can't…yet. I'm sorry. It's too much." I push at his chest.

His body freezes. He drops his arms to his sides and moves away. I bend over, grasping my knees with clenched hands.

"If that's what you want." He tightens his lips into a line. "I don't want to make you do anything you're not ready for."

My shoulders relax as the relief washes over me. I take a deep breath and then another. He's silent for a long time, and I don't know what to say.

"I guess I'll go then." He kisses my cheek and grabs his keys off the desk. "I'll see you at school."

His thinly drawn lips and down-turned eyes make me feel like I've done something wrong, and all the tension I'd just let go screams up my spine. He won't be around until after his shows, and this can't be his last memory of us until showing season is over. I'm probably overreacting. What's wrong with him wanting to kiss me? Touch me? Isn't this what I've wanted all along? It's time to stop being a child. I cut him off in front of the door, grab the front of his shirt and kiss him hard on the mouth.

"Not so fast," I say. His jaw works back and forth.

"You make me crazy." He sets his forehead against mine, our minds in the same place. After a breath, his eyes meet mine. "Are you ready for this?"

Heart racing, I shove him against the wall and press my whole self against him, feeling the power in turning the tables. Instead of pushing away my weight, he grins and wraps his arm around the back of my waist, his other hand on my hip. My heart swells at his welcome and races only a few steps ahead of my brain. I want to kiss him, to feel his need to kiss me back.

I answer him by sliding my hands around his neck and pressing myself harder against him. Through each touch, I send him my gratitude for wanting me. With each kiss, I pray he'll feel my loyalty to him for making me feel wanted.

His keys crash against the cement floor as he slides his hand up the middle of my back. Arching into him, I angle my head back exposing my neck. Flicks of his tongue send waves of wanting and joy through my body. I can crawl inside this moment and stay here forever.

"Does that tickle, Wren? You can tickle me if you want," he says into my neck. He kisses me harder. Taking my hand, he buries it under his shirt. "Slide it down…tickle me." He brings both of his hands around my waist and softly slips them across the front of my sweater, breathing hard into my mouth.

He wants more. The air rushes from my lungs and the room shrinks, and all the air is gone.

"Wait," I say, trying and failing at taking a full breath. "I need to stop. We should stop." I lean on the desk. My breaths escape in the broken spaces between what I want and what I know I should do. His kisses are like a drug I never want to stop taking. But I can't give more. Not yet. "Sorry, I just, I can't." *Eloquent as always.*

Jay falls against the wall and smacks the back of his head on it, the thumps coming one after another in rapid succession. After what seems like forever, his eyes find mine, but there's no kindness in them. His lips pull into a tight grin.

"You shouldn't start things you can't finish."

I stare at my feet and swallow hard. Social media says my body, my rules, but how can I play when I don't know what they are? His stony expression makes me shrink inside myself. And the lack of light behind his smile cuts into my lungs, slicing away any hope of breathing normal again. Beached Whale Girl stands there, taking up all the space. I'm a child. Huge, conspicuous, ridiculous.

"I want to. I just…" My eyes fill with tears. "I'm sorry."

He exhales and cracks his neck.

"Don't cry. I'm sorry if I made you." He pushes the hair away from my face, making me tremble. He's like a magnet, pulling me toward him.

"I'm not crying. I'm just highly allergic to your ability to make me forget my own name." I wipe my face with my sleeve.

He tilts his head and grins. "You make me forget everything but you. You drive me crazy."

"Is that a good or bad thing?" My stomach churns on the uncertainty of his reply.

He kisses me on my forehead and reaches for his keys. "Everything about you is good. That's the problem. See you when I get back." My whole body shakes under the little electrical currents racing up and down my spine.

"Okay." My voice is small. The office door clicks shut, and I feel it in my heart.

*****

Saturday, Granny wakes me up early with French toast and a work order to prune the roses in the front garden. Mom sits at the table, slumped over her coffee mug and some Over 40 Glam magazine.

"Rough night, Mom?" I push the bread around my plate.

Her tired eyes meet mine. "Can't seem to get used to my bed, but I'll be good once I can get some sleep."

I almost say something about her never being in it, but think better before I'm grounded for all eternity. But I know how she feels. My heart longs to be waking up in my old room with nothing to do but flip channels or hang out at Robin's as she and her family vie for the last pancake. Not working for "the family discount," as Granny calls it, sneezing in the middle of thorny bushes, and dodging flying bugs.

When I report for duty, Panayis is in the garden, hard at work on one of the rose bushes. Fengari's supervising from the porch nearby, curled into a patch of sunlight.

While the nights are getting colder, the sun still dominates the November sky, and the days are warm. I'm wearing a long-sleeved t-shirt to protect my arms from the thorns, but no jacket. I search for a pair of gloves but there's zero to be found.

"Great," I mumble. "Who needs gloves, anyway? It's not like thorns exist or anything."

Panayis tosses his head back and lets out a nasally burst of air.

"What?" I ask.

"You could try the barn. There's a whole drawer full of gloves in there." He keeps working on the bush, tediously clipping at the joints. "Third drawer from the bottom."

"Awesome." I grab the least dirty pair of gloves and trudge back to the roses. "I thought you were working in the vineyards today. That's why I'm out here, right?"

"I am, but Granny wants me to make sure you know what you're doing. You took so long, though, I started without you." His eyes stay on the roses.

He slices through branches, hurling the scraps onto the ground. Normally, Panayis works as if every motion is part of a sacred dance between him and nature. This morning, he's cutting sharp and fast with little regard to anything.

"What's wrong with you?"

"Nothing. Just trying to get some work done." He wipes his brow with his arm, then nods to some clippers near the fence. "Do you know what to do?"

"It can't be that hard. You just cut the branches, right?" I lean in to one of the bushes and single out a branch.

He lays his hand across the bush like he's protecting a child in a car crash. "No. You have to look at the plant and determine the best place to cut. Here, like this." He points to a longer shoot sprouting outward from the bush. As he speaks, his voice softens, and his shoulders lower into his normal relaxed stance.

"See the knobs on the branch? Those are called mati. It means eye." He points to his own which light up, his voice animated. "If a branch needs to be cut, you do it right above the mati at an angle, so the branch can see which way to grow. It's all about teaching the plant to flourish in the right way. If you just cut, then the plant has no idea which way to go, and you get a mess."

"Fine, I got it." My voice sounds a little more on edge than I am, but he doesn't seem to notice. I go to work on the bush, careful to clip at an angle and above the knobby parts of an off-shoot. "What if there's a flower?"

"It's okay to trim the pieces that have buds. In fact, the more you trim away the blooms, the more you'll get." His smile likens him to a little kid picking out his first toy. "See this branch? If you cut here, a new growth will be able to shoot out and bloom more toward the sun, which will create more flowers in the spring."

"You know, it's shocking you don't have more friends." My eyes widen as I realize that sounded way ruder than I intended. My dad used to lecture me about how not everyone appreciated my kind of humor.

"Well, with jokes like those, it's shocking you do," he says. I laugh, grateful I can prove my dad wrong.

The sun rises in the sky, and the warmth encourages our banter. He cuts away the decaying summer growth, and I pretend to cut one every now and then for appearances.

"Get that one, there, in the middle." He points to a rogue branch.

As I reach into the bush, my sleeve snags on the thorns. When I try to loosen it, the sharp points slice down my arm.

"Ooh." I bite down hard on my bottom lip as blood swells in the scratches. My arm stings like I've been given a thousand tiny shots. "Damn roses. See? This is why I don't come outside. Dangerous to my health."

"Let me see." Panayis extends his hand. "I think *you're* dangerous to your health." I think he's only half kidding, the way he narrows his eyes. I hold out my arm. "It's not as bad as it seems. Let's go inside and get you fixed up."

Holding my arm, he escorts me to the back porch and into the house, Fengari barking at his heels. The back room has a sink and doubles as a first aid station for the small bumps and bruises that are common in farm life.

"You know, I can rinse off my own arm." I wince at my tone. Trying to soften it, I smile. "It's just, I mean, I'm sure you'd rather be outside. I know you're trying to help."

"Don't be stupid." He gently rolls up my bloody sleeve and smirks. "You don't know what you're doing, and I'd hate for your arm to get all infected and need a ton of shots."

My eyes go wide and I gasp, and he laughs.

"That can happen? See? I am so over roses."

He shakes his head and adjusts the water.

"No, it can't. You'll be fine. It's not that serious. I'm just having a little fun. Since I don't have more friends, as you say, have to get my fun in when I can." He nods to the sink. "Let the water run over your arm to clean it out. I'm going to get a towel and some gauze.

And don't touch anything sharp."

"Ha. Ha." I roll my eyes and wince as the water hits the scratches.

Blood smears into the water and runs down the drain. Eventually it thins and only water dribbles off my arm. I sigh. The last thing I want to do is waste my time in the garden, especially if I have to pay my dues in blood. He comes back and gently presses the towel over the wound.

"Hold that there, and make sure it dries completely." He opens a tube of antiseptic gel and squirts some on the gauze.

"You know, I'm perfectly capable of cleaning this up," I protest again. "I don't need you to…"

"Make sure your arm is clean and dry. Wouldn't want you to lose it or anything." He applies the gauze.

I wince. Again.

"I see you have a remarkable tolerance for pain." He presses the gauze gently to my arm. Against my will, my heartrate flares and my skin fevers under his touch. He's so gentle. His brow wrinkles in concentration, and I have to muster everything I have not to reach up and trace the creases with my finger.

When he finishes, he catches me staring. Instead of saying anything, he matches my gaze. We just kind of stay that way, neither of us able to move.

The rumble of bass and gravel under tires fill the air. A truck engine revs by the garage, and I don't have to check to know who it is. I blink and yank my arm away from Panayis, pressing the edges of the tape around the gauze.

"Well, thanks for helping me." I shoot him a quick grin.

He rubs his hands on the sides of his jeans. "Oh, sure… Have to take care of my apprentice, right?" He clears his throat and steps backward.

"I guess. I'm going to, um, go now. See you outside?"

"Actually, I think you've got the hang of it now." His voice is different, farther away than before. The levity in it just moments before washed down the drain with the blood and water. "I'm going to head over to the vineyards and help out there. Granny will be wondering where I am."

I nod and run upstairs to change my tattered shirt, heart pounding. Out the window, Jay and his dad talk by the offices. We haven't spent much time together since that last night. I grab a random top and throw it on, careful to cover the bandage. I check my hair and skip down the stairs two at a time, making Granny's trinkets and dolls dance with the echoes of my footsteps. I fling open the back door, nearly knocking Jay over.

"Want to get out of here?" He wears a big grin on his face as he holds up a bottle of sparkling wine in one hand, his guitar in the other, and a bunched-up blanket under his arm.

I glance outside, wondering if anyone sees the bottle. My chest heaves up and down from the quick sprint to my room. The fact that his excitement is palpable means I'll be out of breath for the rest of the afternoon.

"Yes. Where though?" I point to the bottle. "And where did you get that?" Slight panic bubbles its way through my uneven breaths. Not only are we risking massive amounts of trouble, a cardinal rule of dieting is no alcohol. My stomach pinches at the thought of any caloric intake.

He winks, grabs my hand and leads me toward the back part of the vineyard, away from the crowd of workers.

"I stole it from the tasting room." He raises an eyebrow.

Despite my efforts to feign shock, a slow smile spreads on my lips. The last time we were together, disappointment filled his eyes. This time I'll do pretty much anything to keep that from happening.

"We can hang out back here, and no one will be able to find us. If they do, we'll say we got lost." He chuckles, his eyes bright with risk and possibility.

If Granny does find us, I'll be grounded until I'm forty. But if she doesn't find us, what else could happen?

"I don't know. What if we get caught?"

"We won't. Besides, you know I'm leaving on that stupid vacation with my parents in a few weeks, and we won't see each other for a while." His eyes flash with a contagious excitement that stirs every butterfly in my stomach. "This might be our only chance to be together."

I glance at the bottle and what might happen when we drink it. I've only ever had small sips of wine at family dinners. The idea of not being in control, not to mention how many squats and sit-ups I'll have to do to make up for all the calories turns the butterflies into a storm of wasps. But maybe that's the point of drinking. To not overthink everything. Forget.

There's a lot I'd like to forget about, too.

Once again, I open the closet in the back of my mind, find an empty box, and shove in all my reservations as far into the back as I can. Being here with Jay is all that matters.

"Okay. Let's do it."

We settle in a spot underneath the birch trees lining the back of the property. I settle myself so the winter sun blankets my back, warming what the breeze chills. Jay pops open the bottle and sits next to me. After a long swig, he burps and hands the bottle to me.

"Classy," I say.

He shrugs. "Sorry." He wipes his mouth with the back of his hand.

I draw a long taste, swallowing both the warm, fizzy liquid and my doubts. And then another. It's like bitter soda, except without the saccharin after-bite. My eyes water as the bubbles scratch my throat. I offer it back to him.

"Have some more."

"I'm good for now." Air presses against my gut, and I imagine my belly expanding to twice its size. He swigs again, and then trades it for his guitar. I bend forward, attempting to hide my bulge.

He strums a few times and clears his throat. His broad chest contracts, and he tilts his head and closes his eyes. Crinkling his forehead, he bites the bottom corner of his lip, which twists his mouth into a sideways pucker. The muscles in his forearm dance as his fingers pluck the strings. I listen and sip from the bottle, waiting to forget.

Soon, the air is lighter and the music twists my heart into a different shape, one that needs another piece to feel whole. I close my eyes. Lying on the blanket, I ride the sound into the sky.

"You doing all right?" His voice is a warm whisper in my ear. I turn my head towards it, eyes still closed.

"I'm so relaxed." My body melts into the blanket.

"You want any more of this?" Liquid smacks against the glass as he swishes it.

"I don't want to get drunk."

"It's probably too late for that." He rests his hand on my belly and then slides it over my hips. You're losing weight. Should you be doing that?"

My pants have been looser, but I can still feel the bulges. Out of instinct, or maybe reflex, I suck in my gut. "Yeah, right. Now you sound drunk!" I laugh and try to sit up, but my brain hasn't landed from flying with the music yet.

"Maybe you should stay horizontal for a minute." He cradles my head and lies down next to me.

The whole point of coming out here was to forget. And to spend time with Jay before he leaves again. The guy who, for whatever reason, thinks I'm pretty enough and skinny enough to want. I open my eyes and roll over so our foreheads are touching.

"Why are you with me?"

"What?" He sits up and swigs from the bottle. I sit up, too, but slower, leaning on my hands for support.

"Why don't I repulse you?" The light is bright and my body trembles the way it does when it makes room for the truth. "Why do you like me?"

He laughs but it comes out a weird sound. "You *are* drunk. Here, have the last drink." He upends the bottle, but I push it away, spilling it down my neck and shirt.

"Jay!" I wipe at the spill with my sleeve.

"Oops." He laughs. "Now you'll have to strip." He tugs at the corner of my shirt.

"It's not funny. Now I'm going to smell like wine. And I'm not taking off my shirt. It's cold."

"I'll keep you warm." He rolls the bottle to the end of the blanket and nuzzles his face into my neck. "It's not that bad, Wren. Just a few drops. Here, let me see what I can do." He flicks his tongue behind my ear and down my neck. "That's gone." He kisses me again, every one going lower. "And that's gone."

I soften at his touch.

"Okay, thanks. I think you got it." I laugh too and push him away.

He licks his lips, meeting my eyes and pressing his mouth to mine. He tastes like the wine. Between the bubbles and the breeze, my head's spinning. I stare at the sky as the leaves dance around us. Jay runs his hand over my shoulder and down my arm. I wince.

"What did you do?"

"Oh." I lift my sleeve and focus on the bandage, but it's floating. "I scratched it when I tried to prune a rose bush. I shouldn't be allowed around anything sharp." I close my eyes and the world becomes a merry-go-round I'm riding upside down. "Whoa."

"Are you okay?"

His hand's on my stomach. Then he's kissing my nose, then my mouth. Am I standing or flying? The only thing that exists is our kiss. His hand slides under my shirt and I'm lost in how his tongue feels swirling around mine.

A deep voice stabs my ears. "Granny is looking for you." Panayis stands over us, his shadow blocking the sun.

Jay jumps up. He says something to him I can't understand and pushes his shoulder. Panayis shoves him back, sending Jay to the ground. Then Panayis is lifting me up, helping me stand.

"What did you do to yourself?" He's adjusting my shirt and wrapping my arm around his shoulder. "She can't see you like this. Come on, let's get you to the house before anyone does."

"I'm fine, Pawn," I say. "I'm only tipsy." I rest into his shoulder and try to find the exit off this ride. "Where's Jay? I need to say goodbye."

"He's cleaning up the mess you guys made. He'll find you later. Now come on, we need to go." He half drags, half carries me to the house and my room.

The third stair from the top squeaks as I step on it, making me laugh, hard. And then I'm ugly laughing—the kind where your face melts into a fun-house painting and your sides hurt. And then tears are streaming down my face with each guffaw.

"I have to throw up," I say between sobs.

"Do you feel sick?" He leads me to the bathroom.

"No, but I have to. I just have to. And I need my journal. Where's my journal?" Panic fills my lungs and chokes me.

"Okay, I'll find it. Will you be okay?"

"Yes, I'll be fine." I close the bathroom door and kneel in front of the toilet.

A few minutes ago, I was in the middle of a beautiful dream, and now I'm hiding from Granny so she won't know I've been drinking and avoiding my chores. I expel all of the jumbled emotions with every wretch and gag. Somewhere in the distance, a truck starts and a thumping echoes in the driveway. There's a soft knock at the door.

"Wren? You all right?" Panayis asks. "There's a book on your bed. Is that your journal?"

Shit. I rinse my mouth and splash my face with cold water. The clouds behind my eyes part, and the room isn't spinning as much as it had been. I open the door, and he's standing on the other side, a mix of concern and irritation on his face.

A cloud of embarrassment floods my cheeks, and I focus on the ground to avoid the judgment in his eyes. As much as I don't want to care what he thinks of me, I can't help it.

"Thank you. You're nice to me and I don't know why. But thank you." I stumble to my room and lie on the bed.

He stays in the hallway and sighs. "Get some sleep. I'll tell Granny you got sick and went to bed."

His boots are clunky on the stairs, and the sound shrinks as he heads outside.

I roll over, away from the sun, and close my eyes. Before I can register that Jay left without checking on me or Panayis had the book where I write my darkest secrets, I slip into a comfortable darkness, my journal safely in my hands.

Chapter 15

The first morning of winter break, a gray sky hovers outside my window, promising no school for the next two weeks. The familiar tug of deadlines and math quizzes loosens as I stretch the morning fog from my body. I throw back the covers and jump to my feet, thinking I might run into Jay while he's working, but then sag back into my covers remembering that he and his family are taking the downtime of the vineyard to find a sunnier climate. There'll be no outings or office interludes, and Jay's in a tropical place surrounded by girls in bikinis who're prettier and probably friendlier than me.

I slide onto the floor and begin my morning sit ups. Since the drinking episode two weeks ago, I've added two more sets to my morning routine and an extra set of stair climbs. Even though I'd thrown up most of the alcohol, my chat group says a lot of the calories are still absorbed, and I can't risk it.

Blurred light stripes the floor and far wall. Since that day, I haven't seen much of Jay around the vineyard, and for some reason keep missing him at school—either he's perpetually tardy or busy. After school, we've only texted, and even those are snippier. Suddenly, the two-week break seems long.

Downstairs, Granny's at the kitchen table drinking coffee. "Good morning, Sunshine!" She's said that forever. I stifle a groan. Hi, not five anymore. "First day of break. What are you going to do?" She sips her coffee out of a brown, chipped mug. She's never liked matching dishes, so most of them are an eclectic collection of sizes and patterns. Somehow, they all seem to go together.

"I don't know." Still blurry-eyed and hair in tangles, I suppress a yawn. "Where's Mom?"

"Still sleeping. Got in late last night." She pours me a cup of coffee.

I groan. We haven't heard from my dad in weeks, and it seems the longer his silence lasts, the more "late nights" she has. I glance at the empty spaces on the wall where our family pictures used to be. Expecting what, I don't know.

Fengari whines at my feet. I bend and scratch his belly as he plops over and stretches. The room suddenly darkens at the edges of my vision, and I can't stop myself from dropping on the floor next to him. I cover by landing with my legs folded in front of me, pretending I sat to keep petting the dog. The way his lip hangs open, he doesn't mind. I inhale a big breath and the world turns back to its normal color. I avoid Granny's gaze.

"I have an idea," she says. "You can help Panayis and Alex set up the burn piles in the back. Now that the vines have been pruned, the piles need to be sorted."

I slump into the fetal position and cover my face with my arms. "It's the first day of break. I kind of want to just hang out." Fengari flips right side up and sniffs my face between my arms, licks them once and trots away. "Some help you are," I say after him and sit up, too. "How is that legal, anyway? Setting things on fire doesn't seem like the safest thing to do around a vineyard." I lift myself from the floor, curl up with the coffee and settle into a corner chair.

"Well it costs too much to haul it to the dump and, besides, it's good for the land. And, there's no better way to relax than to spend some time outside working. You can connect to nature and feel how the world works."

I roll my eyes into my coffee cup. Based on my experiences this last year, I'm fairly caught up on how the world works, thank you.

"Besides, Jay isn't around this week, so maybe you'll get something done."

Heat climbs up my neck and settles into my cheeks, but I'm not sure if it's embarrassment or anger. I sip the scalding liquid and let it burn all the way down. "Fine. Since you've decided my day, I'd better go and get ready."

"Wear layers. It's cold out there." Her voice sing-songs up the stairs as I clomp to my room.

I hope if I stomp loud enough, Mom will wake up and somehow transport us back to our old house so I can feel normal again. She'll make pancakes while my dad complains about how fast the grass grows or something else suburban-y.

Slamming the door, I kick my slippers into the wall. I really, really don't want to be out there. And with Panayis? Ever since he helped me bandage my arm, he's been acting weird. He even bought a new radio for Bubba, and I swear it's so he doesn't have to talk to me. Which is fine. I have my phone to keep me occupied.

Just the same, I can't bring myself to face him after he practically carried me to bed. My face flushes. There's no one around and I still manage to embarrass myself. Another fun way to keep myself occupied for years to come.

I don't know what's wrong with me or why I care so much about what he thinks. He's just a guy who works at the vineyard. Jay's the one I want.

I plod to the back of the property, gloves on and hood up. Panayis is already there stacking piles of cuttings on top of each other. The sun peeks from behind the haze, but the air is sharp with the kind of cold that can slice open an old wound.

Adjusting my shoulders and shoving my humiliation into a little box in my mind, I sidle up next to him. "Those piles are like little animal houses, like in a fairy tale." I keep my voice light.

Ignoring my attempt at humor, he hefts his armload on top of a growing pile and steps back, breathing hard. He wipes his face with the back of his hand.

"Why aren't you wearing gloves? It's freezing out here." I shove my own hands into my pockets like I have to prove it or something.

"Work faster without them. You can get started on that." He nods to his left but keeps his eyes on the ground. His breath comes out in little white puffs. I point to them.

"See, it's so cold, your breath's becoming clouds. Robin and I used to pretend we were smoking when we were little." I shrug. "We thought we were so cool." I shake my head slowly. Because lung cancer is so not cool. He ignores my reminiscing. Wren–0. Humiliation–1.

Where he's pointing, a mass of sticks and branches lies scattered on a tarp. I know they're just sticks, remembering Panayis's lesson about pruning and the mati—how the plant needs to see where to grow next—but they're more like false starts and mistakes needing to be erased. All that work just thrown away because someone doesn't think it's good enough.

"You can start a new pile here." He points next to the one he's working on. Without another word or glance, he turns, crisscrossing sticks.

"That looks like a fun game of Jenga."

Nothing.

"Okay," I say under my breath. I grab a few branches but drop them again. This isn't right. This isn't how he is. I face him.

He keeps working, avoiding any eye contact with me. I move and stand between him and his precious pile, but he turns to the next one. I keep telling myself I don't care what he thinks, but my heaving breath and flared nostrils tells the truth.

"What's your problem, anyway? What did I do to you?"

He stands up straight, his back still to me. His shoulders tense and then forcibly relax as he exhales.

"You did nothing to me, nothing at all." He chucks a handful of branches onto the ground.

I cross my arms and wait until he realizes I'm not going anywhere. "You've been avoiding me ever since that day I tore my arm open on the stupid roses."

He exhales a sharp snort and shakes his head, eyes toward the sunless sky. "Why do you sneak out with him?"

The blatant honesty of his question makes me recoil as the mortification of my not-so-stealthy-self sets in. Fire burns my skin from the inside out.

"What are you talking about?" I move to another section, but he follows and grabs my arm. I whip around, hair wild and swinging. "Why do you care? It's none of your business, anyway." I hurl my words like knives.

"He doesn't care about you," he throws back. "He's using you."

"For what? Friendship? We haven't done any…" I swallow the rest of my sentence. "I'm not talking about this with you." I barely know Panayis and he obviously hates me. "Never mind. You don't understand." I jerk my arm from his grip and step backward.

"Actually, I do, and just so you know, you aren't the only one he has a 'friendship' with." His fingers wink quotations around friendship.

If it's possible, my face burns even hotter, and tears stream like melting ice down my cheeks. The air burns the wet skin, and I wipe at them like I can erase the whole conversation. This lunatic is obviously wrong.

"He wouldn't do that. You're lying." I turn to leave and trip over the clippings. Falling hard on my knees, I throw my weight on my hands, the gloves the only things preventing me from cutting them to shreds. Panayis crouches, reaching to help.

"Are you okay? Here." His voice is softer as he offers his hand, but I swat it away.

"Leave me alone." I push myself off the ground and adjust my clothes, checking for rips in my jeans. "I'm fine."

He stands straight, brows furrowing, head shaking back and forth. "Obviously." He turns back to his work and new pile leaving me alone at last.

I make a bee-line for the house and stop at the porch—too shaken to go inside. Besides, Granny'll send me right back out, Panayis and my aching knees be damned. I pace until I find Fengari napping in a sunny spot. Scooping him up, I collapse on the swing, his warmth calming the shakiness in my core. I resolve to hate the Greek boy with the laughing eyes for as long as I live.

*****

FatKat: I'm not losing weight. No matter what I do, I stay the same.
Cherry: That happens.
FatKat: What? Why?
Girl: It's called a plateau.
Cherry: Your body figures out your tricks and learns how to stop burning as many calories.
Girl: And you don't lose as many calories throwing up as you think you do.
FatKat: That sucks. What else can I do?
Cherry: You could try laxatives.
Girl: I knew a girl who did that and she didn't lose anything. Turns out your body absorbs all the calories before you, you know, and all you're losing is water. I wouldn't bother.
Cherry: Your body will wake up. Just be patient.
FatKat: I guess. I just want one more pound. Then things will be perfect.
Girl: It's always one more pound.

*****

I spend the rest of break, or at least whatever time Granny doesn't have me running around the vineyard, locked in my room and as far away from Panayis as possible. Every time I think about his words, I want to punch something. Which is stupid because his opinion doesn't matter. But what if it's not an opinion? What if it's fact? The last thing I want is to show up at school and have everyone see me as a fool for believing someone like Jay could be with someone like me.

Another solid reason to keep me and Jay secret. But if Panayis knows, how soon will everyone else? I need reinforcements, so I text a 911 to Robin.

A few hours later and practically before she finishes parking her car, I nearly dislocate her arm dragging her onto the porch. Granny keeps a small space heater next to the chairs for her evening tea ritual, and I spark its flame so we won't freeze in the December haze.

I push Robin into the chair and tell her to brace herself.

"What is your issue? Let's go inside; I'm freezing." She wraps her sweater tighter and tucks her chin into her scarf. Grabbing her hands, I sit next to her, partly for warmth but mostly to feel like I'm not alone.

"Out here's better. More privacy. I have something to tell you. Please please please don't be mad."

"Okay?" Her eyes are wide as she nods. "Spit it out." I close my eyes and blurt out the words before I lose my nerve.

"I know I've told you I've been forced to work a lot, which is why I haven't been able to hang out as much, and that's mostly true, but things have kind of gotten more serious with Jay?" I risk opening one eye. She's staring back, mouth half-open. "I didn't say anything because you know how I am. I hate putting my business out there for everyone to judge. Not that you're anyone, ugh, you know what I mean. But now Pawn said that Jay had other friends and I should be careful." I spit as much venom with his name as Draco does when he says Potter.

"Wait. What? Who?" She holds her hand up. There's a small design on the inside of her wrist peeking out of her glove.

"What's that?" I point to her raised hand. She withdraws it like she's touched something hot.

"Nothing. Who's Pawn? Your personalized Uber driver?"

"Yes, the guy I ride to school with. I thought he was, at least, a little cool, but then he started saying all these things." I swallow, anxious to not talk about him. "Did you draw on yourself?"

"Not exactly. And why do you care what some random guy says to you? Unless…" A grin spreads across her face as she crosses her arms and tilts her head, raising a single eyebrow.

"No! He's…it's whatever." I shake my head. Resolve sets in my spine like cement. "Obviously, he's just saying that because he hates me for whatever reason." I ramble on, throwing up all my feelings into a jumble of words at once, like the pile of discarded vines on pruning day.

"Okay, breathe." Her hand shoots up like a she's directing traffic.

139

"First of all, WOW. Now I know why you never text back." She bites her lip as she leans in to whisper. "How serious have you gotten?"

"Not *that* serious, but tongues and hands have been involved." A weird mix of TMI and pride well inside me, but if I can't tell my best friend, who can I tell?

Her eyes narrow as she studies me, then her entire face lights up and her lips stretch into a wide grin. "Wow."

"You said that."

"I know. I just… Is this a good idea?" Her eyes search mine, and she's got this weird look on her face, like she's trying to not make any sudden movements. Of all the ways I thought she'd react, this never crossed my mind.

"What are you talking about?" I cross my arms over my chest. He's someone I like, someone I like to be with. And he likes me, too. Why wouldn't it be a good idea?

She loops her hair behind her ear, and the mark on her wrist slips out again. I grab it and slide up her glove. An outline of a heart the size of a dime is tattooed in the exact same spot we said we'd put ours. She jerks her hand back and tucks it under her leg.

"What is that? That's temporary, right?" My nostrils flare as I clench my teeth, my breaths coming in between bursts of exhales.

"No." Her voice is small, and her eyes are focused on her lap. "Sitta and I, we were out one day, and it just kind of happened. I didn't really know how to tell you."

"You pick up your phone or send me a pic or something. Geez, Robin. That's supposed to be our thing." I stand, shaking too much to sit anymore. She stands, too.

"I'm sorry I didn't tell you, okay? You haven't really been around and it wasn't planned."

"So it's my fault because I had to move? We made a promise."

"When we were ten. I didn't know it was so important to you." Her watery eyes are full of anger, and I wonder how she can be both fire and ice at the same time. "Hey, I came out here because you needed me, not to fight over a silly tattoo."

Her words are meant to comfort me, but they feel like an

innocuous scratch ripping off a scab, and I need to bolt before I bleed all over everything.

"I'm sorry to have interrupted what would've been a perfect day with your girlfriend. Don't let me ruin anything else for you." I stand rigid, brows pulled in so tight, pressure over my left eye threatens my vision. Clutching the opening of my hoodie, I nod toward her car. "You can go. I don't need your help."

"You really need to check your drama level." She picks up her bag and keys, her eyes more water than fire. "Let me know when you do." She turns on her boot heel and slams the gate on her way out.

I stand there until her car is out of sight, standing straight, expression fixed. She's obviously moved on, doing things with Sitta that we'd always said we would do together. It's not that I'm angry she's doing things without me. It's just I thought I'd be involved, somehow. Just like she's involved in what I do. Isn't that what best friends do? I guess I kind of suck at that, too. First Panayis, then Robin. At least I'm consistent.

I'm not letting that happen with Jay, too. I guess I just have to talk to him. He comes back in a few days. I'll figure it out by then.

Now, I'm going to focus on the one thing that hasn't failed me—my diet plan. I press my hand into my stomach pooch and feel my hip bone instead of a tub of dough. I run my hand down my outer leg and have hope one day that will feel the same.

*****

A few days later, the last of break, I sit on the swing under the huge tree as Fengari chases the chickens around the flower beds. The sun's hidden behind the cloudy haze of an early January afternoon. The air smells of pine needles and crisp air, the sound of new music in my ears, thanks to an e-gift card Dad sent me as a belated Christmas present.

"Hey." Panayis taps me on the shoulder. "Can I say I'm sorry?" He stays to my side keeping his eyes on the dog.

I remove one of my ear buds.

"You can say whatever you want, Pawn." I'm so not letting him off the hook that easily.

He snorts and shakes his head. I swallow, immediately regretting calling him by the name he hates. My eyes stay glued to the dog, too, following him in circles as he barks and play-jumps at the chickens, making them squawk and flap their wings.

"I mean, I want to apologize for sticking my nose in your business. I shouldn't have said anything. It's not my place to judge."

I sneak a glance at him. He's grasping the sides of a plate covered in plastic like whatever's on it might explode any minute.

"What's that?" I nod at the plate.

"I made you those cookies. As a peace offering. The ones my mom taught me how to make." He waits a minute, but when I stay silent, he sets the cookies on the ground and heads toward the gate.

I want to say something. To tell him how sweet it is to do that. But I can't because panic lumps in my throat, making it impossible to speak.

I stare at the cookies and want to see forgiveness, love, friendship. But all I see are calories. I'll have to eat them to accept his apology. But I can't. And he'll never understand.

I clench my teeth. *Talk about anything but the cookies.*

"You're wrong," I say to his back. "About Jay."

He turns around, sadness fading from his expression as quickly as it appears.

"I'll prove it as soon as he comes back." I raise my chin in defiance, something I learned from my grandmother.

"I hope so." His voice is soft. I stand, shaking with determination.

"Why do you care anyway? Why'd you get so mad?" I almost feel the heat in his skin as it rises from his neck to his cheeks.

He kicks his shoes at the grass.

"I don't... I just don't want you to get hurt." He moves toward me and I back up, like I can outrun the pain on his face. "You're a good person, Wren, and you deserve to be treated well, not locked away in some secret office hook-up."

My eyes widen at the mention of the office, and I recoil back into the swing. His shoulders slump.

"I mean, whatever you want."

I open my mouth to reply, but the chime of a cuckoo clock interrupts my thought. A text.

Back early. Long story. Meet later?

"It's Jay." The relief in hearing from him swells in me like a million helium balloons, but knots I'd forgotten tighten in my stomach, although I don't know why. Icy tears blur my vision. "He wants to meet later."

Panayis knits his brows and appears to contemplate the tall branches of the oak tree. Hands on his hips, he shakes his head at the sunless sky. When he does turn to face me, his frosty glare tightens the knots in my stomach.

"Alone? In the office. In secret?" A mixture of pleading and exasperation bleed from his voice.

"So what if he does?" I spit my words at him. "Like you said, it's none of your business." My upper lip twitches into a sneer. Beached Whale Girl whispers he could be right. Before she can say anymore, I search for the box in the back of my mind's closet to pack away any doubt, but it's nowhere to be found. *Shut up. Shut up.* "Shut up!"

"Okay. Enjoy your date."

A hot tear burns my cheek. How can I tell him I'm screaming at myself? Rearing backward, I slink off to the other side of the yard so he can't see me cry. When I wipe the tears away and turn back, he's gone.

Of course he is. Why would anyone stick around after that?

I stare at the cookies sitting on the ground. The power to chew is overwhelming, but I have to be better. I scoop up his plate, intent on throwing it in the trash, mind reeling with questions that had no answers. He doesn't know Jay like I do. And he doesn't know me either.

I race to the garbage bins behind the office before I can change my mind. Their sweet licorice and sugar smell makes my mouth water. Fumbling with the latch on the bin, I drop the plate, sending broken porcelain and cookies everywhere.

"Fabulous." I let out an exasperated sigh.

I crouch down to pick up the broken shards of Panayis's peace offering and split my knee on a pointed piece. Cursing my clumsiness, I scoop up the cookies I can reach and lean back against the fence, eyes closed trying to steady my breathing.

Beached Whale Girl's voice whispers again. *None of this matters. You're not pretty enough or skinny enough for Jay.* Panayis is right. Robin is right, and I hate them for it. No one will ever notice me, and I'll never become the kind of girl who could ever call a boy like Jay her boyfriend.

Robotically, I shove an entire cookie in my mouth and chew. Numbness spreads through my body, and Beached Whale Girl relaxes into a familiar routine. *Yes, eat. That is what you need. Feel better. You're fat anyway. It doesn't matter.*

I close my eyes and devour cookie after cookie, not tasting but allowing the chewing and swallowing to comfort me. Nothing matters but the blanket of warmth spreading from my mouth, down my throat, and into my stomach. Until the cookies are gone.

Beached Whale Girl laughs, and the warmth turns to ice. *This. Right here. Is what's wrong with you. How pathetic you are eating cookies off the ground. Do you even see the dirt and germs? Do you really feel better? Because you shouldn't. All you should feel is fat.*

I shiver.

I've been throwing up so often that I don't have to try anymore. I kneel over an old box next to the bins, putting extra pressure on my cut, embracing the pain. My body empties. Lightning strikes explode in my back with every wretch.

This is what you deserve. When there's nothing left, I throw the box into the bin, covering it with papers and bags.

In my room, I record everything in my journal. Then get ready to see Jay.

Chapter 16

This time I'm the first one to arrive at the office. No sense trying to sneak out anymore. As I closed the door, Granny's last words to me rang in my ears. "If you're man enough to do the crime, make sure you're man enough to do the time."

I exhale to shake off the memory and focus on what I'm going to say to Jay. In his case, there's no crime, at least not yet. The door creaks open, sweeping in the icy wind.

"Man, did I miss you." He closes the door, opens the zipper of my sweater and slides his hands to my back, leaning in for a kiss.

I step back and move his hands to his sides.

"What's wrong? Didn't you miss me?" This time he finds my mouth with his. He's so warm and smells like I could matter.

I almost forget I had anything to say. He wraps me in his arms, and I melt into him.

But then Panayis's voice is telling me Jay's using me, and I step backward.

"We need to talk."

He exhales through his nose and wipes his mouth. "Okay. What would you like to talk about?" His tone stiffens my spine.

"Don't you want to tell me about your vacation? We haven't talked the entire break. In fact, we haven't even seen each other since our little picnic. And all you want to do is make out?"

This makes him grin. He wraps his arms around my waist.

145

"Of course I do." His breath tickles my neck. "I miss you, all of you." His eyes travel the length of my body. "Let's make up for lost time." He squeezes me.

Doubt tickles the back of my mind. I mean, shouldn't he want to catch up? Unless Robin's right. I plant my feet firmly to the ground, and push his hands away.

"Jay, are you… Are you hanging out with anyone else? Like we do?" The words tumble out of my mouth before I can suck them back in.

His brows draw together and a full, throaty laugh bellows from deep within his chest.

"Who told you that? Robin again?" He runs his hand through his hair, making the spikes fall like crashing waves on a windy beach. "No, Wren. I mean, I hang out with other people—girls sometimes, but we aren't a thing. Not like you and me." He checks his watch and shoves his hands in his pockets.

"What exactly are you and me?" Time slows down, and the weight of the question presses hard on my chest. I've spent the last couple of weeks waiting for this moment, and now I'm not sure I'm ready for the answer. "I mean, I like this, what we're doing. I just want to know *what* we're doing."

He stares in silence.

"I mean, don't you?"

His soft blue eyes turn to diamonds.

"You want to hear about my trip and why my jackass dad made us come back early?" He falls against the wall and slides down so his legs fold in front of him.

What I want to hear is how much he missed me and why I'm the one apologizing about our botched picnic even though he's the one who left me to find my way back to the house. To tell me Panayis's words were out of jealousy and not truth. But something's better than nothing. And that's a whole other level of intimacy.

After all, talking's way harder than not talking.

"I guess." I kneel down next to him, and he straightens his legs so the sides touch mine. The lady in the grape barrel floats back and forth on the computer screen like a ping pong ball as I wait for him to tell his story.

"Actually, it's not that complicated." He laughs bitterly. "Grades came out, and mine are lower than my dad thought they should be." He gives me sideways glance. "Then your grandmother told my dad about that day we had our outing." He tilts his head back on the wall and stares at the ceiling.

My heart sinks. This is Granny's fault. Which means it's kind of mine. Anger flushes my cheeks. "Shit. Oh no, I'm so sorry." How can she do this to me? I sit on my knees and face him. "She told me she knew over break. She didn't seem that concerned. What did your dad say?" I lace my hands with his—my own issue forgotten.

"He doesn't care about what I want, only what affects his job." His shoulders slump. "I mean, he doesn't care if we date. He just doesn't want me sneaking around with the boss's granddaughter."

"So then, what do we do?" Hope bubbles under the film of the last few weeks of uncertainty.

"Exactly what he said. We date. For real. In public. That way, we aren't making him 'look bad.'" He put air quotes around the last two words. "And we can still do what we do." His hands are firm on my hips, and I let him guide me closer. "And, you can finally stop asking me silly questions." My bubble of hope erupts into a spring of gratitude and excitement.

"Did you just ask me to be your girlfriend?" My heart skips every other beat as the air rushes out of my lungs.

The right side of his mouth curls into a crooked grin. "Is that going to be a problem for you?" He blinks slowly and squeezes my hands.

"Um, no, I don't think so. I can learn to deal with it." I purse my lips together and nod, hiding the smile that's never going away.

"Good." His lips brush against mine, soft at first, then harder and hungrier. His hands run the length of my upper body and around my waist. Just as I feel myself floating away under his touch, he comes up for air, licking his swollen lips. "Can we talk about how skinny you're getting?" He circles his hands around my waist as if he can tap his fingertips together. A small groan escapes his lips as he rests his forehead against mine.

I blush at the compliment. His eyes are no longer diamonds but pools of exotic waters, inviting me in for a swim.

I dive in, head first.

*****

I let the back door slam back at the house.

"Is that you, Wren?" Granny calls from her bedroom. It's unusual for her to be up there so early. More unusual, Fengari's bed isn't in the kitchen. I grunt out a response, but that's not enough for her. "Could you come here for a minute, please?"

I let out a huge, heavy sigh and climb the stairs, stopping at her doorway with as little emotion as possible. "What?"

Either Granny doesn't hear me or she's pretending not to. Her face is smooth with a neutral grin plastered on her lips.

"Come over here and sit a minute." She pats the mattress next to her, and then smooths the sheets. I sit but face the rest of the room and not her. "How's Jay?"

"Really? That's what you're leading with?" I move to leave, but she touches my arm. I lower myself back on to the bed. "Why did you say anything to his dad? You ramble on with your 'can't do the crime' speech and then you decide my punishment?"

She coughs and clears her throat. "Wren."

There's weakness in her voice, a sure sign she knows I'm right. "Too bad for you, then, because we are dating now. He's my boyfriend." I hold her gaze with my own, daring her, although to do what, I'm not sure.

Instead of fire in her eyes, only a soft ember burns. "It's not my intention to cause trouble for you. In fact, I'm helping you." She brushes a hair from her face.

"I'd hate to see how you'd hurt someone if that's your way of helping."

"You're misunderstanding, Wren."

148

Everyone tells me I'm misunderstanding, but I know what I feel. I see Jay's expression when he's around, how his body reacts to mine.

"It's whatever anyway. It's done." I wait a minute but she's silent. "Can I go now?"

"Yes, good night. Remember that I love you."

I don't respond as I head to my room and shut my door. I'll show her. Panayis, too. I'll show them all.

Beached Whale Girl is dead. Long live Skinny V-Neck Girl.

*****

The last Sunday of Winter Break, I stay the night at Robin's house so I can ride with her to school the next day. Mom practically forced me to text her and say sorry for overreacting about her tattoo. That our friendship meant more than one or two relationships, and I need my friends after being so isolated from everything, living way out here. I think she wanted an excuse to not have to tell me why another bag full of evening wear and new lingerie sat by her bedroom door.

In her room, Robin does most of the talking. I stop her only once to ask to borrow something to wear. Jay and I have a big surprise for everyone, and I need an outfit deserving of the occasion. And now I actually fit into her things.

She rambles on about her last week of vacation and how her brothers dominate the house when the oldest comes back from school and how she's sick of sharing her car with everyone and will be glad to have her routine again. She carefully avoids bringing up Sitta, but her frequent phone checking and the way she smiles into it tells me all's well in Loverville. She asks me if I've talked to Jay, but I avoid telling her everything. I want her to be surprised, too. She's so going to be proud that I'm standing up for myself the way she does.

The next morning, she fits the car into her usual parking spot and flips down the visor for a final inspection before making her way to the crowd huddling around Jay's truck. I do the same. This time, the eyes in my reflection are full of a determination that didn't exist yesterday. I raise my chin, set my mouth and shoulders and grab my bag. Without waiting for Robin, I make strides straight to Jay. He sees me coming, smiles, and opens his arms. I strut into them like I've done it a thousand times. His mouth meets mine. Hard. In front of everyone.

"Get some!" Amsel hoots and hollers.

When he lets me go, I adjust my bag, clasp Jay's hand, and stand next to him. I expect Robin to be smiling and giving me a thumbs-up or something. Instead, she's looking at Sitta who's looking at Ashley. None of them are smiling.

Robin passes me and sidles up to Sitta. They lace hands as they turn toward campus and never once turn around. I smile at Jay and shrug. The way he's smiling at me makes me forget all about Robin.

"Happy now?" He squeezes my hand. I return one, and he kisses me again. I scan the parking lot for Panayis, wondering if he saw, then remember I hate him and don't care.

"When's the next party?"

"Who are you?" He winks, and my chest swells so much it nearly bursts.

"I guess that'd be your girlfriend… Can we go to class now? It's a tad cold out here."

*****

"What do you think you're doing?" Robin tosses her book bag on the floor of the bathroom, a clear mood indicator since she's about as germophobic as a person can be.

I've been preparing for this moment all morning. I'm still surprised at how she reacted. I knew she'd be shocked, but angry never crossed my mind. Beached Whale Girl would've apologized for not telling her in advance and probably do something awkward so Robin would feel sorry for her.

But I'm no longer that girl. I will the butterflies in my stomach to be still and turn to the mirror, smoothing the frizz appearing around my face. "Checking my hair?" I reach for my bag.

"You know what I mean." Her hands are balled into fists resting on her hips like she's some angry mom about to scold her toddler. "I told you to be careful."

"I know what I'm doing." I start toward the bathroom door, but she blocks my way. "Do you mind?" My voice catches on the last word. I flare my nostrils, taking in more air then huffing it out.

"Do you? You're my best friend, but I've never seen you act this way. Not once. This isn't you. Why are you willing to risk everything for some guy?"

"Who is risking everything? And I'm the dramatic one?"

She opens her eyes wide. "If the skirt fits." Her eyes go to my borrowed clothes. Tears sting the corners of my eyes, but I blink them back.

"Uh, it's your skirt. Unless you're giving me an ultimatum. Are you saying we can't be friends if I'm dating someone? Hypocritical much?"

"Of course not." Her shoulders droop as she sighs. "I just want you to be careful. If he's really doing what Panayis says, you might get hurt. That's all I'm saying." She moves to the side, letting me pass. Her face is blotchy, and she's wearing the same expression Granny had that night in her room. Little earthquakes well in my chest.

Why is she reacting this way? If she's really my best friend, she'd want me to be happy. The entire world's against Jay and me when all I want is for people to see that I'm finally getting something I want. What makes it worse is she sounds exactly like Panayis. His words echo in my head, and hers feel like a stab wound straight through my heart.

"Why didn't you tell me?" she asks, pain in her voice.

I don't know why, but I want her to hurt as much as I do in this moment. I straighten my spine and throw back my shoulders, clenching my fists to hide their shaking.

"Because I knew you'd be jealous and act like a bitch about it. Just like you're doing right now." I turn toward the door before she notices my lip quivering.

"Wow. When you're back from your trip to Crazy Town, call me.

If I'm around, I'll see if I can help you come back from whatever this is." Her voice is filled with tears.

I lift my chin.

"Yeah, okay." More than anything, I need my best friend. She's the one who knows how to deal with people and high school drama. But she sounds so much like Panayis, the boy I now hate, and I can't deal. "Feel free to lose my number because I won't need any sort of help." I march over the threshold, and the door between Robin and me closes in slow motion.

Before I enter the cafeteria, I pause a minute to stop shaking. At our table, Jay pushes Amsel over to make room for me. He doesn't really need to, because there's considerably more room since Robin and Sitta are missing. I fit in without being smashed.

"Where's Robin?" Jay asks.

I scan the crowds to see if she's come in and lock eyes with Panayis standing at the opposite door. His mouth is a flat line. He darts his gaze over my head. I stare, hoping he'll get the same message I've just given Robin.

"She's probably with Sitta."

He kisses me, tasting like turkey sandwich and banana. When I check for Panayis, there's only an empty spot.

"I guess we're on our own." I kiss him again.

"Get a room, you two," Amsel says.

"Screw you." Jay winks at me.

I swallow a grin and open my lunch. I'm starving, but way too excited to actually eat. My diet plan dictated that I eat half of my sandwich and then go to the bathroom to expel what my body doesn't use in the next few minutes. The last thing I want is to leave the table, but I don't have a choice. Things are finally working out for me, and I'm not about to change anything now.

Chapter 17

A circle of headlights pools through the rows of vines casting shadows on the road ahead. A large fire burns in the center, and an enormous pile of dead branches lies in the back of one of the trucks. Jay's tires bump from the paved street to the dirt road. For days, Panayis and Robin's words have mingled together and echoed in the back of my mind. Tonight, I'm pushing them out. I'm concentrating on not doing anything stupid like tripping over a rock and falling on my face, or worse. When he turns off the engine, I adjust my sweater over my shoulders, preparing to jump into the world of parties and pretty people.

"Why don't you leave your sweater in the truck?" Jay slides his finger down my spine.

"Oh, well, I only wore a tank under it, and it seems kind of cold." Frost circulates in the rays of the headlights on the field.

Jay's curls his mouth upward and bites his lip, grazing my collarbone with the same hand. "You won't need it. There's a fire, and if that doesn't work, I'll keep you warm." His eyes are hypnotizing. "Tonight's about having fun. No fights with Robin, no working at the vineyard, just you and me and a bonfire to keep us warm."

"Okay. It's probably not that cold anyway." It's probably not frost—just smoke from the fire, and whatever else. "Let's go already." I drop my sweater on the seat and, like the proverbial moth, head straight for the flame.

Amsel's speakers belt something about a fun night under the stars with your sweetie, and the group's well on their way to not remembering much about what they're about to do. Maggie sits on the tailgate of one of the trucks, swinging her legs back and forth. She's wearing a flowered top with black leggings and a denim jacket. Higher in the bed of the truck, Robin and Sitta are deep in discussion, except Robin's totally faking. Her laugh gives it away every time. Two can play that game.

"Hi Maggie." I smile extra big.

"Wren! I'm glad you're here." She glances at Robin then smiles at me. She sips her beer. "Want one?" She holds hers in the air. My heart races. Everyone is holding either a bottle or a red cup.

"Um, that's okay." I forgot about the beer. Stupid. I'd been so focused on what I would wear and how it would be at a party with people who don't like me—Robin—that I'd forgotten about the calorie trap. Not only are they the kind of thing that go straight to your ass and stomach, I've never cared much for it. Mom let me try it once, and that was enough for me.

"Too bad, because I've already opened one for you." Jay hands me my own chilled bottle. "Bet you can't keep up with me." He chugs his beer, eyes sparkling in the firelight. Robin's eyes are narrowed, arms crossed. Her expression says she knows exactly what I'm about to do. I suppress the desire to roll my eyes.

"Probably right." Jay's always telling me I need to chill. Despite the calories and the panic threatening to close my throat, I swallow a large gulp. This is what Skinny V-Neck Girl would do. It's what they're all doing. The bubbles burn my chest as they go down.

"That's my girl." Jay empties his bottle, lets out a whoop and throws it into the bed of one of the nearby trucks. The clank echoes after his cry, causing a nearby dog to bark a warning. I freeze for a moment, expecting some hysterical farmer to chase us off with a shotgun or something, and then Jay grabs me by my waist and kisses me hard on the mouth. Maggie laughs too loud. I shut my eyes, pretending this is normal. When he lets go, I gulp down half the beer.

"That's my girl!" Jay shouts into the sky this time, then heads to the cooler for another.

Maggie peels the label off of her bottle, and the other two go back to their fake conversation.

"So, Maggie." I steel my nerves and clear my throat. "Did you see the Gatsby movie? The newer one?" My voice is about an octave higher than normal. She glances backward before answering with a smile that doesn't reach her eyes. "It's so much better than the old one from the 70s."

Beached Whale Girl's laughing in the back of my mind. *No one talks about homework. Nice job.*

"Who cares? They're both hot!" She jumps from the truck and trips over the uneven ground, plowing into my shoulder. Grabbing my arm, she laughs too loud. "The party is starting!" She totters to the other side of the fire and leans against Amsel.

I catch Robin's expression, all puppy dog eyes and a turned-down smile. Screw that. Jay's there with another beer. Handing it to me, he wraps his arm around my shivering waist and whispers in my ear.

"You're so pretty." He kisses my bare shoulder then my neck, sending a different kind of shiver down my spine. I close my eyes, not really believing he's saying those things to me. He pushes aside my hair. "You cold?" He squeezes his arms around mine, making it hard to hug him back.

I inhale his scent and turn my head into my shoulder. He runs his hands up and down my back and then brings his face to mine. Whispering how beautiful I am, he presses his lips to mine, flicking my lips with his tongue. I can almost hear Robin's disapproval, which only makes me kiss him harder.

After, he rests his forehead on mine, running his fingers through my hair. "You up for a moonlit stroll?"

I leave my untouched bottle on the truck bed. Taking my hand, he leads me away from the heat of the fire and headlights into the dark of the budding vines. A few feet in, he turns and brings me close to him.

"I'm so glad you're here." His hands circle my waist then slide under my tank, his fingers spreading across my back. It may be the alcohol, but between the smell of the budding fruit, the earth, and Jay's musky scent, the ground sinks beneath my feet and the air whirls around my head, making it hard to think. I slide my hands up his arms toward his back.

He exhales, his breath smelling like beer. "You're so pretty. I can't keep my hands off you."

He tickles the middle of my stomach, and my muscles tense. A giggle escapes my lips. His lips press hard against mine. He's so tall and warm, but all I can feel are eyes on us in the dark rows of vines. Moving shadows and the sound of rustling branches keep my eyes darting into the distance. Robin's condescension haunts me and it's all too much. I turn away, but he draws me tighter.

"Stop," I mutter into his mouth as he licks my bottom lip. "Jay, that's enough."

His hand reaches the front of my shirt and slips over my bra. "Baby, you're so amazing. Let me kiss you."

Of course I want him to kiss me. Who wouldn't want to be where I am right now? But the more I silence the voice rising to be heard, the louder it becomes. I bring my hands to his chest and push him away.

"I said stop." Breathless, I trip backwards into a shallow hole but catch myself, crossing my arms against the cold.

The beer's made my head fuzzy, and I can't remember why I didn't want him to touch me, because I craved it. But as much as I want him to, it can't be where everyone can hear or even see us. I want him, but not like this.

"What's wrong? You know I think you're hot. I want to be with you." He wipes his mouth with the back of his hand.

"Me, too. It's just everyone's right there, and I've never been to a bonfire and we're missing it." My reasons turn to rambling, and he smiles. I touch his stomach and immediately regret it. His lips press hard on mine, but I jerk away. "I mean it."

"Okay, okay." He steps back, inhales sharply, then spits into the dark. Then the right corner of his mouth slides into a smile. "I love you."

All the words I've ever known leave my vocabulary. I force my wrinkling brow to relax and spread my lips into an upward curve. "Oh."

"Did you hear me?" His words melt into my ears.

"I love you, too." I swallow.

He steps forward and brushes my cheek with his finger.

"Wren? You back here?" Robin emerges from the shadowed vines. "I wondered where you went."

Jay's grin morphs into a sneer but disappears so quick I must have imagined it.

"What do you want? We're kind of busy." I'm face to face with her crossing my arms.

"Just wanted to make sure you're all right. I didn't see you and got worried is all." She glances at Jay then back at me.

"You aren't my mother. I don't need you checking up on me." My hands slide around Jay's waist. "See? I'm fine, even without your supervision."

"Very fine," Jay says.

I try to shoot her a thank you, but she's not paying attention to me. She's scowling at Jay and waving him off.

"I'm talking to my best friend, not you," she says.

He scoffs. "I'm getting another beer. Come find me when she's done." He stumbles through the vines toward the fire.

"Best friend?" I ask "Thought you gave that title to Sitta." It's hard to spit the words, like my tongue's swollen.

"Why are you acting this way? You've changed so much. I hardly recognize you." Robin's eyes brush over my tank top then toward the group. "These aren't your kind of people."

"Why? Because I'm not a cheerleader or in student government, like you? Are you jealous because Jay wants to be with me?"

"Jealous? No. I don't understand why you think you need to change who you are or how you act to get a boyfriend is all. Sneaking around, drinking. You don't do those things."

"I guess I do. And I'm not sneaking around, obviously." I hate that she makes me feel like I'm some lost puppy. "I don't need you or your pitiful friendship if this is how you're going to be around me and my boyfriend." I raise my chin.

"Ugh. Stop throwing that word around like it's some sort of trophy. You didn't win anything."

"I knew you were jealous." A lump in my throat's all that's holding back a flood of tears. "And if you can't deal with me having a guy in my life that makes me happy, then you obviously aren't the friend I thought you were."

Despite the hardened expression I'm trying to wear, my heart twists with regret as soon as the words leave my mouth. They're the kind that can't be taken back. Her face drops, but then she smiles— an empty curve on her shaking upper lip.

"If that's the way you want it. Fine."

"Fine." I choke down a jagged sob.

She turns toward the vines, finds Sitta, and the two of them climb into her car. In the dark, I memorize the entire scene. Everyone's drunk-dancing in the truck beds and around the fire. My shoulders and knees shake with the finality of a friendship-ending fight, but I refuse to let Beached Whale Girl back out of her box.

Jay finds me at the edge of the party and leads me back to the fire, where the music's loud enough to drown out Robin's condescending voice playing in my head. Jay hands me another beer, and this time I clutch it willingly, wanting to forget the vulnerable feeling I had when we were alone in the vines. To forget Robin's eyes when I said I didn't need her. To forget Panayis and his sweet voice and strong arms. To forget that this is my life now, and my family is over and nothing will ever be normal again.

I close my eyes until the pain drowns in the music's beats. Robin's brake lights bounce up and down until she hits paved road. She's gone. I smile at Jay.

"Come on. Let's dance."

Chapter 18

Before I open my eyes, pots crashing and plates clinking pound in my ears. Prying my lids apart, I can practically hear the light streaming from the bare window. With a groan, I roll over and bury my head under my pillow, welcoming silence. Bacon and coffee permeate the dark, inviting me to come downstairs. Instead of making me hungry, the smell turns my stomach. Reaching for my journal under my mattress, I let out another groan and try to count the beers I drank at the bonfire.

I'd had enough to help me forget about my fight with Robin. But I can't forget Jay's groping hands and pressing kisses. His attention excites and terrifies me. I like feeling wanted, but I'm not sure I'm ready for the things he wants to do. If only the effects of the beer were permanent.

"Wren! Come and eat breakfast!" Granny shouts her sing-songy tone from the bottom of the stairs. "Don't let it get cold!" Her voice scratches my spine, leaving shards of glass in my ears. My head pounds in time with my heart.

Downstairs, bacon and syrup mingle with stale beer and smoke from the bonfire. I reach for a piece of toast and nibble around the edges enough to avoid any probing questions about my appetite. Granny places a mug of coffee in front of me and pats my shoulder.

"Where's Mom?" A sharp pain of dread settles in my shoulder blades.

"Had an early meeting in town. You got in late last night." She lets her words hang, waiting for my response.

"I made it back before curfew."

"Oh, I know exactly what time you got here. That god-awful truck up and down the driveway. The birds knew when you got home." She flips the pancakes browning on the griddle.

"Sorry. I tried to be quiet, but I can't help the sound of the truck." I keep my tone as anti-sarcasm as I can, but I can't help an eye roll. Mental note: have Jay drop me off at the road next time. Why she hates him so much is a mystery, but since I want to spend the day in my room with a book, I'm not asking.

"No matter. There's a lot to be done today, vines to be tied and ground to turn over." She sets a plate of pancakes on the table, the aroma an arrow to my appetite.

"Granny, I'm not feeling very good. I'd rather just stay in." The pancake steam races against the coffee's toward the ceiling.

"Nonsense. Nothing better than fresh air to get you back to one hundred percent." Her eyes move over my frame. "Eat those before they get cold. You'll need your energy."

When she turns away, I push away the plate. My phone buzzes. Jay.

Hi. 💀

Memories of his hands and Robin's words swill together in a beer haze. I text back, saying I'm eating breakfast and will text later. Not three seconds go by, and my phone buzzes again.

I miss you. Do you miss me?

And again.

Sorry if I freaked you out last night. I just really love you and want to be with you.

And another time.

I want to see you.

My lips slip into a reluctant grin. He didn't mean to make me feel bad about last night. And this proves it. I text back.

> *I want to see*
> *you, too, but*
> *Granny is*
> *making me work*
> *today. Text you*
> *when I'm done.*

"Someone's getting a lot of attention," Granny says.

I fake a smile and go upstairs to get ready. Granny calls up the stairs.

"You didn't eat anything."

*****

As usual, Panayis is already working when I arrive, bundled up in a hoodie and coat. Spring brings clear skies, but the air's still frigid with stubborn winter frost. Buds will soon be forming on the vines, but for now, they're barren limbs entangled in sleep.

In the row over, he clips stray shoots from the twisted wood, carefully avoiding the wire frames waiting for the vines. His hands smooth their way over the base, feeling for knobs of new growth. The muscles and veins in his forearms stand at attention as he flexes and fists his hands.

"I thought we already did the pruning."

Panayis startles and fumbles his clippers.

"Oh, sorry. I thought you knew I was here." I raise my eyebrows and cross my arms.

"I didn't hear you." He stands sideways, studying the vines and the wires separating us.

"I guess."

Silence.

He's wearing a long-sleeved t-shirt and loose jeans with a bandana shoved into his back pocket, already damp. My breath turns into fog and evaporates. Kind of like my irritation when I'm around him. As irritating as he is, it's hard to stay angry. Anxious to see the smile behind his eyes, I search for something to say.

"The cookies were good. Thanks for making them."

He stands taller, and his demeanor lightens, although his expression stays the same. Glancing at me, he shoves his ungloved hand into his pocket, no sparkle in his smile.

"I'm glad you liked them. Thought you left them on the ground, though. Didn't seem like you wanted them."

"I was angry, sorry." I sigh and step closer, and a stray branch pokes me in the face. "Ugh!" My hand shoots to my cheek. Panayis glides under the wires, his hand covering mine. "I'm fine, just another Wren Special."

He laughs for real this time, moving my hand away from the scratch.

"It's red but it isn't bleeding. I think you'll live."

"Thanks, Dr. P."

His gaze travels from my cheek to my eyes, but his own are darkened by a shadow.

"I meant it when I said I'm sorry. Sometimes, I'm just, you know." I can't tell if he understands, because even I'm not sure.

"If I do go into medicine, having you around will be job security." He presses his bandana to my cheek. "And I know you're sorry. The blood sacrifice on the vine is evidence enough." He smiles and the crinkle around his eyes is back. Something inside me defrosts.

"Well, I have to be good for something, I guess." His hand's still covering mine, its warmth grounding me in a way I haven't felt in a long time. My heart pounds two beats at once. If anyone sees what appears to be hand-holding, rumors will fly and Jay will freak. Thinking about Jay makes my heart skip, and not in the good way.

Too many emotions coming too fast. "Um, we should probably get to work. Thanks for the medical advice, Doc."

He blinks, snapping out of a daze. He lets go of my hand and slides his into his gloves. I follow him under the vines, avoiding the pools of water underneath.

As I crouch, my distorted reflection ripples in the puddle. One side of my face is bloated and fat, and the other side is drawn, cheeks sunken. Panayis steps in the puddle, sending splinters of my reflection to its outer edges.

"What are you doing?"

"Nothing, why?"

He laughs like nothing happened, like we'd never fought. Now, being outside all day isn't such a punishment.

We plod our way down the rows of vines in a comfortable silence, pruning away the stray shoots to make way for better grape production as the weather warms. An unspoken rhythm emerges: I pile as he clips. The automatic movements allow my mind to wander.

It's obvious Jay and Panayis don't like each other—since the first day I saw them together. I know I shouldn't ask, and this is the sort of thing Robin and I would spend hours FBI-ing social media to find out answers. But that's not happening any time soon.

"Why don't you guys like each other?" I keep my eyes on the growing pile of pruned shoots, kicking strays back into the mass. I dare a peek at him from the corner of my eye. He pauses for a split second then recovers back into his rhythm.

"Who?" he asks. The way he moves, I can't tell if he's grinning or grimacing.

"You and Jay. There's obviously something going on between you, and I don't like my friend and my boyfriend fighting. That's all." I clear my throat and throw his discards into a new pile.

"We're friends now? Is that what we are?" A sheepish grin inches across his face and echoes in my chest.

Heat rises from my neck into my cheeks. My eyes widen in surprise at my own embarrassment, which only makes me blush more. I claim interest in the pile of castaway canes, but he touches my arm.

"You don't have to be embarrassed. You just said we're friends, and I like thinking of you that way. And besides, friends don't hide stuff from each other."

"Why are you touching my girlfriend?" Jay stands a few feet away, eyes wild and lips tight, a mix of hate and disgust. I stumble backward into the vines behind me.

"We…we were just talking. No big deal," I say. Jay acts like he doesn't hear me and stares down Panayis. My newly declared friend exhales.

"Relax." Panayis turns to his vines.

"Don't tell me to relax. All you do is snatch whatever you want without any regard to who it hurts." He cocks his chin and stretches his shoulders wide, reminding me of Granny's rooster.

Panayis turns around. "I don't have time to play the Poor Jay Game, so if you don't mind…"

"I do mind. I'm so sick of seeing your face in my business."

"How am I in your face?" Panayis gestures to the surroundings. "I'm out here, working. You're holed up in the back office."

"Hey," I say.

"Sorry." His voice is softer. He steps in Jay's direction. "I'm as far away from you as I can get."

"But now you're on my girl, and I won't allow that. Stay away from her."

I move to intercept Jay, a forced smile on my face. I want the peace we had a few moments ago. I want Jay to hug me and tell me how happy he is to see me and all the things he's texted earlier.

"This is a surprise." I widen my smile.

"Obviously." He grabs my arm and leads me back to the driveway in front of the house. "What do you think you're doing, embarrassing me? You need to stay away from him." He folds his hands over his head. I breathe hard, unsure where to land. We weren't doing anything wrong; I don't know what Jay thinks he saw.

"I'm sorry. Granny makes us work together…" My wave of anger suffocates under a blanket of shame. I made him mad, and this is my fault.

"I don't care. You're going to have to figure out a way. That jackass has been in my face since 7th grade, and I am over him."

"What are you talking about?" The sun is higher in the sky, but a chill races up my spine. I hug my sweatshirt.

"We used to play in the same league, but the coach moved him up to varsity freshmen year. Everybody knew it should've been me, but they took pity on him for some reason. He quit when he couldn't handle it, of course. He's useless and he knows it. That's why he works out here, away from everyone." He spits to the side and then pauses, resting his hand on my cheek.

"I'm sorry, Jay, I didn't know. You played football? He did, too?" But they don't anymore. I don't know why it still matters. But then Robin and I never talked about the time she moved to orange belt when I stayed at yellow, even though we started karate at the same time. Some things just stay better unspoken, I guess.

"Just promise me you'll stay away from him."

Panayis and I had just figured out we were friends, and he's the one person I don't feel awkward around since my fight with Robin. Now the one person who says he loves me wants me to give him up. I narrow my eyes and study him. His skin is paler than normal, and he needs to shave—just like my dad when he stresses. And now he's gone.

"Please, Wren. For me. We're so good together, and I've never felt like this about anyone before. You make me crazy, in the best possible way." He kisses my hand, then my shoulder and neck, working his way to my mouth. My thoughts become fuzzy, and soon I can't tell who made me feel what.

I glance at the rows where Panayis should be, but he's moved to the opposite side, hard at work removing the vines that'll suck the life out of the harvest. New clippings and new piles. I should move on, too. "For you."

"For us." He brings our hands to our sides and threads our fingers together.

"For us." We stand forehead to forehead, connected in mind and body. Ambling toward his truck, our pace slows with every step, neither of us wanting to leave.

"There's a party next week, and we're going." He glares at the hibernating vines. "Everyone can see how together we are." He bites the inside of his cheek and smirks, raising one eyebrow. "And wear something hot."

Chapter 19

The beat of the music dictates my heartbeat before I can even hear it. Cars line the long driveway and spill onto the street. Lights blaze from every window and open door. A group of rowdy seniors play some version of life-sized beer pong on the front lawn, and are only slightly louder than the splashing and screaming coming from the backyard.

This spring's been unseasonably warm, and everyone wants to celebrate shedding their winter coats for something tinier and tighter. There's been a lot of parties this weekend, but Jay picked this one since it's supposed to be the biggest blow out of his senior year.

Jay turns off the motor and the impending summer heat immediately thrusts itself into my lungs, making it hard to breathe.

"You ready?" He jumps out of the driver's side and runs around to help me from the passenger seat.

I tug at the edges of my shorts as if that'll magically make them grow another inch or two. Old habits die hard.

"You look amazing." He kisses my neck. "Don't be nervous. Everyone's having a good time." His hand on the small of my back encourages me toward the house.

"I'm good." I navigate the unfamiliar sidewalk in the stiff wedges I'd borrowed from my mom's closet. She's so into her own thing, she'll never notice they're gone. My feet already ache, though. How she wears these all the time is a mystery. But here I am, wearing them to show up girls I don't care about and impress a guy who already loves me.

Genius.

Every room is lined three-people deep. The beats of the music dominate the conversations, which is probably what everyone wants. More time to empty the keg that's set up in the kitchen. Jay stands close, hands on my hips. He presses himself against me and moves our hips to the music, his mouth searching my neck.

"Jay, people will see." I laugh too loud. Beached Whale Girl cringes, but I force her into silence.

"Let them." His hips dig into my backside, so I step forward, checking for any bystanders. A low chuckle escapes his throat. "All right, I'm going to get us something to drink. Stay here."

Everywhere, couples hold hands, some climb the stairs toward the bedrooms and privacy while others sneak into the hall bathroom. I turn to check out the living room and nearly smash into Robin.

"Oh, hey."

She stares, eyes hard and mouth tight. When she says nothing, I push past her toward the kitchen.

"Good talk."

"What are you doing here? And what are you wearing?" She scowls at my off-the-shoulder blouse and lacey shorts. "Borrow something from your mom? I hear she's making the most out of the divorce. I guess the apple really doesn't fall far from the tree."

"Brilliant, Robin. Talk about my mother. How original. Maybe you can make up some new Yo Momma jokes and gain some popularity." Red anger erupts and hot tears threaten to burn my eyes.

"At least my popularity wasn't earned on my back."

"Screw you, Robin. You know I'm not like that."

"I don't know anything about you anymore." She casts one last glance at my shorts and turns to the backyard.

"Happy spring break to you, too," I say to her back. "What a bitch."

"True story." Jay hands me a full red cup.

I empty it in big gulps, determined to shove Robin into the same box as Panayis. Neither of them have a clue.

"Yes, someone came to party! Let's get you another."

The warmth of the drink drowns Robin's insults. The ocean of anger calming, I force my shoulders to relax and sidle close to Jay.

"Let's just have a good time." I lean on him, and he smiles against my hair. I tilt my face to him, allowing his lips to part mine. I close my eyes as his hand slides under my shirt.

"My thoughts exactly." He releases me and gulps the rest of his drink. Then Amsel's there, chest-butting him, spilling his beer everywhere.

"What's up, Brother?" he asks. "I see you found the keg." He nods to me. "Hey." Before I can reply, he grabs Jay's cup and empties it, then lets out a huge belch.

"Charming," I say.

Jay smiles at me, his eyes on fire with drink and his people. Amsel totters to the kitchen, and Jay follows. People high-five them and shout greetings as they go by, like they're celebrities on a red carpet. No one really says hi to me, but why would they? None of these people know me that well. Being here with Jay is exactly what I want.

A few red cups later, the music changes from Anthem Country to Hip Hop. People gravitate to the pool patio as if the DJ's the Pied Piper. Single people pair off to dance to the mixes. The lights magically dim, or maybe the people just crowd so the shadows seem more obvious than the strung-up lights around the pool.

Jay grabs my hand, and I follow him to the middle of the patio. The bass dictates the movement in my hips. Jay's hand is on my waist, drawing me close to him, our legs intertwining as we sway in unison. I lift my hands to my neck and toss my hair. Jay grabs my arms and draws them over my head. I close my eyes and tilt back my head, letting him control where we move. He spins me around and presses himself behind me, hands riveted to my hips.

Using his grip as an anchor, I buckle my knees and twist low, then straighten my legs so that I'm bent over. Then Beached Whale Girl's there, mocking me for being exactly the girl I used to make fun of.

Like camera flashes, I see myself dancing in too-short shorts, laughing too loud, drinking too much. This is what I want. So why do I feel so exposed?

I straighten and tug on the shorts, adjusting them to cover more skin. The lights spin, and I sway as my stomach bloats with the pressure of the beer. Jay snakes his arms around my waist, trapping mine underneath. He buries his face in my neck.

"You're so beautiful. Let's go upstairs."

More than anything I want to deserve this attention rather than feel like an imposter observing from behind a painted mask. Keeping my gaze straight ahead, I nod.

Upstairs, he closes the bedroom door as I fall onto the bed. The room is dark, except for the light coming in from the window and under the door. I try to count the beers I've had and do the calorie math, but my fingers won't stay still long enough.

Jay lays me back gently on the bed, his tongue lightly flicking my neck and mouth. His hand slides under my top. My legs hang at an awkward angle off the bed, so I bend my knee to scoot myself up, tagging him between his legs.

"Oomph." He rolls over next to me.

"I'm so sorry! Are you okay? I'm such an idiot." I bury my face in his arm. He swallows a few times and, after a minute, he coughs.

"All good. Scared me more than anything." He holds his arms open. "Come here." In the dim light, his crooked smile curves upward. I meet his lips, eager to be lost in his touch. He rolls me over on my back and climbs on top. "Where were we?" His hand finds its spot and runs over my bra.

A sigh escapes my lips, encouraging him to continue.

He slides his hand under me, lifting my torso as he blazes a trail of kisses down my neck. Then I'm arching farther, raising my chin, exposing my neck. There's a release of pressure around my chest, and I realize my bra's undone. Adrenaline pulses through my veins, my heart races and my breath quickens. My eyes dart to the light under the door. Shadows move back and forth outside.

"Is the door locked?"

"Of course." His breath is heavy and his kisses more desperate as he tugs the button on my shorts. His hips move rhythmically against me, his free hand taking mine, trapping it above my head. Robin's words—*on your back*—echo with the thumping music.

I coax his hand to my face, but he slips through my grip and works the button on my shorts again. His weight is heavy and crushes my chest. I inhale but can't take a full breath. I arch to expand my lungs and he moans.

"Wait. I don't know." His kisses force my words into my throat. I can't swallow them, though, and I turn away from his mouth.

"You feel so good. I love you." His mouth trails down my neck to my breasts, licking at my nipples, which betray me, begging him to continue. A deep, breathy growl escapes his throat.

I draw his face back to mine, to keep kissing a while longer. Instead, he rises to his knees and reaches behind his neck, stretching his shirt over his head. Staring into my eyes, he undoes his belt strap with his right hand while his left slides the buckle free.

"Let's talk for a while." I inch backward on the bed, but my addled beer brain leaves me stranded on what to do next.

He matches my crawl. "We are talking, kind of." He cocks an eyebrow and deepens his voice. "Speaking the language of love."

"Wow, okay. No more beer for you." I roll my eyes and suppress a smile, the tension easing in my chest. He grunts.

"I love you and want to show you how much. And this is our last night together until after break. I'll be on that stupid cruise with my family. Let's be together tonight." He slides the back of his hand down my cheek, and I'm pretty sure I'm going to melt off the bed and disappear into the floor.

I want to show him that I love him, to be the girl he wants, and I know he wants this. I lie back as he removes his belt and undoes his pants button. He lifts my top and bra to my neck and kisses me so I almost forget where we are.

When his hands slide to my shorts, *on your back* beats in my ears faster and louder. My heart pounds, my foot shakes back and forth until it feels like it might fly across the room.

"Jay, we shouldn't. I mean, I want to, but…" I spread my top over my body, trying to cover my nakedness.

"I know. Don't worry, everything's all right." His reassuring hands guide my shoulders onto the mattress. More kissing. More touching. But now it's too wet, too strong. Too dark.

I focus on the corner between the ceiling and the wall, following an imaginary line in between the two. He slips my top over my head. I close my eyes as the material slides over my face and keep them that way, focusing on how his fingers send tiny electric shocks over my ribs and waist.

"You feel good." He tears at my shorts and pushes his own jeans toward the floor. He slides his hand between my legs and groans.

"You want this, I can feel it. You won't leave me like this, will you? I'll go crazy and it'll be your fault. You don't want that, do you?"

My eyes jerk open. Just minutes ago, I wanted this. I'd have done anything to be the most beautiful girl he's ever seen. I need that reflection of me in his eyes. But now, his eyes are closed, and I can't see myself. All that's there is the judgment of who I'd be if I can't give him what he wants.

"No." I choke on the word and turn my head to the side. His weight keeps me under him, his breath hard in my ear. There's ripping and a crinkling of paper. The smell of antiseptic.

Salty tears fill my mouth. Somewhere in the back of my mind, Beached Whale Girl's voice is soft, defeated. *It doesn't matter anyway.* I let my body go limp and stare at the lamp on the bedside table. The shade is green.

He pushes into me, and I withdraw inside myself.

When it's over, he rolls onto his back, breathing hard. I don't move. After a minute, he props his head on his bent arm and smooths my hair over and over with his other hand.

"Thank you. So much. You're so beautiful."

In TV shows and movies, this is the part where we lay together and tell each other funny stories, reliving how nice it is to have found each other. My head on his shoulder. I turn onto my side, wanting to feel safe in what I've given him. He straightens his arm in a way that invites me in. For that moment, it's worth it. It's not perfect, but it can be. Will be.

Instead, he reaches for my top and plops it on my head.

"We should get dressed in case someone comes a knockin'." He stands and zips his jeans. After he slips on his shirt, his hand automatically runs over his hair, spiking the tips.

I push my arms through my sleeves, numb and out of words. The beer haze is gone but its remnants fill the air with a putrid stench. He tosses a tissue box from the dresser onto the bed.

"You might want that." He bends down, kissing my forehead. "I love you."

I clear my throat and swallow, staring at the ceiling. "Me, too."

"I'm going to go downstairs. Come find me when you're done, okay?"

I nod and cross my arms over my nakedness as he opens the door. Light and sound flood the room as he leaves. When he closes it, I'm alone with the echoes.

Chapter 20

I'm not sure how many songs play before I find the strength to sit up. I fumble with the button on my shorts, hands shaky and head heavy from the beer. We did what people who love each other do. That's it.

But it didn't feel like love.

I should feel something. Fulfilled in some way. Instead, emptiness consumes the place my heart should be.

The pillows on the bed are still propped in their places, the bedspread wrinkled here and there. I place the tissues on the dresser, needing the room to be like it had before. I pull the chain on the green light, and a halo of yellow shines on the ceiling. Green shadows crawl along the walls. Behind the lamp hangs a cracked mirror, its frame and faded masking tape holding the two sides in place.

The left side of my face angles higher than the right, both distorted by light and shadows, flashlight expressions during a fireside scary tale. My right eye reflects bloated helplessness, and the left is like glass, stark shadows carving its cheekbone. I did everything Skinny V-neck Girl would do. And Beached Whale Girl stands alone in an upstairs room at a party full of strangers.

The door crashes open, the blare of music and light shoving me from my thoughts. Two drunk bodies topple in laughing and kissing.

"Oh, we thought this room was empty." More giggling. Then silence. They stare, waiting for me to leave.

I try telling them the room's all theirs, but the words die in my throat. I must seem like some sort of freak standing there, mouth gulping like a dying fish.

"So, if you're done…" An awkward smile and a nod toward the door propels me to move.

Flashing strands of light make the downstairs a sea of distorted faces, carnival laughter rising up like the bile in my throat. The air is sour with stale beer, and the lack of fresh air makes my head swim. The thumping bass matches the throbbing behind my right eye.

I can't go downstairs and pretend everything's all right. Eyes wide and knees wobbly, I avoid eye contact with anyone between me and the front door. The vineyard is miles away, and it'd take all night to get there on foot, but I can't face sitting next to Jay while he drives me home. And there's no one I can call who won't lecture me or tell me how stupid I am for believing I could be loved for myself.

The weight of my solitude sits on my chest, crushing my heart into a fine powder a strong wind could obliterate forever.

I make it to the bushes lining the front sidewalk before the beer and the bile forces their way out. Some girl laughs and comments on how wasted I must be, her tinny voice coming from some far away TV. Jay's nowhere in sight, probably back at the keg with Amsel. Good. I won't have to explain my leaving.

I keep going until the crunching of leaves is louder than the thumping of the music. Through the drizzle of the incoming fog, an open area with picnic tables and a slide appears; a park in the middle of newly built, cookie-cutter houses. The kind I used to live in with my family. Robin safely across the street.

What is your damage? Beached Whale Girl's whisper grates on my spine.

I let Jay do what he did to me. I thought having sex would make me feel loved, like I finally belong somewhere, with someone. I thought it'd make me better. I straighten my posture. Skinny V-neck Girl responds.

You should go back. He's going to wonder where you are.

But I didn't feel better or even loved.

I dig my phone from my pocket. My lock screen lights up, me and Jay lying on the office floor making stupid faces.

He's not looking for you.

He probably hasn't noticed I'm gone. Somewhere deep down, I know he doesn't mean it when he says he loves me. Another wave of sick gurgles in my belly and shivers up my spine.

It seems so easy for other girls. And none of them would've raced out of the house like I did.

Way to go, Genius.

Tears sting the corners of my eyes, but not from the cold creeping in with the mist. I sit on one of the swings and let my feet drag in the damp sand underneath. After living at the vineyard for so long, it's weird to see man-made nature exist in the middle of stuccoed sticks. Everything beautiful eradicated from this world for a revamped version of nature that suits progress.

Funny what we think about when we can't think about the truth.

I squint past the manicured lawns to see the blotted-out stars beyond the street lights, tears streaming over my lashes, dragging mascara down my cheeks. I cry for the vines and the birds that used to live here.

We used to have swallows that tried to nest on our porch every year, because that's where they'd always come, until the vines were ripped out and robbed them of their home. My dad hammered nails into our porch overhang and mounted a plastic owl to scare them away.

I sob, sorry I didn't understand the birds needed their home until it was too late to help them. *Too late to help myself.*

Tears soak into my top until their bitterness turns my throat sour. My body shakes from the cold and shock, and the swing creaks under my weight. No matter what I do, I'll never outrun Beached Whale Girl.

I leave the park and plod under the streetlights until the houses turn into gas stations and fast food joints. Bubba's parked under a pool of yellow parking lot lights. Panayis and two other boys sit on the tailgate eating fries and laughing. The tension in my shoulders melts. I don't think about what he'll say or what I'll say to him. I just need home.

I wipe the makeup streaks from my face and step into a puddle of light on the opposite side of the lot. I hate for him to see me like this, mascara trailing down my cheeks and shivering in a tear-stained shirt. But I need him to drive me home. There's no way I can explain any of this to Mom, if she's even home. Or worse, Granny.

His eyes shift from his fries toward my frantic waving and he nearly chokes. As he jumps off the truck bed, he says something I can't hear to the others and wipes his hands across his jeans. He jogs to where I stand with my arms crossed in defense of the cold and any human contact. As glad as I am to see him, I can't handle anymore intimacy, friends or anyone else.

"What are you doing out here?" His eyes dart up and down, taking in what must be an awful appearance. "Are you all right? Where's…?"

"I'm fine. I just need a ride home. Can you give me a ride home?" Words pour out of me. The more I talk, the less he can ask. If he finds out, he'll think I'm a bad person, and I can't handle that. Not right now.

"You're not okay. You're shaking." He rips off the shirt hanging over his t-shirt and drapes it around my shoulders. I flinch. "What happened?"

"I was at a party, and then I wanted to leave."

How stupid. Can you hear yourself?

"Hang on. I'll be right back. Stay here." In a minute, he's back with his truck, buckling me in the passenger seat, his friends gone. "I'll get you home."

Bubba's new radio is silent; only the clicking of the blinker and the tires on the road interrupt my thoughts. He sneaks sidelong glances as he speeds out of town. I'm pressed into the passenger door, legs curled and propped against the door. I close my eyes and pretend we're on our way home from school. That the day is bright and homework's our biggest problem.

"Sorry I ruined your night. I didn't know you had friends." I

177

cringe as soon as I say it.

"Nice." Ironic laughter in his voice.

"God, I'm such a bitch." I stare out the windshield. "I mean I never see you hang out with anyone at school."

"To be fair, your attention is elsewhere when we're at school." He flips the blinker and turns left toward home, town lights dimming in the background.

I wrap his shirt tighter. Panayis cranks the heater, and musty air wheezes from the vents.

"I'm a terrible friend. A terrible person." New tears form, and I'm not sure if they're self-pity or sadness. *It doesn't matter anyway.*

"Do you want to talk about it?" Another sidelong glance.

"Not really." The way his forehead wrinkles, he must think I could break into a thousand pieces at any second. I can't imagine his face if he knew the truth. Closing my eyes, I welcome the darkness of the country roads.

"Are you sure I can't help you inside?" Panayis rolls to a stop by the mailboxes. I insisted he let me out at the mailboxes so his engine won't wake Granny. "I want to make sure you're safe."

"You're a good friend. Better than I deserve." I attempt a weak smile. He raises his hand to object, but I interrupt. "I'll be fine. I just need sleep."

"I'm here when you're ready to talk."

"Thanks, Panayis. I'm sorry, for…a lot of things."

The house is dark. I let myself in and climb into the downstairs shower. The water runs over my face and ruined clothes, pain and guilt swirling down the drain. Heat scalds my skin turning it bright red, but the sting keeps away the real pain. I lower the cold water.

I throw my clothes in the washing machine and turn it on, hoping the noise won't bring Granny downstairs. There's a note on the table explaining a plate of dinner is in the microwave for me. On command. my stomach makes a noise reminding me I haven't eaten in a while. Spaghetti and homemade sauce. Without warming it, I rest the plate on my knees as I crouch against the cabinet.

I pick a strand of pasta from the plate and drape it into my mouth. Chewing brings a memory of something comfortable. Another strand. More chewing. Approaching numbness. Three strands, then more, then a handful. I shove the pasta in my mouth faster than I can chew it. I swallow over and over, welcoming the familiar routine. Beached Whale Girl whispers the words of a forgotten evening prayer.

This is who you are. This is what you are. No matter what you try or who you can get to like you, you will always end up here. By yourself.

I open the fridge for more. Nothing. I find the cookie jar and bring it to the floor with me, shoving cookie after cookie into my mouth until they, too, are gone. My stomach bloats in protest. Too much food in too little time. A familiar tensing in my back. In front of the sink, I turn the water on, closing my eyes.

Lightning bolts in my back explode as my punishment comforts me. Lets me know my place.

You tried to climb up the social ladder, but you will always be crouching on the floor alone, where you belong.

Water-logged and exhausted, I clean up the kitchen, toss my clothes in the dryer, and climb the stairs to my bed. My phone lights up with message after message. Opening my closet, I bury it under a pile of shirts I no longer wear. Sleep is the only way to completely block out anything. And I want oblivion.

Chapter 21

FatKat: *I blew it.*
Girl: What happened?
Cherry: You okay?
FatKat: *Ate too much. Again. This is like three days in a row.*
Cherry: Trigger?
FatKat: *You can say that. Nothing's working, I can't get it out of my head.*
Cherry: Do you have someone at home you can talk to?
FatKat: *I have you guys, right?*
Cherry: Not the same.
Girl: You always have us? Need to PM?
Cherry: Reach out to someone. See if they can help. I mean we're always here, but sometimes you need a person IRL
FatKat: *Thanks. I'll let you know.*

*****

Granny knocks on my door. "I brought you soup? And grilled cheese cut into tiny pieces, just like I made your mom. Banana pudding's in the oven, too."

"Thanks. Can you put it on the table? I'll eat later." I close my laptop and sit up.

"Panayis has been by the house no less than six times in the last two days to see you. Want to tell me why you're holed up here in this lovely weather?" She sits on the edge of my bed and feels my forehead. "No fever. Anything you want to talk about?" She gives me one of her famous see-through stares, where it feels like she's gazing right into your soul.

I bite my lip and turn away, pretending I need to stretch. How can I tell her I made a mistake? That she was right all along. What would she do to Jay? Or worse, his dad? He could lose his job, and it would be my fault because I couldn't be that girl. Because I'll always be this. I'll always end up here.

"It's my stomach, I don't know. Just kind of achy and really tired. Drained." I slide onto my pillows and draw my knees up so my feet rest flat on the mattress. Clenching my stomach, I fake a yawn.

"Okay, well that should fix you right up. Grandpa used to say chicken soup cures everything from a headache to flat feet." She raises an eyebrow when I don't laugh and pats my shoulder. "I'll be back with that banana pudding in a bit."

"Can you close the door when you leave? Please?" She clicks her tongue as the door shuts. My stomach rumbles in conversation with the soup, so I open the window to let out its aroma.

Panayis is in the roses below, adding mulch and turning the soil. I duck before he sees me and dive for my bed, the springs in the frame squeaking when I land. Holding my breath, I wait for him to call out. When he doesn't, I roll off my bed and unearth my phone from my closet. Mr. Pickle stares at me from the floor, so I grab a pile of folded shirts and drop them on his face.

Lying on my floor and ignoring all the texts, I scroll through social media apps, one pic after another of filtered selfies and plates of food. More fake life for fake people. With one last swipe, I swipe through a bunch until my eye catches a group of people holding red party cups. I scroll back up and stop. It's from three days ago.

My heart quickens and my breaths go deeper. I inhale and hold it to steady the panic circulating in my veins the way ants crawl over a melted piece of candy. Jay and Amsel stand in the middle of the frame, surrounded by Maggie and five or six other girls—one of them Ashley. Everyone's eyes are golden and blurry, smiles smeared too big on their faces, cups launched in the air.

Jay's hand is around Ashley's waist, hers is on his thigh like she's depending on him to stay standing. I close my eyes and fill in the rest of the night after I'd left. After those few texts, he probably forgot I'd been there at all. I search to see whose account posted this. Robin. Even she didn't care where I'd gone. I swallow the bitter taste gathering in my throat.

I slide the picture up so I can see the comments.

Sic party!
Lit! 🔥
New girl already? Man-whore dumps slut and levels up. Fuckin' stud.

My chest rises and falls with shallow breaths until darkness crowds the corners of my eyes. I half throw, half slide my phone under my bed and roll onto my stomach, balling my fists under me to press out the hunger, letting the emptiness consume my entire body.

*****

This last week I'd milked being sick well enough that Granny let me stay in my room. But now that week two of break has arrived, she's decided the only cure for my health is fresh air and sunshine, like I'm some heroine in a Gothic novel. When she lets it be known if I want coffee or breakfast, I'll have to "walk my skinny butt downstairs and get it myself." She's obviously delusional; regardless, when I see her drive to the east part of the property in her old El Dorado, I slink into the kitchen's corner chair with a hot mug as Mom reads over the morning paper.

She's wearing sweat pants. Not the kind with a matching jacket or rhinestones on the butt, either. Real ones. Her hair is tied on top of her head, and her skin is makeup free. She's Mom before the move. A sweet feeling curls its tendrils around my insides, hope blooming wherever it touches. I haven't yet figured out the definition of love, but I'm pretty sure whatever existed between Jay and me isn't it. Maybe she'll know what to do. I nod toward the paper.

"How are those things still delivered? Don't people internet out here?" I test the cup with my lip and flinch. Still too hot. Mom picks up the paper and fluffs it like they do in old movies.

"Says here some kids threw a party in town. Music so loud the cops had to shut it down." She peeks from behind the paper, eyebrows raised. "Please tell me you were there. I want all the deets!"

Straight-faced, I shake my head. "I will tell you only if you promise never to say deets again."

"Fine, whatever you want, Dear." She pats the chair next to her, an invitation to move to the table. I do and set my cup in front of me, turning it round and round by its handle, mesmerized by the illusion of the liquid inside staying the same.

"So? Spill." She tiny claps in front of her chest. I resist the urge to roll my eyes.

"Mom? How do you know when you're in love?" More turning, more still coffee. She covers my hand with hers, a combination of mine and Granny's, blending generations in the creases.

"Oh honey, you're way too young to think about love. Just have a good time." Her eyes drift into a far-away place. "Otherwise you'll end up like me, beating bushes when you're old, trying to find something that sticks."

"But you...have sex with them, right? The guys you date?" I risk peeking at her. She slumps in her chair, flushed around her neck and ears. "I mean, even though you don't love them?"

"Well, now that kind of love is even more complicated." Her eyebrows draw together and small lines form in between them. She purses her lips into an awkward smile. Patting my hand one last time, she stands and carries her cup to the sink. "If you want my advice, just have fun. That Jay sure is cute, and so is that other one hanging around here all the time. You're too young to think about being with one guy. This isn't one of those TV shows you and Robin binge every weekend. This is real life."

She kisses me on the cheek on her way to her room and closes the door. No, this isn't one of those shows. If it were, I'd turn into a vampire and eat the guy making my life hell or sing some sort of ballad with my friends who all magically know the words to the song in my head and the choreography to match. Then I'd finally have life figured out.

In this life, I have to go outside this afternoon and the one after that and be nice to the guy who just wants to be my friend. Who deserves way more than I can ever do for him to make up for all he's done for me. I have to go back to school and face all the people who saw me throw up outside the party and speed away like some sort of freak. I have to sit next to my ex-best friend in math as her life goes on without me.

And worst of all, I have to tell Jay I never want to see him again.

Chapter 22

First day back to school. Everyone'll be talking about prom. Dates, themes, dresses. After parties. I shudder and grab my bag from my chair, happy to be back to oversized shirts and no makeup, even if this time I really do want to be invisible.

Panayis stands outside Bubba's open passenger door, leaning against the side, holding a travel mug, dusty boots crossed at the ankle. Before I can close the gate, he's there offering to hold my bag.

"I can carry it." I flinch when his hand brushes against my arm and have to force myself to breathe normally. He draws his brows together and steps back, both hands up. I sigh. "Sorry, I guess I'm just grouchy. Not ready for school again."

"Which is why I bring you caffeinated gifts. Ever had Greek coffee?" He offers me the mug. He doesn't mention anything about that night or the two weeks since, and I'm grateful.

"Figures you have your own coffee." I shake my head. He laughs, and I bite my lip to hide a grin.

"It's a tad stronger than what you're used to. There's also a little sugar to help with the bite." In an overdone accent, he adds, "But not too much."

I settle into the seat, fasten my belt, and cup my hands around the mug. "I usually drink my coffee black." I clench and release my jaw, flaring my nostrils in search of air. If I can't handle easy banter like this, how am I going to get through an entire day?

"That's why I put in sugar. Trust me. You want a little something sweet."

The truck ambles down the drive, and I sip from the mug. The coffee's strong and hot, and the sugar counteracts any bitter aftertaste.

"This is pretty good."

He smiles as he turns onto the main road. Although I like the coffee, knowing we're barreling toward all the people I never want to see again, it rolls in my stomach. "Did you make it?"

"Yeah, it's easy. There's a special pot to boil it in. I can show you sometime."

I nod. "Thanks for the pick me up. I need it." I ignore his questions hanging in the air and fumble with the radio to find something to fill the space.

"Are we going to talk about your choice of clothing at all? I mean, I'm no fashion expert or anything, but it's not what you usually wear." He nods to the flannel shirt I borrowed from my grandpa's clothes, still hanging in my closet.

"What? I'm bringing back 90s grunge." I can't tell him why I'm wearing an old man's shirt as a dress.

He raises his eyebrows but says nothing. I sigh. The less of me that's visible, the better. I rolled up the long flannel sleeves to my wrists, and the tail of the shirt rests comfortably at my knees. My leggings and tall boots help cover up what I can't show the rest of the world.

I spent the last two weeks tallying all the consequences everyone else would have to face because of my mistakes—the perfect form of punishment, my own version of self-flagellation. I settle into the seat for another blame spiral, but Panayis interrupts my thoughts.

"Drink up, we'll be there soon." He turns up the radio.

I wish Robin and I were road-tripping, making fun of pop songs like we used to. Instead, I'm bouncing on old shocks in a rusty farm truck, staring out the hand-cranked window, wishing I could disappear.

"I hope you're not suffocating all day." He nods to the boots. "It's supposed to be pretty warm."

I nod at the irony. I'll be suffocating all right, just not in the way he means. I shake my hair so it covers my face and slink further into the seat, missing the peace of my room.

The school appears. Before the party, my gut performed tumbling maneuvers to make any gymnast jealous with the anticipation of seeing Jay. Today, it's doing different kinds of leaps. Like Bubba lurching into the parking spot, my stomach lands right in the middle of my throat.

Thankfully, Panayis parks at the opposite end of the student lot. Across the way, the usual people huddle around Jay's truck, music loud and girls giggling.

"You going over there?" He nods toward the group, his Adam's apple bobbing up and down.

"No, I'm going to class. The bell's about to ring, anyway."

The corner of his mouth turns up slightly. "I'll come with you, if you want." I nod.

We stop in front of the cafeteria. It occurs to me that I have no idea how he spends his time at school or who the two other boys were that night.

"Where are you headed?" I ask.

"I have math first, so I usually hang out in the lunch room until school starts." He shrugs. "It's close."

I nod again and peer inside. The same boys are seated at a table near the window. "Your friends are there."

"Who, them? Yeah, they're from a club I belong to. Nice enough, I guess."

I hardly know anything about his life. I sigh, tears welling in my eyes. "I'm a terrible friend. You've been there so many times for me, and I, well, I barely know you."

He brushes a tear from my cheek. "You keep saying that. Stop. I'm sure one day I'll do something catastrophically stupid, and you can come to my rescue."

"Did you just call me stupid?" I laugh but it comes out more as a sob and I playfully punch him in the arm. He holds his hands up in the shape of a T.

"Time out! No, of course not. I was calling the…lamppost stupid." He nods to the one by the building across from us. I cough out another laugh. "We're friends, remember? No one keeps score around here. I'm sure you'll be there for me if I ever need you. That's the way it works."

"I guess that lamppost is pretty stupid." I press my lips together. "What club are you in?" I sniffle.

"FFA, of course." He laughs.

"Of course." I return my own weak version of a laugh.

"Hey." His smile fades to serious. "If you need me today, for anything…" There's steel in his eyes I've never seen before. He sees the true me behind the mask.

Beached Whale Girl recoils at the recognition. A raw, but pleasant sensation works its way up my spine, making me want to stay and bolt at the same time. Before I can do either, he smiles, lessening the intensity in his gaze.

"See you here after school?"

I nod and shake off what must be the millionth tear I've shed these last two weeks.

"It's a deal." After the cafeteria door closes behind him, I head toward the English building bathroom. No one but underclassmen use it, so it'll be a safe hide-out until class starts.

Two minutes to the tardy bell, I round the corner, and Jay's waiting outside my English class. I've imagined this exact scenario a thousand times since that night. Every one ends with me parading off to some victorious sounding 90s song while he lies on the ground, in tears, with the full understanding of how he made me feel like a receptacle, an object to be used. In every fantasy, he begs my forgiveness as I toss my hair, never to be bothered by him again.

But then he smiles, and my insides freeze and shatter into a million pieces.

"There you are." He's leaning against the wall, hands in his pockets, his crooked grin pasted on his face.

The usual rush of heat rises in my cheeks as his hand brushes against mine. Shame and desire swirl together like two coats of oily paint. Now I'm doubting my own memory. I mean, I didn't exactly yell or fight him off. Somehow, I summon the courage to speak.

"You found me." My hands shake, but my voice is stronger than I thought it could be. He kisses my cheek. The same tingle is there, confusing me even more. How can I let him touch me when I hate him?

"We got back super late last night. I've missed you. Feeling better?" He rocks on his toes then heels. "I figured that's why you left. Did you have the flu?"

I shrug and run my tongue over the roof of my mouth and swallow. My breath jerks like an old truck backfiring when it shifts gears.

"Why didn't you come by the truck this morning?"

"Didn't feel like being around a bunch of people. I don't know." Pressure mounts in my chest, the air weighted down with humidity and lies. I stare at his mouth—his lips move, but I can't hear anything. "I'm going to go. Don't want to be late." I clutch my bag to my chest.

"Always the A student." He flashes what should be his trademarked smile, and I swallow a sneer and smile instead. I can't start anything here, in front of everyone.

"Got me there."

"That I do. See you later. We need to talk prom." He winks like I'd just won some massive prize, and it's all I can do to go through the door and not sprint for the bathroom. I haven't eaten much except that stupid coffee with sugar, and I'm sure it's attaching itself to my gut as I wrench my notebook from my bag.

Instead of lecturing, the teacher passes out a worksheet. I stare at the words until they're just symbols on the page. My whole self trembles from deep inside my chest. I've spent the last two weeks building a wall around myself, like a tourniquet on a bleeding wound. But apparently, it's made of straw. And one kiss blows it down.

*****

When the lunch bell rings, the small storm forming in the pit of my stomach intensifies. Morning debriefs with Robin are long gone, and I'd rather retake all of high school math than go to the cafeteria. I should've asked where Panayis would be, but again, I'm too self-absorbed to think of that.

Guess it's Library-ville for me. Better to be alone with the books than to deal with the whispers behind my back. Like they know more about what happened than I do. Just that one day on Robin's feed proved that.

Whispers and rumors morph into gigantic, life-destroying stories. Labels are applied and my reputation defined in one high-five. My stomach churns at the thought of everyone in the cafeteria throwing sideways stares and knowing nods like they're auctioning off my virtue. Because they don't know the truth, even though I'm wearing it all over my face, accessorized by this oversized flannel shirt.

The library will be my sanctuary, a quiet place to settle the storm and get lost in the lives that lived in the pages of books. Except there's two things I don't know but find out at the same time. One, Jay's waiting for me in the hall. Two, it's entirely possible for your stomach to flip and sink at the same time.

"Hey." His hands are shoved in his pockets, and his ankles are rolled so he balances on the sides of his shoes. Cute Boy Pose 101. Does he practice this stuff? I raise my hand in a small wave. "I waited for you."

"I see that."

He reaches for my hand, but I fake an excuse to adjust my bag. His expression changes.

"What are you wearing?" He flicks his finger over one of the creases in the flannel at my elbow.

I shrug.

"Are you ever going to tell me where you went? I looked for you, but..." His voice trails off as if it's following me down the sidewalk and to the park that night.

The truth boils in my stomach. Beached Whale Girl's screaming to be heard, but I can't. Not here in front of everyone. Like with what happens to girls who scream the truth. They're labeled as hysterical. Weak. Angry. Instead, I stand up taller, shake my hair from my shoulders and adjust my Skinny V-neck Girl mask. And even though my knees tremble and my stomach turns, I meet his gaze.

"It was late, and I was tired. I couldn't find you." My voice is flat, nearly robotic. I'm doing my best to appear bored.

He nods, giving me a sideways glance, his brow creased in puzzlement.

"After, you know. I missed you." He grabs my shirt by the buttons and tugs.

Panic rises up my spine and threatens to strangle my lungs. I'm pretty sure everyone in a ten-foot radius can hear my heart thump against my ribs. With every crash, Beached Whale Girl pleads, but my tongue fills my whole mouth. I concentrate on breathing. In and out. I push against him with sweaty palms and step backward until I hit the wall.

"You okay?" The crease between his eyebrows deepens. He runs his hand over his hair, his nervous habit, eyes scanning the crowd.

"Yeah, I just need to go to the bathroom. Go eat your lunch. I'm going to the library to work on homework."

He nods, his lips pursed in question. Before he can ask it, Amsel jumps on his back.

"Hey, Wren, where've you been? Have fun at the party?"

The word "party" slashes me like a paper cut. But they go on like the world never changed colors. Amsel fake punches Jay under the chin.

"I'm starving. Let's eat!" He jumps off and jogs backward to the cafeteria.

I hug the flannel tight around my body and scurry as fast as I can to my new bathroom without drawing more attention, my heart pounding in my ears. I imagine Jay's high-fiving Amsel over his conquest, telling stupid jokes. He'll eat his sandwich and not think about me again until he wants to.

I raise my hand to push open the door when it flings open. Maggie and another girl burst out, laughing.

"Oh, hey, Wren." Maggie's smile fades to a thin line across her face. "Have a good break?"

I force a smile as fake as she is and squeak out a hello. After a furtive glance, she turns to her friend and nudges her with her elbow. They giggle together and slither away. The other one asks if I'm the one from the Snapchat story the night of the party.

My mouth drops open. Flashes of me grinding on Jay while we danced, chugging beer from a red cup, and making out all the way up the stairs make me gag. Instead of going into the bathroom, I run, head down against the flurries of high school gossip. Through the quad, around the cafeteria, one foot in front of the other, inhaling and exhaling. Bile rising. Feet taking steps until concrete turns to dirt and soil turns to grass.

In the shade, and completely alone, I half-sit, half-collapse under the bleachers. Closing my eyes, lightning spasms ready in my back. Distant voices yell and laugh and compete with the wind through the slatted seats. Relief is coming.

Release and the sweet pleasure of my muscles tensing becomes all I can think about. I've stayed away from drama for sixteen years and don't know what's changed so much that I end up alone, under the bleachers in the middle of my own sick. Self-respect is the price of my popularity, and I don't even have that anymore. Not that I ever did. A cynical laugh comes from somewhere, and I realized it's my own voice.

I open my eyes when the spasms stop. Red streaks the mess of bile and coffee in front of me. The world shifts off-balance for a moment. I rest against the post, breathing deep. In and out. It's probably just from being so upset. I make a note to ask my chat about it. See if it happens to them, too.

I could be sitting next to Jay, talking about the awesome football season and how great the baseball team's going to be. People do it all the time. Turns out I'm not one of them. I just found out too late. A tear rolls down my cheek. Then another. My shoulders shudder and my back buckles. I'm in a deep pit and no one's coming to help me climb out.

The bell rings in the distance. I stand and smooth out my flannel shirt-turned-dress. I rinse my mouth with my bottle of water and spit, careful not to splatter any on my boots. I straighten my bag and march one foot in front of the other to math class and my ex-best friend. The one person I need more than anyone else. And the one person who will never want me back.

Chapter 23

While the weekdays consist of thickening scars derived from high school wounds, weekends have become a peaceful respite from the noise of fake laughter and competing early morning parking lot music. Instead, the humming of the farm equipment accompanies the melody of the songbirds.

I click off my alarm two minutes before it's set to ring, the light casting gray streaks on the walls and sideways shadows on the dolls lining them. I've never understood why the sun saves its best colors for the evening. Seems to me it'd have more energy for pretty things early on.

The house is silent—Granny's probably already in the vineyards barking at her crew. God knows where Mom is. My stomach gurgles, and I move my tongue around my mouth and swallow as much saliva as I can generate. Familiar tension creeps through my ribs and squeezes my lungs. Sitting up, I slide my journal from under my pillow and hold it close to my chest. Its slick, cold cover pressed against me pushes away the dread. I draw in a deep breath and release it slowly, letting the air and spit be enough nutrition for now.

The aroma of bacon and griddle cakes waft through the cracks of the old house, and my stomach churns. I move around my tongue and swallow again. Tucking my legs under me, I open my journal to an empty page and record my food allotment and exercise routine. The more I write, the less I shake.

*****

I settle into the soft pillows of the porch swing, journal resting on my lap, eyes closed and listening to the breeze rustle in the leaves. Thirty minutes to lunch. As I mentally slice the apple into wafer-thin pieces, a shadow cools my face. I feel his presence before I open my eyes.

"Sleeping? What would Granny think, wasting such a beautiful day?" Panayis slopes against the porch wall, arms crossed in mock condescension.

Normally around other people, I make sure I sit straight so my stomach doesn't spill over the top of my jeans. I keep my legs just right for maximum thin-thigh potential. Around Panayis, all of that kind of slips away. I mean I don't care what he thinks, which is probably why it's easier. I bite down on a smile and draw my eyebrows together.

"She would think that some people are over achievers and other people need to be left alone on their day off." I shield my eyes with my free hand.

He moves so that his shadow blocks the sun.

"Yeah, yeah, just messing around." He stares at his shoes. "I wanted to see what you were up to today. Feel like an adventure?"

There's twenty-eight minutes to lunch, and I need to eat before Granny comes in for hers. I have to be done and out of the kitchen or risk something deep-fried shoved at me. But I can't tell him all this. And he is fun to banter with.

"If it requires sunscreen or special footwear, I'm not interested." I cross my arms in mock stubbornness.

"I don't know about special footwear, but you might want an apron. Thought you might like to finally check out my amazing cooking skills and help me make lunch."

A stone forms where my apple's supposed to go in twenty-seven minutes. I know how much his cooking means to him, keeping his mom's memory close and all, but the idea of being around food that I hadn't planned sends razor blades swimming in my stomach. A cold sweat glazes my skin.

"I'm going to make pastitsio, a kind of Greek lasagna." His eyes shift to my journal for a split second. Instinctively, I hug it to my chest. "It's all good for you."

"Well, I did have plans to read the Bell Jar and wallow in complete country isolation until three, but I guess I can make a last-minute adjustment to my overwhelmingly full calendar." I can probably fake Normal for an hour or two. And there's always the backup plan for unwanted calories. It hasn't failed me yet.

He scrunches his thick eyebrows and scratches his chin the way detectives do in black and white movies. "And what are you doing after three, or should I ask?"

"I'm afraid that's above your security clearance. If I tell you, I'd have to do something involving chinchillas, lip gloss, and the blood of the fallen."

His lips are a flat line as he deliberately closes and reopens his eyes.

"Reading, then?"

I can't tell him the truth, that I'd be locked in my room working on crunches and ignoring the box of cookies in the comfort food stash I keep in the back of the armoire. I push away the desire for the peaceful feeling repetitive chewing and swallowing gives me. My mouth fills with saliva at the thought. I could chew, taste, swallow and not feel anything. No one could ever know, though, and for some reason, I think I'd pretty much die if he ever found out. So reading it is.

"Pretty much."

He shakes his head as a slow grin spreads across his face. I laugh. Can't help it.

"Top secret reading," I add.

"Whatever works, I guess. You'll come?" He glances at my journal.

I slide my hand over it as if he can read through the closed cover, my heart beating a little faster. The idea of all that food, the carbs and sugar alone make me cringe. But Panayis has been there for me in ways that no one else has. Not even Robin. Especially her. And the night of the party. I'd probably still be trudging home if he hadn't found me. How can I say no? A sour taste creeps in the back of my throat.

"Sure. Just make sure you have a fire extinguisher handy. You never know when I'm around." I stand, and the world flips upside down and goes dark. Before I can find my balance, two strong hands grasp my arms, anchoring me to the ground.

"Hey," he says. "You okay?"

I blink until the world comes into focus. "Yeah. See? Total klutz." I pretend to smile. "Must've gotten up too quickly."

"Sure." The tone in his voice suggests he thinks differently. I avoid his gaze. "You need some good Greek food. That'll make you feel better. Do you need a minute?"

I straighten my shoulders and release a heavy breath. It's only an hour or two. "I'm good to go whenever you are."

Maybe Normal and I aren't such good friends after all.

The side door of Panayis's house opens directly into the kitchen. Faded pictures of kindergarten graduation, report cards, and recipes cover the cabinets. A large embroidered picture of the Lord's Supper dominates the rest of the wall space. A table barely large enough for four is tucked in the corner underneath.

"This is where the magic happens." He reaches up and turns the ceiling fan to low. A faint aroma of warm spices circulates in the air.

"Is that you?" I point to a picture of a scrawny boy buried in football pads and a helmet running toward the goal post with a ball tucked under his arm.

He busies himself setting out pans and measuring cups. "I'd tell you but then we'd need the chinchillas again."

My lips curl and I laugh in spite of myself. I peer closer at the picture. A familiar tightness clenches my chest.

"Is that Jay running with you?"

"You mean behind me? Yeah. Good eye." A glint of superiority echoes in his eyes.

"Competitive much?" I raise my eyebrows and lower my chin for dramatic effect. "Didn't think you had it in you."

He shrugs and piles ingredients from the refrigerator onto the counter. I try not to stare at the meats, cheeses, and cream. "You miss playing?" My voice cracks a little, and I clear my throat to cover.

"Not anymore." He pours olive oil into a pan and waves his hand over the counter. "There are more important things. How good are you at dicing?"

I tuck myself into a corner at the table and run my hand over the smooth plastic, covering an intricately woven tablecloth underneath.

"Unless you mean playing craps or something, not so much. I shouldn't be trusted with sharp objects, remember?"

"You make a solid point." Panayis wags a knife in my direction.

I groan at his joke.

"I'll tell you what. There are dishes in that cabinet and silverware in the drawer underneath." He points with the knife. "You set the table, and I'll start over here." After dicing an onion, he works the meats and onion together in the heated oil while I set out plates and cups.

Panayis stands over the stove like a mother does over her sleeping child. His hands caress the wooden spoon and pan as he stirs in spices and more ingredients. I tally the calories as he scoops a small bit into a spoon.

"Here, try this. Close your eyes." He holds the spoon over his open palm and lifts it to my mouth. Instead of opening my mouth, I reach for the spoon, my hand grazing his. I jerk it back, nearly dropping the mixture on the floor.

"Oh, sorry. I just, I didn't think you wanted to feed me and..." I'm starting to rethink the lobotomy.

"It's fine. You're fine." An easy smile lights his eyes. "Just taste it. The filling. Meat and spices. That's it."

I close my eyes and let him lead the spoon into my mouth. Intense flavors of savory garlic and tangy tomatoes with hints of cinnamon float on my tongue.

"That's amazing!" I open my eyes. He's stands still, spoon in the air, his mouth curled into the biggest smile I've ever seen.

"Wait until you try it with the noodles and béchamel sauce."

"What kind of sauce?"

"It's cream and cheese. Hand me that box of noodles."

There's no way I'm going to survive this food. I'm going to have to run laps around the property for days. But he's so happy, and it smells so good. I push back my shoulders and promise myself I'll deal with it later.

"These are huge." I hand him the box.

Opening the box, he holds a noodle to his eye like a spyglass. "My mom used to call them Water Hose Noodles." He drops them in the boiling water.

"You must've spent a lot of time with her for you to learn all this." I tilt my head to the side. He stops stirring and frowns for a fraction of a second, but long enough for me to see it.

Brilliant. Bring up how much he misses his mother.

"I mean, of course you did because she's your mom and why wouldn't you spend time with her and I'm going to stop talking now." I hide my face in my hands, heat creeping up my neck.

"It's okay. I know what you meant. Yeah, I liked to watch her cook. She said it was how she showed us love. Making her recipes feels like she's still here, in a way."

I prop myself against the counter, my head against a cupboard.

"All my mom cooks is out of a box, if she does at all anymore. And Granny cooks, but it's her reward system. Work hard, get fed." A bitter taste sours the back of my throat. I have two mom figures in my life. Panayis lost his mom years ago, and he's closer to his than I am to either of mine. Food's caused so much trauma in my life. But it brings him healing. "Weird how food can mean so many different things to different people. Much more than just sustenance."

He stops stirring, his expression one I don't fully understand. His hazel eyes burn deep pools of green, his mouth pressed together in a slight grin. I realize I'm talking about why people eat while he's explaining how he misses his mom.

"Sorry, I'm being dumb. It's cool that you have this part of her."

"You're not dumb. Seems to me you're right."

"Thanks." Tension oozes from my body, and for the first time in weeks, a real smile pulls at the corners of my lips. I bite my bottom lip. "You have a gift for taking the awkward out of what I say."

"I speak Wren. One of my many talents. Now try this sauce." He pushes a full spoon toward me, and I reach for it gladly.

An hour later, the timer goes off and he sets the pastitsio to cool. I set out napkins and silverware on the table, making two places across from each other.

"The table's beautiful. But it's missing one thing. Come on." He leads me to the flowerbed on the side of the house. Warmth radiates from him, drawing me closer like some magnetic pull. I step toward the blooms.

"Let's put some flowers on the table. You pick them out and I'll get them inside."

"Still don't trust me with scissors, I see." I wink.

"No, it's not that. I'm out of bandages at the moment, so I'm playing it safe." I throw an arm punch, but he ducks, laughing.

"All right, Dr. Smarty Pants, how about those?" I point to lilies. "They're my favorite."

Panayis cuts several blooms and hands them to me. "Then lilies it will be." He opens his mouth then closes it again.

"Were you going to say something?"

He tilts his head as his eyes settle somewhere far away. "No. I mean, yeah. It's just, those were my mom's favorite, too." He clears his throat. My eyes widen.

"Oh my god, Panayis. Why didn't you say anything?" The burn in my cheeks spreads to my scalp, and I make a mental note to research ways to stop turning red every other second. "You didn't have to cut them for me. You should've said something!"

"It's fine. Good to see you enjoy them, too." He rests his hand on my shoulder. "It'll be nice to have some on the table again. It's been a long time."

I rest my hand on his, and it occurs to me I didn't flinch when he touched me. With a squeeze, I follow him inside and observe him arranging the lilies in a milk-glass vase that matches the plates. He places the pastitsio at the center of the table, along with a salad he's made.

"See? Perfect," he says.

"An excellent spread. I don't want to ruin it, but I'm starving." I blink, shocked that came out of my mouth. This is the most normal I've felt in a long time. Even before that night.

"Let's eat." He dishes us each a slice and spoons salad onto the plates. "You first. Tell me what you think."

The creamy sauce makes the cinnamon sweeter and the meat more savory. And the noodles are light enough to carry all the flavors together. I close my eyes and relish how two such different tastes can complement each other so well.

"I think this is the best thing I've ever tasted. It's…everything."

His face breaks into a wide grin. "I knew you'd like it." Hunched over, he digs into his food, his fork poised like a shovel. I lower mine to my plate as he scoops bite after bite. With his mouth full, he asks, "What?"

"You may not be a football player anymore, but you still eat like one."

He cranes his neck and swallows. "Eat with a lot of football players, do you? Oh right." His body stiffens as he drops his fork, which clanks against his plate. "Sometimes I forget who you're dating." The levity from a moment ago is now a fleeting memory. Icy chills compete with the heat in my stomach from the food. I sniff. He lets out a sigh and pushes his plate away. "I knew he'd work his way in somewhere."

"Don't. Why are you saying that?" I wrap my arms around my middle and rock back and forth in little movements. He runs his hand through his hair and slides it down his face. Panic sets in.

What are you doing? You shouldn't be here, eating. Even Panayis knows you're damaged.

"You know what? You're right. I'm sorry." His shoulders slump. "Let's just eat." His attempt at a peace-making grin is more disguised pity.

The food churns in my body like metal being devoured by fiery acid. The familiar urge to rid myself of the claustrophobic clamp around my core returns, and a blanket of sweat covers my arms and neck. Concern flashes across his face then disappears with the wipe of his napkin across his lips.

Say Something. You're ruining the whole thing.

"Doesn't matter anyway. I think it's kind of over."

He raises an eyebrow. "Oh really. Does he know that? You guys seemed pretty Not Over at school." His eyes go right through me. I press my lips together and wrap my arms around my middle again.

"Why do you even care?" My throat tightens and my heart pounds. I want to sprint to the bathroom, but Panayis's glower pins me to the chair.

"Do you want to talk about it?" His voice is quieter.

I swallow hard, and sip my water to stall. "Talk about what?" Beached Whale Girl stares from behind the mask, begging him to stop.

"Why you turned green when Jay came up, maybe?"

"There's nothing to talk about."

"Then why are you breathing like you just ran a marathon? I know something happened, Wren. I drove you home that night. And you haven't been yourself since." He reaches over the table, a silent peace offering. "You can talk to me."

I push myself away from the table like I can push away the conversation, but he doesn't give up.

"Someone hurt you." His eyes widen. "Did *Jay* hurt you?" His hands clutch handfuls of his hair as he stands, his chair slams into the wall behind him. He brings his hands down to his sides, his fists clenching and unclenching, jaw locked. My head shakes back and forth, each movement another denial.

"Panayis, it's my fault. I didn't say anything when…"

He turns toward the wall, his back to me, breathing hard. I'm frozen, like the slightest movement will send him through the door to confront Jay. I'm paralyzed in my own inadequacy. The room's energy shifts, and he's silent.

He meets my gaze, his eyes as sad as mine are terrified. The only sound is the hum of the refrigerator. Even the clock stops ticking, as if time had paused. I choke out a whisper.

"I didn't say no enough."

As my body shakes with culpability, I cover my mouth with my hands, but a sob escapes. I bow my head and squeeze my eyes shut, tears falling to my feet. My choices have hurt so many people, and I can't handle seeing the disappointment on his face, too.

He exhales heavily, his footsteps firm on the linoleum. When I open my eyes, his feet are in front of mine. I close them again, afraid of what's coming next. His finger touches my chin, lifting my face toward his. I shift my eyes to the window where the Delta winds shake the trees beyond the panes.

"Can you look at me? Please?"

I step backward and cross my arms, needing space even it's a feeble attempt at protection. From what, I'm not sure.

"It's okay. Everything's going to be okay." His eyes are clouded with sorrow.

I squeeze my eyes shut. Things will never be okay again. Breath comes in uneven bursts. There's no way they could be. He reaches for my hand, and I let him. He clutches it to his chest and rests his forehead against mine.

"Listen to me." His voice is a whisper. "Saying no one time is enough." He holds my head close to his. "You don't deserve to feel like this." He cups my face in his hands.

My legs can no longer hold the burden I've been carrying on my shoulders. My legs buckle and together, we slide to the floor. I curl into a ball, my arms wrapped around my knees. Somewhere far away, he's telling me I'm all right.

As my mammoth tears soak his lap, my shame turns into something sharper, something hot burning in my lungs. With every breath, the idea that maybe I'm not the one that should feel ashamed becomes clearer as my breathing gets heavier.

Sometime later, I wake up under a crocheted blanket and a pillow where Panayis's lap had been. The sky has turned from bright blue to shaded amber, and a small lamp shines in the opposite corner of the room. I stretch my kinked leg muscles and follow the sound of clinking dishes into the kitchen. Panayis folds the remnants of our forgotten meal into plastic containers.

I don't know what to say, so I sit at the table and rub my swollen eyes.

"You woke up." Panayis sets a glass of water on the table for me and sits, the same places we'd been before.

"Yeah, sorry." I focus on the glass. "I don't know why I fell asleep."

"You were exhausted, I guess." He reaches over the table and touches my hand. "We never really ate. You hungry?"

My stomach cries out in favor of a snack. He smirks.

"I'll heat some up."

Several hours later, as I stare at the sky from my bed, I realize I left my journal on Panayis's table. I hadn't thought about my diet plan the entire afternoon. I reach for my phone to text him but curl up instead. I'm so relaxed, my stomach finally satisfied. There's always tomorrow.

Chapter 24

I'm dreaming of light before her hand touches my shoulder. The room is dark, but Granny's outline is unmistakable against the light in the bare window.

"It's the middle of the night. Is everything okay?" I yawn, still recovering from my tear-stained hangover.

"Everything's fine. Come on, get dressed."

Fengari jumps onto my bed, pawing at the covers. I push him away, dragging the sheet over my head. Granny pokes at my cheeks through the sheet and laughs under her breath. I flip it back and a rush of cool air assaults my face. She scoops the dog under her arm, his wagging tail beating the back of her jacket like an off-beat drum.

"I want to show you something," she says.

"Fine. It's not like I can sleep with dog breath in my face anyway." I unweave myself from my covers and slide into the jeans I'd left on the floor.

"I'll meet you downstairs." Her boots echo down the stairs.

The living room's dark except for the moonlight shining through the open front door. I move closer, threading my tangled hair through an old hair tie. Granny's seated on the cement steps, staring at the vines lining the driveway. Fengari pants at her feet, eager for whatever adventure she's planned. When he hears me, his tail beats backwards and forwards as he runs in circles around my legs.

"All right, dog. I see you." I scratch behind his ears. The white circle on his backside wiggles as his tail wags. "What are we doing out here in the middle of the night?"

Granny stands, adjusts her long sleeves and kicks her rubber boots against the porch. "I want to do a sugar check, see how long we have until harvest." She calls Fengari and heads for the gate that leads to the acres of ripening grapes. "Come with me."

"Um, isn't that easier to do during the day? When there's actual sunlight?" I follow her into a row of vines. They're heavy with bulbous berries, and the full moon shimmers on the leaves, casting silver shadows over the entire vineyard.

Ignoring my question, Granny continues deep into the vines. Fengari darts in between the rows and then sprints after another darker shadow skittering among them. I shudder at the thought of what it can be.

"Granny. Wait up!" I have to jog to keep up with her steady gait.

"A good harvest waits for no one." She shakes her finger in the air. "And I love it out here in the moonlight." She holds her hands shoulder-high, palms turned upward. "It's like getting my battery recharged."

I roll my eyes. She stops in the middle of the vineyard. We're surrounded by rows of thick leaves and feelers that resemble curling ribbon searching for a place to anchor. The air's thick with heat but still smells crisp from the fruit and soil. I stare at the stars to keep from feeling closed in.

"Granny, why are we out here?" I stifle a yawn.

She busies herself with one of the grape clusters, squeezing and tasting a grape, and then repeats the process with another bunch.

"You know, we wait all year for these little things to produce just the right amount of sugar so they'll make the best wine. We wait for them to ripen from a little green ball to a lush purple grape."

I throw back my head and sigh into the stars. This is worse than her turning one of my jokes into a lecture. Especially in the middle of the night.

"Granny. Is there something you want to tell me? Am I the grape in this scenario?"

"See? The smart one." Her mouth twists upward as she pinches off another grape and pops it into her mouth. I can't help think about the time Dumbledore eats one of Harry's Every-flavored Beans and gets earwax. Their faces are the same. When she finishes, she scrapes the ground with a nearby shovel.

"What do you want me to know, Granny? It's late and I'm tired."

"I know this year's been tough, moving way out here. Missing your...family." She moves close enough so the moonlight reflects on her skin and dances in her eyes. "And then taking on a suitor, to boot."

"Granny! Who says that?" My eyes practically bug out of my head.

"My point, Wren"—she lowers her chin at my name—"is that you've done a lot of growing this year, maybe even changed colors." She plants the shovel and scoops out more dirt, making a decent-sized hole.

"Changed colors? What are you saying?" I just want to go back to bed and not talk about anyone's colors.

"All I'm saying is that you've grown up this year, but you still have more to do." When the shovel hits something solid, she unearths a wooden chest, no bigger than a child's jewelry box, and holds it out to me. My jaw drops.

"Is that the infamous treasure chest? I thought you made that up." I reach out, almost afraid to touch it in case it evaporates. Her eyes narrow as her lips turn up at the edges.

"Everybody thinks that." She taps her temple with her index finger. "Sometimes it pays to be a crazy old lady!"

Shaking my head, a whispered laugh escapes my lips. The box proves heavier than it appears. The blackened gold latch seems to match the key on Granny's shelf. Her words come back to me, promising me I could have the treasure one day, and a buzzing excitement plants itself in my core.

"The key on the kitchen shelf. Does it really open this?" I inspect the lock more closely. "Why is it buried if you have the key?"

She taps at her temple again but says nothing.

"What's in it?" My excitement bends toward frustration.

"One day, when I'm gone, you can open the box and see for yourself. Until then, it'll be here. Waiting for you." She places it back in its hole, and reburies it, tapping the dirt with her boot.

Closing my eyes, I wipe at my forehead with the palm of my hand. "What the heck, Granny? You wake me up in the middle of the night and drag me out here to just show me where this infamous treasure is and then leave it here?" I start toward the house, but it's so dark, I can't tell which way to go. I end up circling right back to where she is. I huff in protest. "I don't get it!"

Granny's back to her grape clusters, testing one or two down the row as she roams. "Like I said, you have a-ways to go…like these grapes here. Do you know what makes the grapes so sweet?" She turns and raises her eyebrows, an unspoken invitation to follow.

Arms crossed and eye rolls at the ready, I accept my fate. I'm so not getting out of this lesson. "No."

"It's the sun. One of the reasons grapes do so well here is because of the summer heat." I raise my eyebrows and purse my lips, waiting for the big revelation. "All summer long, the heat is relentless, forcing the fruit to ripen." She nods once, lips turned down in finality.

"Heat equals pressure equals getting over yourself. Got it." I give her a thumbs-up and an enthusiastic nod in hopes of seeing my bed again sometime soon.

She ignores my comment. "And it's up to us, the farmers, to make sure the grapes get the perfect amount of heat, otherwise, the fruit'll shrivel up." She snaps her fingers and makes a fist. She's inches away from me, her silvery eyes a deep lake, her voice a river. "Every one of us can tolerate different amounts of heat, just like the grapes. When we can't get to shade, it is up to us to find someone that can help." She wraps her arms around me and holds me close, talking into my hair. Instead of resisting, my shoulders drop, and I melt into her embrace. "Do you understand me?"

"I think so." Although I'm not sure I do. Suddenly, a vast empty feeling opens in my chest, and my limbs are heavy. I wrap my arms around her waist, hoping for something I can't name. With one last squeeze, she grasps my shoulders and straightens her arms so we're eye to eye.

"Do you? Because I think it's time you reconsider who you spend your time with."

"What do you mean?" Every muscle in my body tenses.

"You'll be spending your time here and only here. At least until you can get through the day without raiding your grandpa's closet or crying yourself to sleep. You're practically a ghost. I'm worried about you."

Relief and dread wrestles the emptiness in my chest. On one hand, I now have the perfect break from the Jay situation, but on the other, there's just no way I can ever fix the mess I made.

"Come on. It's the middle of the night for goodness' sake." She pats my shoulders and jerks her head toward the house. Fengari trots at her heels as she treads through the maze of vines. I trip along, doing my best to memorize the steps. Trying to keep up with her makes me feel five years old again, like playing dress up in her too-big shoes.

*****

After Sunday dinner, which is actually at two in the afternoon, Granny sends me out to clear the driveway of weeds. It'll be time for the harvest soon, and trucks and vans full of temporary help will flood the property.

"Can't I weed tomorrow? It's a hundred degrees outside." I carry my plate of pushed around food to the sink and fill my water bottle.

"It's good for the complexion. Makes your cheeks rosy."

"Well, I'll need a bigger hat, because I don't tan. I cancer."

"Use mine!" Her voice is sing-songy. With a grunt, I pluck hers off the rack and plod out the door.

Granny, 1. Wren, 0. Again.

Clover weeds creep through the cracks of cement, and I scrape them out with a tool that looks like a screwdriver and a forked tongue had a baby. I know I'm supposed to be angry I'm being forced to live out my grounding on the chain gang, and I've complained loudly enough about it to maintain deniability, but secretly I'm kind of relieved to have a reason not to deal with being Jay's girlfriend, even if it's pretty much in name only.

Just as I find a rhythm in the scraping and swiping, the rumble of Jay's truck scratches the gravel road. I pause the song pounding through my ear buds, but the thudding of blood in my ears is all I hear.

I don't know how to act around him. At school, my shoulders tense at every corner and doorway. In the library, I jump every time the turnstile clicks. Yet I can't bring myself to break up with him. Without him, I'd be alone, and too many people have already left my life. Now I'm stuck in some weird simulation of sitting in a hot frying pan yet not jumping for fear of the fire.

The tires slow and the engine quiets. Footsteps behind me, I keep sweeping my hands over the same spot, trying to figure out what to say. When his shadow consumes mine, I raise my chin. He's wearing a dark gray tank top and shorts. Peering at me over his sunglasses, he bares his teeth in the most unwelcoming smile I've ever seen.

"Hey, Baby." He yanks me into a bear hug, trapping my arms at my side and sending my hat to the ground.

"I'm all sweaty." I glance at the porch, hoping Granny or someone will be there. No such luck.

"Uh-uh, don't try and get out of this. I haven't seen you in forever. You're coming with me." With his arms limiting my mobility, we stumble to the office.

Inside, the air is thick like I'm inhaling through a towel fresh from the dryer. Jay flips the switch on the wall cooler.

"We shouldn't be in here. I'm grounded, remember? They'll hear the air and Granny wanted me to clear off the driveway before—"

Jay's lips are on mine, silencing me. His hand presses on the back of my neck, his tongue in my mouth. Kissing used to mean he desired me. More than anything, I wanted that feeling again. And it feels good right now. That's not a bad thing. His arms and mouth tempt me to silence the inner voice saying he's not choosing me, just my body.

Every time we're together, he's touching me, pulling me into an embrace or a kiss, or more. We never talk about anything except how much he hates his dad or where the next party is or the antics of some random drunk at last night's party.

"Jay, stop." I put my hands on his shoulders.

"Come on, you're such a good kisser." He wraps his arms around my waist and jerks back. "You're so bony. Look at you." He flicks his tongue along my neck as he shoves his hands in my back pockets.

Just a few months ago, hearing Jay tell me he thought I was pretty or skinny meant everything. But now those words are knife wounds, weakening me as my heart bleeds onto the floor. And that is a bad thing. Because I want more than that. And what I want matters.

His touch creates a whole other level of wanting to be sick. I push at his chest.

"Jesus, Jay, I said stop! Is that word not in your vocabulary, or what?" My nerves race against my anger.

Frustration flashes in his eyes. His face contorts as his nostrils flare—his new expression—one used to calm a trapped animal. "What's wrong? You like it when I kiss you. Don't you want to be with me?"

The tingle left on my lips spreads to my cheeks. I breathe in the syrupy air, hoping to find relief from a ribbon of the manufactured cool winding its way around the room.

"Why can't we talk? Or, you can help me outside. Maybe show Granny we can do regular things. Then we can hang out. Like a real couple." I ramble, trying to find the spark that'll ignite something non-physical to help run the harvest. "We hardly see each other, and it'll be nice to, you know, hang out."

The reason we haven't been together much is mostly my own doing, but hopefully I hid that well. It seems all I've done this year is hide. And I don't want to anymore.

"Come on. Neither of us wants to be outside, and I would much rather not talk, if you know what I mean." He twists his fingers through my belt loops and directs me toward the wall, but I side step him. He throws his arms up and laces his fingers together on top of his head, muttering and pacing in circles. Resolve weakens my knees, but I'm determined to make this work. It has to. I stand straighter, hoping my voice won't betray me.

"Jay, I don't want to right now." I unclench my fists and lift my chin. "This isn't what I want."

"But what about me, what I need? You're my girlfriend. It's what we do." He props himself against the wall, thumbs hooked in his pockets. Anger anchors my spine, and something inside me snaps.

"Girlfriend? Am I? I'm your girlfriend? How exactly am I your girlfriend?" I repeat the word as if saying it will give it new meaning, but every time, the meaning slips farther away, like a language I've never learned. "We don't do anything together except meet in here or go to parties and slip off by ourselves. You're always off with your friends doing whatever it is you do, and when I am around, everyone ignores me, like I'm some pet that should be kept in the corner." My entire body shakes with the truth.

"You've got the nagging part down, don't you?" He plops in a chair and twists the seat back and forth. "We haven't seen much of each other because you've been dodging my texts. Or you're always in the library. How is any of that my fault? I have needs."

"Yeah. I'm aware of your needs. How can I forget?"

"What does that mean?" He looks at me like I'm a large stuffed animal he's given up on winning at the fair.

"What you did!" I choke on the words and swallow a sob. Backing into the wall, I slide to the floor, my knees too weak to hold me up anymore. A bead of sweat trickles down my spine. "That night."

"What did I do? What are you talking about?"

Betrayal washes over me like a lukewarm bath. I inhale a jagged breath, tears in full-assault mode on my cheeks. I feel everything all over again like it just happened. But I can't say it out loud. That I didn't want to have sex that night. That I thought I did but changed my mind, and now it's too late and everything is broken and I have to fix it so there's some worth to all this.

I still want to believe that I'm wrong. That maybe I did want to, and all the books I've read are wrong and that really is the way love feels. That maybe it'd be easier to live in his shadow so I don't have to see mine. My breath is uneven and broken between sobs.

"Are you going to tell me?" His voice is softer now, confused and bitter.

"That night you, I mean, we…at the party." I wrap my arms around my knees, resting my chin on top. My eyes stay fixed on the floor, afraid to see the expression on his face.

"Exactly. That's what I'm talking about." The satisfaction of his memory lilts in his voice. His chair squeaks as he stands. I squeeze my legs tighter to my chest.

"For you, maybe. But not me." His expression is new. Is it disgust? Boredom? Whatever it is, it's not love. "I'm not doing that anymore. Not with you." The second it comes out of my mouth, I regret it. His whole being erupts in rage.

"Not with me? Then with who? Who else are you fucking, Wren?" He punches the wall above my head and kneels so his face is inches from mine. Shards of spit spatter my face like shrapnel. "You are mine, you hear me? If I see you talking to anyone, especially that piece of shit, Panayis, we are going to have a problem."

I'm wrong. I can't fix this. I wipe the tears and spit from my cheeks and crawl to my knees. Slowly, I drag myself to standing.

"Not that I owe you this, but there's no one else. You're the only one that I ever…did that with. Please, don't threaten me. I just, don't want to anymore. It's not right."

He stares at me for what seems like an eternity. A million possibilities of what might come next rattle through my thoughts. I inch closer to the door. The same thing my mom did when my dad lost his temper.

In two strides, he's there first, swinging it open so it crashes against the wall, making the building shake. I stand glued to the wall, shaking with relief as he flies through it. His truck door slams and the engine roars to life. Tires spin in the gravel, rocks pelting the cement driveway. Music thunders and shakes the windows. I stay there until even the boom of the bass disappears down the road.

I close the door and slide down the wall, gulping for air. My phone buzzes. A text from Jay.

You can forget about prom. But this isn't over.

With shaky hands, I shove my phone in my pocket and turn off the air conditioning, glancing at the house every few seconds to see if Granny's coming outside. I'd tried to make myself as small as possible, taking up as little space as I could while Jay dominated the tiny office with his expectations and anger. But it doesn't matter how tiny I make myself. According to him, I'll always be the big mistake.

I'll always be the one that doesn't understand how he feels. His arrogance leaves no room for anyone else's opinions but his. I'm no more than a tool to him, like the rusty one I'd been using to scrape weeds out of the driveway.

A sickly knot tightens in my stomach and a cold tingle travels my spine, making me shiver. I'd put all my hope of being loved into one person, and he doesn't know the meaning of the word, nor does he care.

I need a break from all the drama and blame. I just want to be numb.

Granny always keeps several cartons of ice cream in the outside freezer. She insists they be kept out here and not in the house. Less impulsive snacking, that way.

The irony.

I pick one, not caring about flavor, and close myself in the room Jay almost destroyed—a fitting place. Sitting on the floor, I open the carton. A thin layer of chocolate sticks to the lid. I sit it on the floor and stare at it like a convict stares at an executioner's gun. I run my finger through the liquefying cream on the lid, letting it drip to the floor. With a start, my lips upturn into an ironic grin. There's no spoon.

I dig two fingers into the middle of the carton, but it's so frozen. I suck on my fingers to warm them, hoping that'll melt the chocolate treat faster. Sticking them back in, I manage a small chunk, but I can't shovel it into my mouth fast enough. It falls onto the floor, pooling into a sticky mess before I can scoop it up.

You can't even get this right, can you? How idiotic can you be?

I bang my head against the wall and let out a wail, low and guttural, then high and shrieky. Someone raps the door. I clasp my hands over my mouth, muting the scream boiling in my throat. Another knock, then the door creaks open, a sliver of light blooming on the floor.

"Wren? Is that you?" Panayis sticks his head through the door. "I thought I heard... What are you doing?" He shuts the door behind him and kneels beside me, Granny's hat in his hands. His eyes graze the open container, where pools of chocolate form at the edges and condensation spills like tears onto the floor.

Adrenaline drives my actions before my brain can catch up. I sit on my frozen fingers and shake my hair to hide my face.

"Are you okay?"

"You ask me that a lot. Have you noticed?" I stare at the ground.

"Why is that, do you think?" He crouches next to me, back against the wall.

"Were you going to eat that?" He keeps his eyes on the melting ice cream and pushes the lid farther away with his foot. Waves of humiliation and heat wash over my ears and forehead.

"I don't have a spoon." My voice is almost a whisper, yet the words ride the waves of heat in the stagnant air.

He chuckles, but there's no joy in his laugh.

"Exactly." A dry sob escapes.

"Did you already put it in your journal?" He nods and presses his lips together. Pounding quickens over my left-eye, and sweat peppers my upper lip and scalp.

"What are you talking about? How do you know about that?"

"You had me go find it for you that one day, remember? The day I took you up to your room? And you left it in my house that day." His voice trails after the memory.

Another stellar moment in my past year. I cover my face with my hands, too embarrassed to exist. "It's private," I mutter through my hands. "That is supposed to be private."

"Well, first of all, there's no 'This is My Diary-Keep Out Because I'm 12' sign on it. Second, I didn't mean to. It was open when I found it. When I saw what you'd written, I couldn't help but check to see how long you'd been recording everything. I'm sorry I saw it, and I feel bad for spying, but I can't change it now."

A dark calm emerges in my chest and spreads through my core and into my arms, like the eye of a hurricane. I straighten out my legs and close my eyes, my arms like noodles at my sides. Silence spreads with each breath. Even though Jay has seen my body, he's never seen me this naked.

"Is that how you lost all that weight? Because you can stop now." His hand hovers over mine. I flex my fingers, letting him know it's there, if he wants it. Instead of threading our fingers together, he rests his on mine. A giant tear rolls down my cheek. "I'm worried that maybe it's getting out of hand."

"Is that why you made me lunch? Trying to fatten me up? Like some sort of trick?" I face him, lips trembling.

"No, we were hanging out, not worrying about anything. Nothing else."

I narrow my eyes and stare.

"Food can be, I don't know, fun? Happy? Something other than whatever you're doing with it."

"And I ruined that, too." I crumple again.

"You didn't ruin anything. If I remember correctly, I'm the one that did the ruining. Sorry about getting mad when you mentioned him."

I lower my head and a tight grin stretches my lips into a flat line. "That's right, you did. And you can say his name. He isn't some dark lord that will gain more power or anything. He's just a guy."

He laughs for real this time.

"Are you sure he's just a guy? Seems to have quite the following, if you ask me. He got your attention." His gaze lingers on mine, and a new kind of warmth spreads through my body. I shake my head and clear my throat.

"Well, we can check my arm for a dark mark later. Can we just chill, for a minute or two? Suddenly, I'm exhausted."

"For a minute. Then we have to finish the driveway before we both get yelled at."

A crease forms between my brows.

"That's why I came out here, actually. Sent in as reinforcement."

"Of course you were."

We sit in silence until the ice cream melts into a pool of milky froth. Standing, Panayis plops Granny's hat on my head, and we go back to work.

Chapter 25

Dog breath. And then whining. I open my eyes. Fengari's sad eyes and nose peek over the side of my bed. I roll onto my back and sigh. Early summer sun sears the room through the window. Definitely need to ask for a shade to block it out. After all, summer break is coming, and we're not moving anytime soon. More dog whining.

"What are you doing in here, Runt?" I reach to scratch his ears, but he backs up to the door. More whining. He toddles back and forth like he wants me to follow.

"All right, all right." My body's sore from all the lifting and swinging and moving I've been made to do. I flex my feet under the sheet and feel the twinge of another long Sunday. Being grounded sucks, but at least I'm exercising without being obvious. The more I do, the less I hear about being in trouble. And I think Granny likes that Panayis and I have finally made peace.

Harvest can be any time between the next few weeks or two months from now, depending on the grapes' sugar content, so today we're tasked with stacking crates at the end of each row of vines. We've found a good rhythm in our work—like we're two ice dancers pushing and pulling each other in a routine. Balancing because of each other.

Jay makes me feel like I should be grateful to be with him. Like I'm holding on to hundreds of pounds while he waits for me to drop it so he can blame me for breaking them. I definitely prefer a counterweight to an anchor.

But this is Panayis. He's not that kind of partner.

Since the incident in the office, Jay called once or twice promising apologies if I'd only take him back. Even mentioned prom is "back on the table." I shudder. Like that's happening. He left some droopy daisies and a note taped to my locker asking to be forgiven, but with finals coming up and work around the vineyard, I have every excuse to avoid him.

Panayis keeps trying to convince me to call Robin and make up with her, but I can't bring myself to do it. First, I need to be free from Jay and his mess for good—finally do something that might make her proud to call me a friend again.

Fengari nudges my leg and circles the doorway. As I yank on my shorts and t-shirt, I'm not assaulted by the usual pancakes and bacon aromas, staples of a pre-harvest morning.

"They must've gotten an early start, huh? Let's let you out."

Instead of running down the stairs to the door, Fengari bursts across the hall into Granny's room, whining by her bed. Something clicks. No coffee smells. No baking breads.

The hall doubles in length, and I laser focus on Fengari's face. Staring at me. Staring at her bed. My heartbeat scalds my ears. My breath comes in rolling waves, my chest heaves like I just ran twenty miles.

The wood floor creaks in the hallway under my bare feet. And even though the cool of the downstairs mixes with upstairs heat, my blood chills.

I shiver.

My feet sink into her cloudy carpet. The hum of the tractors and the Spanish voices of men shout directions on the other side of the windows. Laughter. Far away. Because my heartbeat. And Fengari, whining. Little soft grunts.

Her hand hangs limp off the side of her mattress, gray-white under the sun and age and work. It's so still. She's not breathing. Somehow, I'm at her bedside. Her head tilts at an awkward angle over her shoulder, her mouth open like maybe she started to yawn and stopped mid-breath. Just. Stopped. Her eyes are open and fixed.

Her hair sprawls over her pillow, silver threads coming loose from the bobbin. It's a good thing she doesn't dye her hair, because hair doesn't stop growing, and she'd never be okay with roots.

I clasp my hands over my mouth, eyes wide. All my breath flees like I've been punched in the stomach. And I want to give it to her. She should have my breath because she needs it more than me. Fengari needs her. The workers need her. The vineyard needs her.

I need her.

There's sobbing in the distance. My legs are wet with tears, and I'm kneeling. Fengari nuzzles his head under my arm, using his nose to wrestle my hand on his head. I pick him up and squeeze him so tight I'm not sure if he's whining from fear or grief. Staring at her hand, I know it'll never prune another rose bush, never hang out the side of her El Dorado grasping at the breeze. There'll never be another chocolate cake for dinner or banana pudding when I'm sick.

Hands are on my shoulders lifting me up. They carry me to my room and set me on the bed. Panayis tells me to stay here. He heard a scream and came inside.

A scream? How stupid. Granny hates screaming in the house.

He says small breaths and he's going to make a call. He'll be right back. More footsteps on the stairs.

The dolls from my room stare, their vacant expressions giving away nothing of the scene unfolding across the hall. I stare, wondering what'll happen to them. Where they'll go. Where I'll go. Their eyes as empty as the future.

*****

Someone brings me tea at the kitchen table. The steam floats into oblivion. I've never seen a dead body before, let alone someone I know...or love. It's not like on television with people pretending to be dead or blown up bodies on the news. Something about the skin seems plastic, moldable. Except it isn't. Everything's so still.

Voices bounce off the walls and people bounce off each other, trying to make room for a stretcher. I imagine all their legs are part of one large body, inching her out the house and into some far away cave.

A blanket's draped around my shoulders, and Mom's crying on the back porch. The sound scratches my ears like nails on a chalkboard. A fresh cup of tea in front of me. The handle's too hot. It's been microwaved. Granny would've hated that.

I'm in the living room, away from the path of her body. Panayis is talking. I shouldn't see it covered in black plastic. The clock over the piano stopped ticking, its pendulum stuck at an awkward angle, the hands at three and seven. It's lunch time and I haven't eaten anything.

*****

The house is quiet again except for the phantom footsteps creaking the upstairs floorboards. Or maybe it's Mom making the bed or picking out clothes for Granny.

Outside, tractors hum once again and cars zoom past the house on the main road. People are still driving to the grocery store, talking on the phone, complaining about cell phone bills, and picking up their kids from school. Even the grapes continue to sweeten.

Life moves on without her, and now I have to as well. The entire year Mom and I have been here, I resented Granny butting in and her stupid mantras-turned life advice. Now, I'd give anything to smell her homemade bread or see her hand waving out of her stupid old car as she speeds down the dirt roads.

Over the sink, Granny's key gleams in the sun, its metal warm from the rays. It burns my hand a little but I don't care. Upstairs, in her closet, a jewelry chest houses silver and gold chains and old earrings she'd been saving "in case." I choose a longer silver one and thread it through the key and close the clasp around my neck.

I tuck its weight under my shirt and press it close to me. Granny showed me where her secrets were buried and, when it's time, I'll dig them up. They'll be her legacy.

Chapter 26

The phone doesn't stop ringing for three days straight. When neighbors drop off sympathy food by the truckload, Mom greets them at the door then shoos them away respectfully, miraculously managing to clock in for parental duty. Even though everyone's pulling extra hours preparing for the upcoming harvest, someone has to oversee things. Farm life stops for no one.

I'm heating up another green-bean surprise for today's lunch—a safe task since I can't do too much damage with the microwave. I pretend the beans are worms, writhing in mushroom chunks and gray goo so I won't eat them. There's so many people milling around the house, there's hardly any privacy. Since I can't expel what I eat, I just…don't.

"How's it going?" Panayis stomps his boots on the porch rug, and then makes himself at home at the table. He's all smiles, but his eyes scan the room. Since the day my journal magically turned up on the porch, he hasn't mentioned anything about it, but I know he checks for it when he thinks I'm not paying attention.

"Good. You hungry? I have this lovely casserole of lumpy vegetables and slimy sauce if you're interested." I offer him a spoonful, and he wrinkles his nose.

"Thanks, but I'll just grab a sandwich from the truck later. Hey, do me a favor, never go into marketing."

"Noted." I replace the spoon and sit in the chair across from him. Mom comes in, sniffing out the casserole's aroma.

"More casserole?" She reaches for one of Granny's mismatched plates in the cupboard. I press the key to my chest, the metal against my skin a solid reminder she's not completely gone. Panayis clears his throat.

"Mrs. Newmann, you ready to rethink my assignment to the fields? I think I'm needed in here more." He winks at me and waits for her reply. I narrow my eyes.

"I'm perfectly capable of heating up casserole, thankyouverymuch." I cross my arms and shift in my seat.

Mom shakes her head as she spoons clumps of beans onto her plate. "You two." She sits in her usual chair and moves her fork around. The smell sends waves of nausea through my body, so I cover my nose and breathe through my mouth as casually as possible. "As much as I would love some of your cooking, Panayis, you've made yourself fairly indispensable out there, especially with all the seasonal help coming on."

"Whatever you need." He tilts back in his chair and folds his hands behind his head. "You hear that? I'm indispensable."

"Great job, Mom. Now he won't be able to fit his big head through the door."

"On second thought, maybe you're onto something." Mom slides the fork from her mouth and pushes away her plate. Panayis smiles even bigger. "I think it's time you go back to school, get into a normal routine again. I mean, as much as possible."

My stomach practically drops through my chair onto the floor. Panayis sits up, his smile frozen in place.

"Mom, no. I need to be here. Helping." I stand, fists clenched.

"School's almost over, and you're so close to senior year. You can't afford any failing grades." She flattens her lips into a straight line and raises her eyebrows like she's been around the entire year and knows my life.

"Let me at least stay home until after the funeral. Please." My voice shakes, but I swallow and clear my throat.

"You know the school won't excuse absences without a good reason," she says.

I can think of at least ten. There's no way I can deal with what's waiting for me. Stupid smirks and whispered questions behind my back. Jay lurking around every corner.

"We could say I'm sick." It comes out more question than statement, and I immediately know I've lost. Should've joined debate when I had the chance. I slump into my chair.

"It's settled. You're going tomorrow." She eyes her plate and sighs. "If I can eat this every day, you can brave an education. Besides it's better to get back to normal as much as possible." She picks up her fork and scoops a mouthful; her eyebrow raises. She doesn't have a clue about my education. I flare my nostrils and shake my head.

Panayis stands. "It won't be so bad. You can dee-jay Bubba's radio on the way. I'll let you listen to whatever you want." He smiles reassuringly.

"Thanks, but that's only getting me to the parking lot. What about the rest of the day?"

"Guess we'll find out."

*****

The next morning I wait for Panayis and Bubba by the mailboxes so I can avoid more of Mom's feeble attempts at convincing me how awesome my day's going to be. I ditch the muffin she forced on me in the garden. Some lucky critter will eliminate any evidence, I'm sure. He rolls to a stop and honks. I jump about three feet in the air and the nearby birds squawk in protest. When I climb in, he hands me a travel mug.

"One order of Greek coffee to go." He shifts into drive and pulls onto the road.

"Thanks. I can't believe she's making me go." I sip from the mug, and my other hand covers the key around my neck as we pass the rows of vines. I can almost see her, Granny, out there in her rubber boots and huge hat, shouting directions and taking lunch orders.

"How're you doing?"

"Okay, I guess. I keep thinking I hear her in the kitchen or rustling around in her bedroom. She said she'd haunt the place, but I'm pretty sure it's just my imagination."

"Well, if anyone can come back and haunt you, it's her. Yia-yia always said ghosts come back during a full moon." His eyes dart from the road to me and back again. I sit up straight.

"What did you say? Full moon?" I do the calendar math in my head.

"Well, it's not official for another day or two, but yeah."

I tuck my leg underneath my body and face him, the first real smile I've managed in days. He narrows his eyes.

"What are you getting yourself into, now?"

I lift the key from around my neck and show it to him.

"What is that? Did you find Narnia or something?" He grins, and I give him my best Are You Serious face.

"No, I didn't find a closet that would transport us to a magical land. Like I'd still be here. This was Granny's, and she gave it to me." Holding it to the light, its colors change as it dangles from the chain. He extends his hand, and I pile it in his palm, the key resting on top.

"She buried a small chest in the vineyard and left it to me. I've been planning for the perfect time to go, but wasn't sure when. Until now."

"What do you think is in it?" He inspects the key at a stoplight then hands it back. My fingers brush his as I grasp the key. He sits a little straighter as the back of my neck heats. I loop the chain around my neck and tuck it in my shirt.

"I don't know. Honestly, I thought she made up the whole story. The key lived over the sink in the kitchen. She used to tell me stories about it, and I never thought she'd be crazy enough to actually bury something out there."

"This is Granny we're talking about."

"Point taken." We both nod. "Anyway, the full moon was her favorite. Even took moon baths, whatever that is." I shrug, and he smirks. "So, if there's one this weekend, it's the perfect time."

He's silent for a minute, then shifts in his seat. Maybe it's too weird for him.

"Prom's this weekend." His voice is quiet and he keeps his eyes fixed on the road. Dread fills my lungs, and I blow out a breath to get rid of it. Of course he has a date. I'm stupid to think he's not going.

"Oh, right. I'd forgotten all about it. If you're busy…" I half-choke, half-cough and straighten my leg to face forward again. The school looms in the near distance.

I'm careful to focus on what's left of my coffee and the peeling nail polish on my pinky as we inch through the parking lot traffic. He's quiet until he parks and turns off the ignition. Before he opens his door, he faces me.

"I thought you'd be going." His eyes are fixed on his knee. I nearly spit out my sip of coffee.

"To prom? Why would you think that?" Like mandatory attendance around these people isn't bad enough, I'd intentionally insert myself in that situation? I set the empty mug in the ashtray turned cup and receipt holder. His eyes meet mine.

"I didn't want to assume anything. I know things are complicated for you with…everything."

"You can say his name, you know. It's not a summoning spell." I unbuckle my seatbelt and dig my absence excuse for the last couple of days out of my bag.

He tilts his head. "Don't be so sure about that. There's something off about him."

"Okay, no more movies for you. Come on, I need to get this note to the office."

Once the note is turned in, we say our goodbyes. His math class is on the opposite side of campus from my English, leaving me on my own. Head down, I make my way through the crowds hoping everyone I want to avoid is still in the parking lot. With any luck, I can be safely in my seat before the warning bell even rings.

As I round the corner, a crowd of people—Jay's people—start cheering. Jay stands in the center, his guitar strapped over his shoulder. Amsel's standing next to him holding a pizza box, shouting my name like some football chant.

It's like being punched in the gut and all the air is sucked from my lungs. I clutch the key around my neck, eyes darting back and forth.

Jay strums his guitar and clears his throat. Everyone hushes each other. He saunters toward me, his left hand moving along the neck of the instrument and his right strumming the strings. He's belting some song about girls like you and backwoods love as he circles me like a shark, and I'm chum in the water. His off-key singing is nearly drowned out by everyone's obnoxious screaming.

First, my lips tingle. Then it spreads through my arms and numbs my fingertips. I swallow but my throat is dry.

Jay ends his circling and kneels in front of me. With a final flourish, he ends with his hand in the air. Amsel steps forward and opens the box. A pepperoni pizza with a question mark made out of olives stares at me. On the lid, written in red:

I know this is cheesy, but will you go to prom with me. Olive u!

Then the world goes dark.

Chapter 27

Sirens.

Flashing lights.

So cold.

*****

There's too much light. A machine beeps. Something's strangling my arm. I reach for Granny's key around my neck, but it's not there. I suck in a breath.

"You're awake." Mom's holding my hand. The warmth of it makes the cold everywhere else that much worse. A shiver bursts in my lungs and spreads to my fingers and toes.

"Where's my key? I need it." I pat the bed in case it fell.

"It's with your other things. Don't worry." Mom squeezes my hand. Another chill.

"I was at school."

Jay's song and Amsel's pizza flood my memory. I turn to vomit, but nothing comes. Mom holds the kidney-shaped bowl for me anyway. Trembling and tangled in a web of wires, I curl into a ball and hug my knees.

"Want to tell me about it?" She tucks the blankets over my shoulders. Her eyes are red and watery, and she's not wearing any makeup. One of Granny's old work shirts drapes her shoulders. I tuck my forehead into my knees and groan.

Tell her what, exactly. That I passed out because I can't deal with being near the one person I'd sacrificed everything for? Everyone? And end up in the hospital for it? How stupid. I try to sit up, but the room flips over. Mom guides me back to the pillow and smooths my hair away from my face. My jaw quivers and my teeth clack.

The curtain slides open and a young woman in purple scrubs and matching lipstick enters carrying a tray. She sets it on the counter. I can already smell what I don't want to have.

"Brought you something to eat. Thought you might be hungry." She adjusts the pinchy thing on my finger and the beeping stops. I hug my knees tighter. "What would you like first, the turkey sandwich or the applesauce?" Her blonde ponytail bounces as she moves. I cringe.

"I'm not hungry." I rub my tongue across the roof of my mouth, but there's no moisture to swallow. Plastic wrap crinkles behind my back, and hospital deli meat mixes with the antiseptic smell of the room. My heart clanks against my ribs.

"I'm sure that can't be true." Her voice is a nasally shotgun, firing words into the walls like shrapnel. "When's the last time you ate anything, Sweetheart?"

My eyes plead with Mom for help, but her expression says she's not on Team Wren. I roll onto my back and count the ceiling tiles.

"I gave you that muffin this morning." Mom's voice is an octave higher than normal.

One, two, three…

"Oh, I'm willing to bet Miss Thing didn't touch one crumb. Isn't that right, Honey?" She winks at Mom. I'm breathing harder now.

Four, five, six, seven…

She wraps her fingers around my wrist, but I yank my arm away.

Eight, nine…

"Wren! Please. Tell us what's going on." Tears solidify Mom's plea. Nurse Purple Nurple raises my bed so I'm sitting at more of an upright angle.

"I have to insist you at least try and eat something." She shoves the applesauce in my face. I turn my head toward Mom and exhale through my nose, mostly to lose the sugary smell. "If you don't feed yourself, we'll have to do it for you. And that's not pleasant."

TEN. A bomb of noise explodes in my brain. Everything is fuzzy and clear at the same time.

"What does applesauce have to do with anything? I fainted, that's all. Jay was singing this awful song in front of everyone, and they all think…" I stop. I can't talk about that night. I can't tell my mother I'm no longer a virgin. Not the way it happened. "I'm fine now and want to go home."

"You didn't pass out because someone sang you a bad song, Sweetheart." Purple Nurple pats my knee.

I seriously want to strangle her.

The curtain moves again, and a gray-haired man in a white coat barges in, a young girl with a clipboard two steps behind. She's writing furiously.

"I'm Dr. Walker. How's our girl?" His voice is louder than Nurse Nurple; it nearly shakes the walls. Mom opens her mouth to answer, but I hold up my hand. If I'm ever going to escape, I have to show them I can handle myself.

"I've been saying I'm fine and want to go home. I got embarrassed and fainted. I'm sure I'm not the first. I mean, read any Victorian novel, am I right?" I huff a laugh, but no one else smiles. I cross my arms and scoot lower on the bed. "Tough crowd."

Mom sighs. Dr. Walker sits at the end of the bed.

"Is there any chance you might be pregnant?" he asks. My eyes practically bug out of my head.

"What? Why? No."

"What's the date of your last period?" His eyes search mine. They're kind, but I hate him anyway.

I don't remember. Before the party? My vision shifts and the room goes gray for a split second. Mom inhales a sob.

"Sorry Mom, but I have to ask." He nods to her then settles his gaze on me. "Are you sexually active? If so, what kind of protection do you use?"

Mom's staring at the floor, a stream of water sliding down her cheeks. I clench my fists, drawing the blanket into knots and rock back and forth. The shaking comes back in waves, like thunder after lightning.

I open my mouth and close it again. If I tell them, everything is going to change. Everything Granny's worked for, her legacy, could be at risk from my stupidity. But if I am…what they say… I have to.

Safety is a sentence away, but I can't say it.

"What is it?" Mom's voice is quiet, calm. "Be honest. No one in here is going to judge you." Her mouth presses into a tight smile, and she nods as she wipes the tears from her face.

I shouldn't have to think about it. It's too much. I squeeze my eyes shut. I cover my face with my hands and gag on the humiliation and panic swirling in my body. Everything's happening so fast and he has so many questions and I just need a minute to think.

"You didn't pass out because you were embarrassed. You're malnourished. From the sores inside your mouth and the broken blood vessels on your cheek, I'd say you've been throwing up your food for some time. Is that right?"

I know I shouldn't do it. It never should've turned into this. Other girls eat whatever they want and stay rail thin. I haven't shopped in the same aisle as them since grade school. I need a rigorous routine. But discipline's turned into obsession. Before, it was a way to deal with extra calories. Now it's the only way I can survive the day.

"If you keep this up, your heart could give out. And if you are pregnant, your baby's life is in danger, too. Your organs will shut down. You will die." His words are cold, like a shiny metal slide in the winter, and I follow it all the way to the bottom.

Mom's hand covers mine, her other rubbing up and down my arm. A sob escapes my throat. I can't do this alone anymore.

"Only one time. And I didn't want it—it shouldn't count. I didn't know. I don't know how, but I didn't. I'm so sorry."

Mom's hand falls from mine. Tears well in my eyes and cascade onto my cheeks.

"What was only one time?" Dr. Walker asks.

"Once. At a party. With my boyfriend. I mean, he's not my

boyfriend now. When he… I didn't want to, but he did anyway." Mom sinks into her chair, but is silent. The world feels smaller.

"Are you saying you were sexually assaulted?"

"No. It's not that. At first I wanted to." I swallow. Mom's face is strained, but she nods for me to go on. "But then I didn't, but he kept going."

"Did you tell him to stop?" Dr. Walker motions to the writing girl, and she slinks out of the room.

"Yes, but the music took over everything and I probably said it too quiet." The cuff around my arm tightens, making me jump. "I tried pushing him away, but then it was over." His scrubs are the same green as the lamp from that night.

"Oh, Wren." Mom's voice is a whisper bleeding into my heart. Tears slide down my cheeks.

"Okay. Thank you for being so honest." Dr. Walker stands, his hands resting in his coat pockets, and faces Mom. "You have a very brave daughter. You should be proud." He nods at me.

She's blinking a lot, which means she's processing, but she smiles and nods anyway. I feel a lot of things, but brave isn't close to being one of them. I wipe at my eyes, but say nothing.

Writing Girl reappears and nods to the doctor. He rests his hand gently on my arm.

"Because a crime may have been committed, as a mandated reporter, I have to notify the authorities," he says. My throat tightens and I close my eyes. This is exactly what I didn't want. "They'll want to ask you a few questions, but it will be up to you and your mom to decide if you want to press charges." His voice softens. "You did the right thing. All that matters now is that you take care of yourself so you can get well."

Mom clears her throat and wipes her cheek with the back of her hand. "It's a good idea to talk to them. You'll feel safer."

I can't remember the last time I felt anything close to safe. A shiver dances up my spine and I nod.

Dr. Walker motions to his scribe. "Order inpatient therapy for three days and then a referral to a specialist. She'll also need nutritional guidance and another blood draw in the next week."

"Inpatient? The funeral. I can't miss it." I squeeze Mom's hand for backup.

"She's right. My mother, her grandma, passed away recently, and the funeral is tomorrow. Is there a way to keep her home?"

There's some lengthy discussion in the hall about schedules and open doors at all times—which blows—and daily counseling appointments, but ultimately Mom convinces the good doctor to agree to let me go home on a trial basis. In other words, one dietary mistake, and it's rehab for me.

Before I can leave, there's more tests and I have to be interviewed by the police. Mom stays with me the whole time while a nice detective named Olivia asks me a bunch of questions about that night, especially what I did after. She explains because it's been so long and I washed my clothes, it's highly probable the only evidence is my word against his. My pregnancy test comes back negative, too, making it likely no charges could be filed even if I wanted to.

Mom is quiet during the interview, but the disappointment etched on her face says this is far from over.

*****

I'm lying in bed staring at the stars through my window. I can't see the moon, but its light is bright, making the sky a shimmery silver-blue. A small knock comes at my door—unnecessary given the new open-door policy.

"Are you awake?" Mom whispers. She'd been quiet the entire way home, if that's what you'd call it. Basically, she stared at the road, turned toward me with her mouth open, closed it again, then turned back to the road. All the way home. Now she wants to talk. I guess it's now or never.

"You can come in." I scoot back against the wall as she climbs onto the bed with me. Personal space has never been her strength.

"I owe you an apology." She nods, but mostly to herself.

I blink. Not the words I expected. We need to talk—sure. Are you insane?—absolutely. An apology?—never.

"Why?" I flip onto my side and face her.

"I should've been there for you. And I shouldn't have made you go to school today." She lies down so we're face to face, like we used to. "I think you tried to tell me once, but I was so wrapped up in my own drama that I didn't hear what you needed."

"That's okay."

"Thank you for saying that, but no, it's not. I'm not the only one going through a divorce, and I forgot that. This is embarrassing to admit, but after your dad left, I felt so ugly and worthless, I made a lot of bad choices trying to feel good about myself again. I saw you doing the same thing, but because I couldn't acknowledge my own issues, I couldn't admit yours either." She wraps my hand in hers and clutches it to her chest. I let her.

I offer a weak smile. I hadn't really thought about her pain, either. She's Mom, after all, and supposed to have it together. It never occurred to me she might be making things up as she went along, too. My grin spreads to my eyes.

"I guess we both suck." I shrug one awkward shoulder, the other trapped, holding up the rest of my body, which suddenly feels very heavy.

"I suck more than you this time." She raises an eyebrow and presses her lips into a downward smile. "Which says something, because at sixteen, you're supposed to be Queen Suckage in the house."

I stare at her, fake anger wrinkling my brows, until we both break out in laughter. Mine turns into a yawn.

"You're tired. You've had a day, huh?" She brushes my hair from my cheek. "Let's get some rest. We have a long day tomorrow."

"Okay." I search her face for a clue of what that might be and, for the first time, see the worry lines and dark circles around her eyes. It occurs to me she might still be making it up as she goes along. For some reason, this comforts me.

"Mom?" I swallow.

"Mmhmmm."

"Will he be at the funeral?" I don't think I'll be able to sleep if I know I have to face Jay and his family. Her back goes rigid. Then she smiles at me, fire burning in her eyes.

"Don't you worry about that boy coming near you again. Tomorrow is about honoring Granny, and I've made it clear he's not to be anywhere near the service or the house." She nods reassuringly. "And I'm sure his parents are too embarrassed to show their faces, if only out of respect for your grandmother."

I sigh and my body relaxes for the first time all day. After she says good night, my phone buzzes. It's Robin. I swallow to keep my heart in my chest.

I heard. I'll be there. Can we talk?

Chapter 28

The next morning, I wake in the stifling heat, sheets shoved to the bottom of my bed. The air's thick as it moves and makes room for me to sit up. Outside, the sky's a crisp blue and white at the edges, not a cloud anywhere. The vineyard's crawling with moving hats and gloves and voices in and out of the rows, readying for harvest. With such intense heat the last week or so, it could be any day. But there's no work or school for me. Today is Granny's funeral.

I reread Robin's text. The weight of missing my best friend presses against my core. So much has happened in the last few months, and we've been so cruel to each other. What I said to her at the bonfire. What she said to me at the party. How we both avoided each other since. I wonder if we'll ever be the way we were again.

I've always pictured burials taking place in cold, rainy weather, where everyone wears black overcoats and huddle under enormous black umbrellas while some stranger rattles off a Psalm or a random poem. But today is the hottest day of the year, and the umbrellas provide shelter from the unforgiving sun.

Turns out even those are a romantic notion better left in movies. Panayis cements his hand to the back of the vinyl folding chairs they give Mom and me to use while everyone else crams under two tarps-turned-makeshift tents on either side of the grave—the only relief from the blazing heat.

Mom sits next to me, wiping her eyes every few seconds. There's no sign of my dad, just a tacky floral arrangement he sent to the house. It even has one of those ridiculous ribbon messages tacked to the front of it. When I saw it, I knew—he's gone for good.

Robin and her mom stand in the back, making awkward, flat-lipped smiles when our eyes meet. I clutch at the key around my neck.

Once all the words are said and all the hugs are given, the crowd, unable to cease their own momentum, disperses to their jobs and families and farms. Those that can make their way to the mounds of funeral food and company at home.

Mom turns away as they lower Granny's casket into the ground. She likes to imagine the dashes in between the years on the headstones mark happy lives, and I smile at her concentrated expression as she reads each one.

As the casket descends into its dark home, I sit in the last folding chair, refusing to give it to the grounds crew wanting to pack up and eat their sandwiches.

Finally, I make my way to the car—Granny's El Dorado—where Robin's waiting. She's dressed in a dark sundress, her hair is cascading fire down her back.

"Hi." Her expression's somber but her eyes are hopeful.

I nod, unsure of how to start a conversation with someone who used to know everything about me. A million things come to mind, but nothing out of my mouth. She's quiet for a moment as she studies the trees and odd assortment of flowers on the graves.

"I'm sorry about Granny," she says. Panayis's words about people apologizing hangs between us, and I half laugh, half sigh. She cocks her eyebrow. "Am I not supposed to say that?" Her expression turns to horror, and she covers her reddening face with both hands. "Ugh, I'm so dumb."

I laugh for real this time. She peers at me through latticed fingers and returns a sheepish smile.

"Hey, I'm the awkward one, remember? Don't steal my lines."

In two steps, we're hugging, talking over each other with apologies and promises and explanations.

"I'm so sorry, I was so mean and I don't know why."

"No, what I said. The worst." She holds my hands and presses her forehead to mine. "Everyone's talking, and I should've known better. I should've come to you."

"It's not your fault. I was so ready to be Miss Independent. I wanted you to be proud of me for making my own choices for once. Who knew my choices would suck and you'd call me out? I promise I'll never not talk to you again."

"And I promise never not to talk to you again." She wraps her arms around me and I do the same. "What are you guys going to do?"

"I guess we'll stay at the vineyard for now. Mom's been around." I make a face. "Kind of annoying, really." I grin, thinking how I've gotten used to country life.

"We have a lot to catch up on." Her eyes twinkle with determination. "Especially since Jay's horrid prom-posal."

I cringe. "I'm sure it's going viral as we speak." Images of me falling to the ground over and over flash before my eyes. I shudder.

"Actually, it's not." She jockeys her eyebrows. "When I heard about it, I told everyone if they didn't delete it off their phones immediately, their prom reservations might accidentally be lost in the Student Government void."

"You did?" A weight lifts from my shoulders as I exhale. She shrugs and shifts her weight from one foot to the other.

"I figured I owed you after the party. You were in real trouble, and what kind of best friend would I be if I didn't?"

A glimmer of light rises in my chest, like the morning sun peeking over the horizon. I tilt my head, tears welling in my eyes.

"A lot's happened."

She clears her throat. "Well, let's talk about it at the house. I'm starving, and there's bound to be tons of food." She squeezes her eyes shut. "I shouldn't have said that. I'm so so sorry." She hangs her head and sighs. I swallow and force a smile.

"Come on, let's get our moms and get out of here."

*****

Groups of tables line the back lawn surrounding the large oak, and heaps of food rests under nets, waiting to be devoured by the hungry funeral-goers. I haven't binged since the ice cream incident, but I still don't trust myself not to throw up when I eat, so I avoid the lawn. Mom brings a small plate of fruit and chips to the porch for me. I pick at them while people come and go. Robin and I sit knee to knee on the long pillows of the swing, each waiting for the other to start the conversation.

"This is awkward," she says, and laughs. I automatically relapse into passive mode, waiting for Robin to lead.

"Sorry." After the initial stuttering, Robin catches me up on the old neighborhood's gossip about the old lady who moved into my old house.

"She stands at the front window and yells at all the kids skateboarding in the driveway. I swear they do it just to annoy her."

I can totally picture it—the boys jumping off the cement wall around her lawn. How many times I stood at that same window, signaling to Robin across the street with flashlight Morse code? I exhale, as if the act could wipe away the memory like some mental Etch-A-Sketch.

"Are you okay?" She pushes her knee into mine.

"I have something to tell you."

And I do. I tell her everything. About what happened. About Jay's reaction. About walking home. About the hospital. She sits silent and still the whole time, tears rolling down her face. When I'm done, she wipes her face with the back of her hand.

"I don't know what to say… I didn't know. What a bastard." She embraces me, smothering me in arms and sundress and hair. "I'm sorry I was a crappy friend to you. I should've been there."

I push her hair out of my face and smooth my own ponytail over my shoulders when she lets go. "Sorry, but the Craptastic Friend Award belongs to me," I say. She raises her eyebrows. "I'm sorry. You've always been my best friend, and I never should've shut you out. Can we just agree that I get to wear the Worst Friend in the World tiara and move on?" She smiles and stretches her arms for another hug. "And also agree that it's too hot to hug?"

"Fine. But we take turns wearing the tiara."

"Deal. Want to get something to drink? I'm melting into a puddle and need to hydrate."

She nods as we peel ourselves off the swing's cushion.

The workers in the vineyard move methodically down the aisles, cutting grape bunches and throwing them into the bins. Panayis is there stacking crates. He pauses to wipe his face and waves. I smile and wave back.

Robin gestures toward him and smiles. "You two seem to be getting along."

I claim a sudden interest in the floor as my cheeks redden. "He's been a good friend to me." At the end of the porch, a butterfly floats in and out of the hydrangeas. "He just works here, and we got to know each other, that's all."

"Okay." Her hands shoot up in surrender. "Just a friend, got it." She smirks. "He's kinda cute."

"Is he? I hadn't noticed."

"Mmhmmm. I'm proud of you."

I clutch the key around my neck. Things are finally starting to feel right again. A new sense of purpose and strength emerges from a part of me that feels like it's waking after a long winter.

"I'm getting there, too."

*****

Later that night as I lie on my bed, my phone buzzes. It's Panayis.

Today was a day, huh?

You noticed, did you?

Only after the video went viral.

Ha. Ha.

So. No prom, then?

No. No prom.

And it's a full moon.

Indeed.

What are you going to do instead? 😈

Want to come with me?

Someone needs to hold the flashlight.

Chapter 29

When the house is finally quiet, Panayis and I set out with our shovel, retracing Granny's steps from the night she'd shown me the chest. The bright moon lights our path. After turning left where I should've turned right and tripping over a crate in the middle of a row, we find the spot. Granny's hand shovel and gloves are still there. Grief flickers inside me, and I inhale a breath for courage.

"How far down is it?" Panayis wipes a bead of sweat trickling down his neck. The heat still hovers, making it hard to stay dry.

"Not sure. Last time, Granny dug for a while."

"Well, give me the shovel." He holds out his hand.

"I can do it." I push the blade into the ground, but he covers my hand with his.

"I know you can. But you did just get out of the hospital. I'm only offering if you'd like my help. I'm more than a pretty face, you know." He winks and steps back. I give him a thankful smile, but I have to do this on my own.

More than a few shovels full of dirt later, I'm breathing hard on my knees, lifting the box out of the ground and brushing off the lingering lumps of clay.

"Are you going to open it here? Or wait and do it back at the house?" He kneels beside me. It has to be here. Under the moon the way she wanted. I know it.

"Let's do it." I cross my legs underneath me, sitting the chest in front of me. He gasps, his eyes bulging.

"You're sitting in dirt. You realize that, right? Where the bugs live?"

I nod, too absorbed in opening the chest to care.

I remove the key from around my neck. After I fumble with the lock a little, the latch gives. Eyes wide, I lift the top.

The inside's lined with tinfoil and is mostly empty, besides a few folded pieces of paper and a black velvet box the size of my palm.

"What's up with the foil?" he asks.

"Who knows." But the borrowed moonlight reflects from inside the box, providing enough light without the flashlight and giving everything a silver glow. A moon bath gift.

I rummage through the papers. There's some old carnival tickets clipped to a picture of a young Granny in front of a funhouse mirror.

"Oh." I hand the picture to Panayis. "She's so young."

"You look like her. Never really saw it before."

"You think so? Let me see," I say. He hands me back the picture. Her once-full lips curl into a smirk, right hand propped on her hip. "I don't know. But people have told me that before."

Panayis rolls his eyes. "You certainly have her stubbornness."

I punch him in the arm, and then turn back to the chest. I pick up a copy of her "world famous" applesauce recipe. "I didn't think she had it written down."

"Now you can make it, if you want."

"I guess." I stare at the stars, shiny bits of light freckling the dark, and sigh, a tightness forming in my chest. "Why did she leave me an old picture and this recipe? I don't get it."

"There's more in there. Maybe once you see everything, you'll know."

I shrug, already tiring of this last game of hers. The hope I'd kept bottled up begins to fade.

I pick up a quartered piece of paper, its frayed edge suggesting it's been ripped out of a large journal. Granny's writing fills the front and back. A note. To me. Panayis's blanched expression matches my reaction.

"I can't read it. You do it." I sit back on my hands, soaking in the light.

He reads aloud:

> *I have a confession. I didn't really find this chest under some magical grapevine. I did find the key, though, but in the old barn, not in the dirt. But your face lit up so much when I told you that story that I knew I had to do something so you wouldn't be disappointed.*

"I was, like, seven when she told me that story. I would've understood." I huff. He raises his eyebrows. "Fine, go on."

> *After all, everyone needs a little magic in their life, no matter how old they get. Anyway, the same afternoon you left to go home, I went to the craft store and bought this silly chest and took a hammer to it. Added on a coat or two of stain, and you had your mystery chest. The trouble was finding the right time to show it to you.*

I remember barely being able to see over the kitchen sink and peering through the bottom of the glass shelf to see the key. Over the years, I've imagined all sorts of things that could be in the chest.

Years ago, I thought there might be a tiara that belonged to a long-forgotten princess, and she left it for me to claim my rightful throne. As I grew older, I thought that maybe she'd found old pirate money and locked it away. But really, what she left me was a part of her. The part that loved me so much, she made a childhood story come to life.

> *When you came to live with me last summer, I knew it was time to let you open the box, as it were. Someone has to carry the family secrets, and I knew if I gave it to your mom, it'd end up in a drawer somewhere, never to be seen again. And before you go rolling your eyes or throwing away the recipe (I know you hate it—you can't fool a fool), there is something else in here that I want you to have. Inside the little box is a locket that my mom gave to me. I hope that when you open it, if you haven't already, you will see the beauty that runs in our family the way I do. All my love, Granny. P.S. If you throw away the recipe, I'll know and come back to haunt you.*

Panayis folds the paper in its original shape and hands it to me.

"Oh, Granny."

"You okay?" His hands on my shoulders steady me.

"Yeah." I blink back tears and reach into the chest with shaky hands. Lifting the velvet box, I pry the lid open. Moonlight shimmers against a shiny silver circle suspended on a chain. My thumbs are too clumsy to work the tiny latch, so I hand it to Panayis. "Can you open this? My hands aren't working right now."

He does. A grin forms at the corners of his mouth. He shuts his eyes and laughs. Without saying anything, he hands me the locket. Probably me as a fat baby and then a school picture or something.

But instead of some picture hacked within an inch of its life, two perfectly round mirrors are perched on either side of the locket. On the left is my reflection—dark circles and gaunt cheekbones. On the right side, the moon shines from its place in the sky, reigning over the ritual.

It occurs to me that the moon is small and large at the same time. A new moon isn't incomplete because the rest can't be seen. It's always there, part of the whole that already exists.

"Do you see it? What she means by the beauty she sees?"

"I get it, but…" My voice trails off as I trace the new angles on my face. "I look really bad."

"Don't you get it?" His glassy eyes reflect the watery light. "You're the beauty she sees, saw, in the world. Not because of your appearance or what you eat or don't eat." He scoops my hand in his. I flinch at his honesty. "I think it's like why I learned to make my mom's recipes. You're a part of her, and she's a part of you."

I choke back a sob and clutch the locket so hard that it closes, its snap echoing in the leaves. He gently opens my fist and scoops the locket into his hands, hooking its chain around my neck.

"In the Greek tradition, when someone dies, we say may their memory be eternal."

"Yeah, your dad said that to me and my mom." I press my hand to the locket against my chest and close my eyes. "Thank you." Although I'm not sure if I'm saying it to Panayis or Granny. Maybe both.

We amble back to the farmhouse in silence, each busy with our own thoughts. At the porch, I turn to him.

"Thank you for coming with me. You always seem to be around when I need you."

He draws the right side of his mouth into a lopsided grin and blushes.

"That's what Granny was trying to get through that thick skull of yours." He taps his temple. I raise my eyebrows and lower my chin. "You don't need me." He brushes his fingers across my chin. "But I'll be here when you choose me." He kisses my cheek and, before I can say anything, turns and saunters down the driveway, a new lightness in his gait.

Chapter 30

The tractor lights slice through the vines, casting shadows on the swing under the large oak. Harvest's a twenty-four-hour operation now, a race to collect the fruit into crates before the sugar content is too high. When things are crazy like this, I've learned to pause a moment and gather my thoughts. So much has happened this year. I've spent so much time sorting things into other kinds of boxes, keeping order and erasing things I couldn't deal with. Talking with my therapist, I've learned I forced myself into another type of box, limiting how I see myself.

I thought Jay's love could silence Beached Whale Girl, but he only made the agony worse. Love isn't something he's capable of, at least not now. I'd deluded myself into thinking I could be someone I wasn't, wearing tiny clothes and punishing myself for not understanding my own feelings. I got so used to wearing pain, wrapping it so tightly around myself in the hopes of feeling secure, only to suffocate the very happiness I longed for.

I'm not perfect at it, but I'm learning to see bingeing for what it is—a way to control how I feel about all the loss in my life. And even though it's clearer now, it's an ongoing battle to give up the behaviors that comforted me for so long. There are times when I miss it. Crazy, I know. But I hear it gets better.

A rumbling of tires over gravel dominates the birdsong coming from the branches. Familiar dread rises, an angry tribe of wasps churning in my gut. I don't know when the love I had for Jay turned to fear, but here it is, the ugly truth. I dig my phone out of my pocket, ready to call for help if I need it.

I close my eyes and focus the grounding energies from the tree into strength, the way I've practiced. His shoes plod on the pathway and stop. If I open my eyes, he'll be there, all sad eyes and worried expression—hunched shoulders and curled feet, his apology pose. His hands'll be shoved in his pockets and his speech slow and purposeful.

I've seen this performance so many times. I know my usual part in this Greek tragedy, but today I'm rewriting the script. I steady my breath, my heart settling into a normal rhythm.

"Wren." He slurs my name like a drunken prayer. He's been drinking. "I wanted to say I'm sorry. I get so caught up in what everybody expects of me. It's so much pressure. You understand." He slides his feet forward, hands at waist-level. I stand and cross my arms.

"Stop." I press my lips together and narrow my eyes, trying to see the Jay I used to see, the one I thought I loved. He's smaller to me, a child searching for his lost blanket. I wait for the walls to build up around my heart but, to my surprise, there's no sense of fear.

"You aren't supposed to be here. You aren't welcome here anymore."

Some switch flips, and his eyes burn with anger. "I didn't do what you said. I couldn't." He snarls and grabs my arms. "You don't know what you're saying." His stale beer breath permeates the air. My heart skips and I swallow hard. Raising my chin, I shake free and step backward.

"Jay, you can't be here." I gulp my breath.

"Everything all right?" Panayis steps into the ring of light near the office.

"Get the hell out of here, Pawn." Jay stands straight and clenches his jaw. "This doesn't concern you. All you've ever done is mess with her head."

"Jay," I say. He turns back to me.

"I've got this, Wren." He emphasizes my name like he just saved me from touching a hot stove. Rage burns in his cheeks, his sorry puppy façade gone. "He needs to understand that he can't control you. After I beat that message into his head, I'll deal with you." He steps off the path and cuts over the lawn so that only the white-washed fence separates them.

Panayis hurdles the fence and closes in on Jay, stopping only inches from his face. His mouth tight and eyes wide, he exhales through his nose like a bull preparing to charge. He opens his arms and tilts his head like he's inviting Jay into a violent hug. Jay laughs.

"What do you think you're gonna do, Pawn?" Jay spits at his feet.

"Guys!" I push between them. "Knock it off!" I try coaxing Jay backward, away from Panayis.

"Let him come. I'm tired of him treating you like shit. He's needed a lesson in manners for a long time."

"You kiss your mother with that mouth? Oh right, she's dead." Jay pushes me onto the grass. He charges Panayis, knocking chests with him, forcing him backward.

Panayis catches his footing and retaliates by swinging. His fist connects with Jay's cheek, sending him reeling to where I'm trying to stand up.

"Bitch move." He points at Panayis and spits blood. Then, I'm in front of him, grabbing his shoulders and shaking him.

"Hey!" He reluctantly turns his gaze to me. Panayis huffs behind me. I pivot to see both of them. "Panayis, go to the porch and wait for me there. You need to leave."

"Not until I know you're going to be okay," he says. Jay scoffs.

"I'm fine."

He lumbers toward the stairs, away, keeping his eyes on Jay the whole time.

"I'll be right over there." He points to the porch.

"Okay, Pawn," Jay says.

"Shut UP, Jay! I don't want to hear any more of your crap. I am over it." My chest heaves as I hold open the gate for him. "Now, I need you to leave. Seriously, have a nice life."

He blinks, blank-faced. "You can't make me leave. My dad runs this shit-show."

"Maybe I can't, but the restraining order can. Try me." My nostrils flare in defiance.

He leers at me like he's deciding which insult to hurl, but then spits instead and pushes past me. Gravel spins under his tires, a large dust cloud trailing his speeding truck onto the main road. Then he's gone.

I close my eyes, counting my breaths until my heart rate returns to something resembling normal. Closing the gate with shaky hands, I smile at my small victory. I touch the locket around my neck.

"I'm really sorry." Panayis paces on the porch, hands clasped over his head. I climb the few steps to meet him. When he turns to me, I raise my hands to stop him. "I snapped. I don't know why, I never do that. Just seeing him come here with more lies. I lost it." He sniffs and wipes his forehead.

"You were right the other night. I don't need you to save me, Panayis. I had it under control—have myself under control."

Pain and frustration haunt his eyes. "I know. I mean, of course you did. I'm really sorry." He reaches for my hand. "Is this okay?" he asks. I let him entwine his fingers with mine. They seem to fit perfectly.

"I think you should go, too. Tomorrow's another long day." As much as I want to explore this new feeling, I need to process what happened. Part of my therapy is to write everything down the way I feel it happen. Then, in session, I go over its accuracy. It's not easy, but it helps.

"As long as you aren't mad?" He squeezes my hand. I shake my head and he smiles. "Oh, I almost forgot. I have something for you." He reaches into his back pocket, revealing a small rectangular package wrapped in brown paper.

"What is it?" I accept it as he places it in my palm.

"Open it," he says. I rip off the paper. "I thought you needed a fresh one."

"You got me a new journal." Warmth spreads inside me and water collects at the corner of my eyes. When I blink, a lone tear slides down my cheek. He wipes it away with his finger. "Pretty good right hook." My voice is barely a whisper.

"Yeah, my hand is killing me." He holds it up and winces when I touch it. A bruise clouds his middle knuckle.

"Guess Dr. P is the patient now."

His lips slide into a sheepish grin, and I bite my own to stifle a smile.

"Come on, we can ice it." Through the dark window, I can almost see Granny waiting for us at the table, sipping her tea. "And never do that again."

"No problem. We Greeks are lovers, not fighters." He wraps his arm around my shoulder, my head falling perfectly in place on his chest.

"And users of terrible clichés."

After his hand is iced to my satisfaction and I'm convinced it's not going to swell, I escort him to the end of the porch. On the middle step, he turns and faces me. He's quiet, studying me. Remnants of Beached Whale Girl stare back. It shocks me to learn I don't care if he sees her. He accepts all of me, even the ugly parts. And that's beautiful.

I lift my chin, and he meets me half-way. When our lips touch, fireworks don't go off. Birds don't sing. But my connection to him is strong. Kissing him feels like flying and landing all at the same time.

"Remember when I said I would be here when you were ready to choose me?" he asks, our hands and foreheads touching.

"Yes."

"Good choice."

After one last kiss, he drives Bubba down the driveway. I stay there until the taillights fade onto the main road. I pick an apple off Granny's salad tree and bite into it, its flavor a crisp promise of fall. Normally, I'd record the calories of however many bites I can handle, but that's not who I want to be anymore. It'll be a while before I rid myself of my bad habits, but that's okay. I take another mouthful, close my eyes, and savor its tang.

When the apples are ready, they'll usually be picked and processed for Granny's applesauce. She'd spent so much time grooming her tree to produce so many distinct types of apples only to merge them together, losing what made them unique in the first place—preserving them in chaos. I like them better on their own. I'll protect and even pass on Granny's recipe someday, as she wished. But as for me, I'm going to keep things natural.

THE END

RESOURCES

Crisis Text Line
Text "HOME" to 741741 for immediate help.

National Eating Disorders of America (NEDA)
Call 1-800-931-2237
or visit
www.nationaleatingdisorders.org for more information.

For help with sexual assault, contact RAINN
1-800-656-HOPE (4673)
or visit
www.rainn.org to chat online or for more information.

Acknowledgments

When I was in my late teens, my mom decided she was going to purchase several acres of farmland with the world's oldest house smack dab in the middle of the property. Everything creaked. The ground was nothing but rocks. Over the next several years, she donned her overalls and muck boots and spent hours sifting the dirt, creating her own flower beds, growing stuff both edible and aesthetic. She cooked incredible meals in her ancient kitchen, all the while singing (off-key) to the old standards while her puppy chased the gophers and chickens. It was her heaven. It was my…well, let's just say it motivated me to move sooner than later. Like Wren, I prefer my critters where I can see them. This story is set in a place very similar to the farmland, and Granny is very much based on her. My mom died just as I was finishing the first draft, and her influence is on every page.

Thank you to my little family for all your support while I toiled away on this project. Special thanks to my husband, John, for picking up all the slack so I could spend time sitting in a corner making weird gestures and clacking away on my keyboard for hours, sometimes days, at a time. Also, Panayis would not exist without you.

And to my children, Megan and Matthew, I appreciate your enduring the incessant discussion about the fictional people in my head. To Megan, especially, for not rolling your eyes too hard at all the squeals that may or may not have escaped from me when Taylor Swift sang about how to get the girl (#teampanayis!). A special shout

out to Matthew for reading and re-reading pages and telling me which parts should be burned immediately. Kids are great for that.

A heartfelt thank you to my teen beta team: Alex, Amelia, Athena, and Danielle: Your feedback and screams of "WHY IS THIS ME?" kept me writing and editing when I wanted to quit. And to the rest of my students at Ben Holt who answered random questions about teenagery things and listened to paragraphs of awkward writing. I cannot repay you for stealing those precious minutes. Except maybe with cookies. See me after class. And to my main peeps at Holt—Jeff, Kyle, Leslie, and Liz—for your cheerleading. Special shout out to Mr. Peabody—you know who you are—I owe you a mint julep.

While the property in this story is like my mom's, hers was originally a walnut farm and only had enough grapes for the family. In order to get the facts about how vineyards work and the growth cycle of grapes, I turned to the experts. I cannot thank Maria Karapanos and her father, Nick Panagakos, for their time and knowledge. Your patience with my questions and countless photographs is appreciated more than you know. Like my mom, Nick passed away before I could thank him publicly. May his memory be eternal.

Thank you to all the brave people who have come forward to tell their own stories after reading Wren's. I'm deeply grateful you have trusted me with them and I will cherish them forever. You are the reason I wrote this book. I have my own reasons for telling this story, as well. It is my wish that it gives people courage to step out of the shadows and claim the love and respect they deserve.

Keli Vice, my first CP, you helped me see the forest from the trees. Eliza Turrill and Dante Medema, my Write or Die Bitches! I can't thank you enough for suffering through a million random messages, texts, emails, and phone calls and always coming through with the right thing to say.

This book would not exist in this form without the invaluable feedback and advice from Michelle Hazen. Her insights and enthusiasm kept me excited to dig in over and over again. And of course, the team at Lakewater Press deserves the utmost gratitude.

Kate Foster, my lovely editor, thank you for having faith in Wren's story. And Rebecca Carpenter, my undying gratitude for making sure the story took its best shape—your copy-editing skills are unrivaled.

Over the last few years, I've come to know some incredible people in the greater writing community. I have relied on the kindness of strangers-turned-family for the last three years, and your input has been invaluable.

Lastly, I want to acknowledge all the Wrens in the world, male or female. You are brave and strong, and your stories matter. I believe you.

About the Author

Deborah Maroulis is all about the words, words, words*, and she's lucky enough to be surrounded by them all the time. By day, she's a not-so-mild-mannered high school English teacher and junior college writing instructor. By night, she's a world-creator, dream-giver and then dream-crusher for the characters in her stories. She lives in Northern California with her husband and two children, whose dreams are very much intact.

*Hamlet, Act 2, Scene 2

To keep up to date with Deborah's author news visit her website:

DeborahMaroulis.com

On Facebook: byDebMaroulis

On Twitter: @yaddathree

On Instagram: deb.maroulis

CPSIA information can be obtained
at www.ICGtesting.com
Printed in the USA
LVHW041507170519
618250LV00001B/168

9 780648 347255